Praise for *Shooting Star*

'Peter Temple ratchets up the tension in his inimitable style . . . Temple's clever plotting and economic prose means the tale barrels along . . . He remains one of the best thriller writers in the world'
Sunday Express

'Temple provides plenty of surprises, oodles of Aussie atmosphere . . . *Shooting Star* hits all the right buttons'   *Evening Standard*

'Temple is a master of the complex plot and his characters leap from the page fully realised in a taut, action-packed thriller'
Sunday Telegraph

'Gripping, well-written and sad'   *Literary Review*

'Pace and plot, along with a stylishly cool approach to prose push him above the rest'   *Daily Mirror*

Praise for Peter Temple

'Peter Temple is deservedly the leading light of Australian crime fiction and it's time the rest of the world caught on . . . This is crime writing at its very best, and discovering Peter Temple has been the highlight of my year'   Mark Billingham

'Peter Temple's prose is brusque and tender, according to need, his characterisation subtle yet strong, and his themes urgent and universal. Put simply, Temple is a master'   John Harvey

'Temple writes . . . with an almost hypnotic pull that makes it impossible to skip a word, skim a page or stop for superfluous things like eating, drinking or sleeping'   *Daily Record*

'Peter Temple can write, make magic with words . . . an exceptional blending of first-rate crime fiction and literary sensibility'
Washington Post

Peter Temple is Australia's most acclaimed crime and thriller writer, and is the only author to have won the Ned Kelly Prize five times. He received the 2007 CWA Gold Dagger for *The Broken Shore*, while his ninth and most recent novel, *Truth*, was awarded the 2010 Miles Franklin Award. Peter Temple lives with his family in Ballarat, Australia.

Also by Peter Temple

An Iron Rose
In the Evil Day
The Broken Shore
Truth

The Jack Irish Novels

Bad Debts
Black Tide
Dead Point
White Dog

PETER TEMPLE

Shooting Star

Quercus

First published in Great Britain in 2008 by Quercus
First published in Great Britain in paperback in 2009 by Quercus
This paperback edition published in 2011 by

Quercus
21 Bloomsbury Square
London
WC1A 2NS

A CIP catalogue record for this book is available
from the British Library

ISBN 978 0 85738 351 8

Printed and bound in Great Britain by Clays Ltd, St Ives plc

10 9 8 7 6 5 4 3 2 1

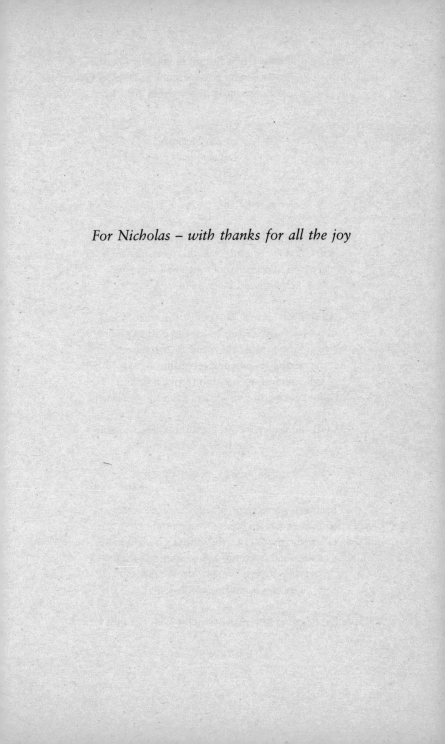

For Nicholas – with thanks for all the joy

THE HOUSE was in a street running off Ballarat Road. Doomed weatherboard dwellings with rusting roofs and mangy little patches of lawn faced each other across a pocked tarmac strip. At the end of the street, by the feeble light of a streetlamp, two boys were kicking a football to each other, uttering feral cries as they lost sight of it against the almost-dark sky.

Outside number twelve stood an old Ford Fairlane. I went up a concrete path and onto a springy verandah. The front door was open and, at the end of a passage, I could see a glow and hear the television, a game show, shrieks and shouts.

I looked for a bell, found a scar where one had been, knocked.

A figure appeared at the end of the passage, then a dim light came on. It was a big man, spilling out of a singlet, fat face, long straight hair falling over his eyes, wearing a plastic neck-brace. He didn't move, said nothing, just looked down the corridor at me.

'Mr Joseph Reagan?' The trick was to sound like someone from Tattslotto with good news.

He wiped a finger under his nose. Even in the gloom, I could see that he didn't have a ticket in the lottery.

'My name's Frank Calder,' I said. 'I'm a mediator.'

'What? Whadya want?'

'I help people having disputes.'

'Sellin'? Don't wannit.'

'Your wife's asked me to talk to you . . .'

'What?'

'Your wife's . . .'

It was like pulling a trigger. The man lurched forward, came down the passage at a run, arms held out like a wrestler, a fake wrestler on American television. I waited till he was almost on me, lunging, roaring, an out-of-control alcohol tanker. Then I stepped left, helped him on his way by grabbing his right forearm and swinging him. The roar changed to a different sound as he went through the rotten wooden verandah railing, falling into a mass of dead and dying vegetation.

I went down the stairs and inspected Mr Reagan. He was rolled into a ball, groaning, tracksuit pants ridden down to show the cleft of his buttocks. I stepped back, balanced myself, began to take my right leg back.

This is not normal mediation practice, I thought, but perhaps there is a place in dispute resolution for the solid kick up the arse.

The verandah light came on. A woman was in the doorway, young, exhausted. She was holding a child, its red hair like a flame against her cheek.

'Well, I'll be on my way then,' I said. 'Just called in to remind Mr Reagan that he owes Teresa twenty-five thousand dollars. She'd appreciate any loose change he can spare.'

I went down the path. In the street, the boys who had been kicking the ball were standing wide-eyed.

'Go to bed,' I said. 'Or hold up the corner shop.'

They drifted away. I hope to Christ the car starts, I thought. Men like Joe Reagan often sought to redress slights with hunting rifles they had lying around. I turned the key. The Alfa started as if it never did anything else.

'Small bloody mercies,' I said. 'Bloody small mercies.'

I drove off, trailing clouds of exhaust smoke. At the corner, waiting for a chance to turn right, I thought about life, how the wide vista of childhood shrinks to a passage in Footscray with a man in a plastic neckbrace charging at you.

I WAS suffocating, someone sitting on me and holding something over my head, saying, 'Die. Just die.' I woke up, gasping, on the couch in the sitting room, an old unzipped sleeping bag pulled up over my head. My breath had condensed inside it, wetting my face.

I put my legs over the side of the couch and sat with my face in my hands. When I lifted my head, I saw the dry black blood on the insides of the fingers of my right hand. For a moment, I was blank, alarmed. Then I remembered the lid of the tuna can gashing me.

I got up, went into the bathroom and took off my clothes. Under the shower, eyes closed, shaving with care, I made resolutions, not many but major. Half-dressed, I went into the kitchen and took two vitamin B complex tablets, big ones, like horse pills.

When I came back into the sitting room, pulling on a shirt, Detective Senior Sergeant Vella was sitting on the sofa, popping a can of beer.

'Jesus,' I said. 'How'd you get in?'

'Through the front door. Open front door. Where do you think you're living? Druggie kicked an old lady to death for a VCR just around the corner.'

'A VCR, that's motive. Not much motive around here. Drinking before lunch now?'

Vella took a big drink, looked around, and said, 'That's right. About eighteen hours before lunch. It's 6.30. P fucking M.'

I went to the window and looked out through the blind. 'Right,' I said. 'Evening. Testing you. Now, day of week and date?'

Vella picked up a book from the coffee table. He examined it like an object from a lost civilisation. 'What the fuck's this?' he said. '*A Guide to Propagation.* Any sex in it?'

'Manual of sex,' I said. 'Cover to cover rooting.' I was putting on shoes. 'I've got a horticulture class to get to.'

'Career number five. How's number four going?'

'Terrific. Had a really productive session last night with a man owes his wife twenty-five grand in maintenance.'

'Mediation,' Vella said thoughtfully, a frown on his

6

long face. 'Get someone to hold them down, hit them with a spade.'

While I looked behind the sofa and found a jacket, I thought about how I had almost kicked Mr Reagan. 'Precisely the attitude that drove me into civilian life,' I said. 'You spend many hours trying to convince deranged people that no harm will come to them. Eventually, they believe you. Then your colleagues kill them.'

'On the subject,' he said, 'the inquest's put back another two months.'

'They're hoping I'll die first. Of old age. Either that or they're having trouble putting out the contract.'

He drank half his can, wiped his mouth. 'Today we heard they want to make negotiation civilian. Put it with the shrinks.'

'A really good move,' I said. 'Lateral thinking. Must have called in Dr de Bono. That shrink who sucks off the post-traumatic stresses, she'll be good lying on the lino in her bra and pants talking to some psycho on speed wants to waste his whole family.'

'The reason I'm here,' Vella said, 'is that Curry comes sliming around today, says to tell you, subject to certain conditions, he'll back you for one of the jobs.'

I scratched my head. 'Tell Curry I'll take the job subject to certain conditions. One is he comes around here and kisses my arse, say around lunchtime every day. Two, he goes on permanent undercover public toilet duties. In a school uniform. With short pants.'

'I'll tell him,' Vella said. 'Tell him how you don't need the money.'

'What conditions? Change my statement, is that a condition? You the messenger boy now? Doing the swine's bidding?'

He stood up, a gangling figure. 'Fuck you. Got to go. A family not seen for two days. Been in Benalla, where some arsehole knifed an eighty-two-year-old lady.'

'A family. Lucky man. On the subject of family, Marco good for a loan, you think? Say ten grand.'

Vella's brother-in-law, Marco, owned the block of units I was living in. He owned lots of things, horses, table-dancing clubs, people.

'In another life,' said Vella. 'What happened to the payout?'

'What there was of the payout,' I said, 'I gave to a charity for bookies. Bookies and barmen. The double B charity. See a briefcase?'

He didn't look around, pointed a thumb over his shoulder at the passage. I found it and we went down the stairs together. It was cold outside, sky grey with dark patches like oil stains. Much like the oil stains the old Alfa was leaving on the concrete driveway.

'My brother-in-law's not going to like this,' said Vella, looking at the marks.

'Marco doesn't get around here much,' I said. 'Your sister know he's fucking her F-cup cousin in that unit in Brighton?'

'E-cup. At least it's in the family,' Vella said. 'Don't tell my sister.'

I got in, tried to start the car. Angry whine. It wouldn't start.

'Man and machine,' said Vella. 'In perfect harmony.' He drained his can, dropkicked it towards the street. It bounced on a parked car.

'Do that in your street?' I said. 'Kick beer cans onto cars? I'm coming around to piss in your neighbour's letterbox.'

'Feel free,' said Vella. 'A bouncer. Well, ex-bouncer. Presently awaiting trial for throwing a bloke across King Street. Landed on a parking meter.'

'The one on the other side,' I said. 'The tiny Quaker.'

I tried the starter again. It whined and nothing happened. I waited, tried again. Reluctantly, the engine came to life.

'Saturday?' Vella said. 'Come and eat. With a knife and fork. Remember?' He mimed eating with a knife and fork. 'That's provided we don't have some pressing murder in Wangaratta or fucking Moe.'

I mimed gnawing on a bone. 'Real men eat with their hands,' I said. 'Kill it and eat it.'

Vella shook his head. 'Kill a home-delivery pizza,' he said. 'Stalk a pizza and take it out with your bare hands. Eight, around then.'

I gave him the thumbs up and took off. Slowly. Five minutes from the college, at an intersection, ahead of me a class and then a date with the teacher, the mobile made its mad-bird noise, changed my plans, changed many things.

THE SECURITY system guarding the home of Pat Carson, patriarch of the Carson dynasty, began with a three-metre-high boundary wall. Then you drove into a gatehouse in the wall and a door closed behind you and ahead another door shot up from the ground and you were going nowhere, not until someone somewhere had looked at your picture from at least four angles and pressed a button. Once out of jail, concealed spotlights revealed that the boundary wall wasn't the only obstacle intruders faced. Four metres or so inside it was an elegant stake-pointed steel fence several metres high. It was entirely possible that the grassed area in between was patrolled by Dobermans and their handlers.

Three Mercedes, one small and two big, were parked in front of the landing-strip terrace that preceded the huge neo-Georgian structure. I parked the shabbier but sexier member of the Axis Powers in front of them.

A man called Graham Noyce was waiting for me. He was in his early forties, short and pudgy, snub nose, fair hair giving out in front. Once a lawyer and an adviser to politicians, he now worked for the Carson family as some kind of fixer. I'd first met him after an affair in a distant reach of the Carson empire, a shopping-mall branch of a women's underwear chain called Cusp. The unhinged husband of an ex-employee took three staff and four customers, all women, hostage. In the beginning, the man, a plumber called Tony, wanted his wife and the manager, who was on leave, brought to him. The idea was that he would get them to confess to having a lesbian affair. I got him to let me sit in the front part of the shop on a white plastic chair, and I managed to talk him out of the confession-extracting scheme.

OK, he said, a million dollars, cash money, delivered by a Carson, no one else would do, plus a helicopter and pilot on the shopping centre roof. That or he'd kill the women one at a time, starting with the fat one who reminded him of his sister, the fucking bitch. Sounds reasonable, I'd said, let's talk details. In the midst of a discussion ranging over many topics, including religion, trust and the ability of lingerie to inflame and deprave, I broke off to get two cans from the machine across the way, outside the jeans shop. Just me in the shopping mall, air-conditioning humming as it pushed the dead air around, all the shops evacuated, the workers and the gawkers and Hepburn and his killers down at the police line. I went back into the lingerie shop, popped my can of Sprite, got reasonably close, tossed Tony his Diet Coke, underhand.

Tony relaxed, took his trigger hand off the shotgun to catch it, and that was the end of the matter.

Five hours after it began. Your face and your shoulders ache dully for days, tension clotted in the muscles.

Noyce put out a hand. Firm but not too firm.

'Frank. Thanks for coming at short notice. Pat appreciates it.'

We went through the front door. I touched its surface, at least twenty coats of black paint, each one almost rubbed away by hand before the next was applied. Inside, the amount of space was alarming: a sparsely furnished hall the size of an art gallery, then a softly lit passage two hospital trolleys could pass in. At its end, a full twenty metres away, a rose-wood staircase rose in a gentle curve.

Pat Carson's study was halfway down the passage. Noyce took me in without knocking. It wasn't a bookish room but a clubby room, a big panelled room, six or seven armchairs, small tables, family photographs and portraits on the walls. Behind a desk the size of a billiard table, closed wooden internal shutters behind him, sat a man, old, had to be in his eighties, square face, deeply lined, full head of charged white hair brushed back.

'Mr Carson,' said Noyce, 'this is Frank Calder. Frank, Mr Pat Carson.'

I knew quite a lot about Pat Carson, a man who went from penniless immigrant builders' labourer to millionaire property developer before he was forty. In his time, he had been accused of beating, bribing or threatening everyone in the building unions, top to bottom, of being the most ruthless figure in the industry, the worst person an honest union man or a subcontractor could ever meet, the most sinister person in construction. But a Royal Commission in the seventies couldn't prove that, couldn't find a single witness to testify to acts more reprehensible than bullying and intimidation and vague mentions of future favours.

Pat Carson waved a big parcel of bones at me, a hand that had known work. As he raised his head to inspect me, his neck skin tautened and, for an instant, he could have been the older brother of the man standing at the fireplace.

'A soldier once, they tell me,' he said. 'And a policeman.'

I nodded.

'Don't know whether that's a good combination for a man. Havin' either of them jobs, for that matter. You know my sons? Tom.'

Standing in front of the fireplace, dark-suited right arm draped along the mantel, Tom Carson moved fingers at me. He was in his sixties, tall, with close-cut grey hair, curved nose presiding over a severe face.

Tom was the visible Carson, the elder son, the public face of the country's richest private company, a man who dined with prime ministers and premiers. Lately, his picture had been in all the newspapers because he was taking Carson Corporation public, ending fifty years of utterly private ownership. He reminded me of someone I'd served under, a man who liked to witness pain. Not inflict, just watch.

Another man, younger, mid-fifties, sat forward in a buttoned leather armchair, extended a hand. 'Barry Carson, Frank,' he said, a genial voice, a light, boyish voice, a voice to put you at your ease. We shook hands. 'Thanks for coming,' he said. He had no grey in his fair hair, dyed probably. There was a hint of the voluptuary in his face, the fleshiness, the hooded eyes behind round fine-framed glasses.

Barry pointed to the chair next to him. 'Sit here, Frank.'

I sat down. Noyce took a seat beside the desk.

'Tell him, Graham,' said Pat Carson.

'We've had a kidnapping,' Noyce said. 'Today. Tom's granddaughter. Anne. She's fifteen.'

'That's police business,' I said.

'No.' Pat shook his head. 'No.'

'I can't help you,' I said. 'These are life and death things.'

'My daughter, Alice, was kidnapped in 1990,' Barry said. He wasn't looking at me, eyes on something behind his father. 'She was eleven. Getting out of the car in the garage of our house in Power Avenue. Two men. They left a note saying no police or your daughter dies. Wait for ransom instructions. But we did call in the police. How can you not call the police? That's how stupid we were. So we had all kinds of police arrive, state, federal, name it. They said they wouldn't interfere with the handing over of the ransom, wouldn't do anything until we had Alice back.'

He looked at me, sat back, crossed his legs at the ankles. He was dressed for golf; I could see a burr on a dark cotton sock, a burr from Royal Melbourne, perfectly at home on a twenty-five-dollar sock.

'For two days, nothing happened,' he said. 'Then the police said they needed public help, the media had to be told. We went along with that. The story was on television that night, radio, front-page news the next day. At about 10 a.m., we got a phone call. All the voice said was: "Didn't listen, rich bastards.

Now she dies." The next day, Alice turned up at a house in the Dandenongs. The kidnappers had taken her into the forest to kill her but she got away.'

I knew nothing about the Carson kidnapping. But then, in 1990, I was in hospital with multiple fractures, a ruptured spleen and a punctured lung. End of career number one.

'I'm sorry,' I said. 'I didn't know. I was somewhere else then. What happened today?'

Noyce coughed. 'Anne lives here,' he said. 'She goes to school with the daughter of Lauren Geary, the estate manager. To Moorfield. They're the same age. The head driver takes them to school, drops them and picks them up. Inside the school grounds. He's not supposed to stop anywhere – going or coming. Turns out he's been coming home via Armadale, letting them go into a record shop for fifteen minutes. Nobody knew that. He's supposed to be a professional.'

'Like the person who hired him,' said Tom Carson, gruff voice, smoker's voice, but quiet. I could imagine that in his life he had only to move his lips for people to fall silent. 'Professional fucking something.'

Noyce's expression didn't change but a breath drew in his nostrils, clenched them like buttocks.

Pat coughed, a come-to-order sound.

'Today was sport, late pick-up,' Noyce said.

'Carmen says she stayed in the front part of the store, Anne went down the back. There's another entrance at that end. To Gawler Street. It was crowded and when Carmen looked for her, she was gone.'

'What time?' I said.

'Carmen came back to the car at 4.50.'

'Kidnapped. What says that?'

'Someone phoned my office,' Tom Carson said. 'Just three sentences, repeated several times. Sounded like an American voice, the girl says, a strange voice.'

'Saying what?'

'We have the girl. Do nothing or she will be killed. Wait till you are contacted.'

'There's a recording?'

'No.'

'Number displayed?'

Tom turned his gaze on Noyce.

'Callbox in St Kilda,' Noyce said. 'Only unvandalized callbox in Fitzroy Street.'

I said, 'You got that from where?'

Noyce shrugged. 'We have these people. Jahn, Cullinan, security people.'

'You've got Jahn, Cullinan,' I said. I looked at Pat Carson and the Carson boys and at Graham Noyce and they all registered that I was looking at them. 'You've got Jahn, Cullinan and you give me a call?'

'Don't trust 'em,' Pat said.

'Mr Carson, they protect presidents, kings. Marcos, Shah of Iran.'

'Most of those dead too,' Pat said. 'Don't trust 'em.' He shook his head dismissively.

'Jahn do the corporate work,' Noyce said. 'Family security is handled in-house.'

'Or not fucking handled,' Tom said.

Noyce swallowed and his face pinkened. He wasn't happy being Tom's scapegoat.

'What time was the call?' I said.

'Just after five,' said Noyce.

'That's at least two people,' I said. 'Probably three, maybe more.'

'How's that?' said Barry. He'd been far away, looking at his hands, flexing his fingers. Something to do with golf, perhaps, thinking about the shot he was about to make when the mobile rang with the bad news.

'Can't get to Fitzroy Street from Armadale in ten minutes in peak hour. Two to get the girl, one waiting in St Kilda for a signal to make the call. Three at least, probably more.'

'Why two to take the girl?'

'I'm assuming there's a vehicle involved. Big ask for one person to force a fifteen-year-old out of a crowded store, get her into a vehicle, maybe have to go around to get into the driver's seat.'

'It doesn't matter how many,' said Pat. 'Three, thirty-bloody-three, doesn't matter.'

I leaned forward and looked into Pat's eyes. 'It matters,' I said, speaking softly. 'That's why you need the police. Put plainclothes cops into the area. All low-key. Someone would have seen two people and a girl in the store, getting into a vehicle in Gawler Street. Get descriptions, might even get a number, bit of a number. Maybe someone saw the person make the call in St Kilda. Person using an electronic device on a payphone. You'd notice.'

Pat raised his big hands, palms outward. 'Frank, listen, son. Last time, that's what happened. They did all their bloody police things. And we almost lost the child. The police didn't save her. She saved herself. This time, we're just payin'.'

'Give the cops another chance,' I said.

Pat shook his head. 'No. No. They had their chance last time. Afterwards, nothin'. They got nowhere. What they ask now, we're payin'. It's only money, it's nothin'. The child safe. That's what we want. That's all.'

I didn't want any part of this and Pat Carson saw it in my face. Perhaps he saw other things in me, too, the way I had learned to see things in people, to read their bodies and faces, know their eyes.

'And what you ask, we pay too,' Pat said. 'Your

rate, forget your rate. When the child's back, tell Graham the fee. No argument from anyone. Cash, bank cheque, any way you bloody want it.'

He'd read me. He knew I'd hear the rustle of the money in the packet, salivate over the prospect of its chewy, salty, crispy taste. He'd looked at me and he'd read me.

But I didn't want to be readable. Better to spend more time in Footscray fighting with men in plastic neckbraces than be read by rich people.

'For doing what?' I said. 'When they tell you what they want, give it to them. What happens after that is anybody's guess.'

I looked at Noyce. His eyes were on Pat. I met Pat's eyes. 'Graham can give it to them, Mr Carson,' I said. 'A cab driver can give it to them. Send the girls' driver. The man's got an interest in getting it right.'

The room was silent. I'd said no. Time to excuse myself. Hope it goes well. I could go, but I couldn't say that. I couldn't say anyone can do it and then use the word hope. Although hope was what it would come down to.

'Thanks for comin', Frank,' Pat said. His lips moved, not a smile, some outward sign of a reflection on life, on himself perhaps. 'Usually, the money talks. Not for you. I respect that in a man. Particularly a man who's been a policeman. Goodnight. Graham will see you're paid for your time.'

I sat. Pat and I looked at each other. His eyes were the colour of first light in a dry country.

'If it goes wrong,' I said, 'it'll somehow be my fault. And I'll blame myself too. For not having the brains to walk out now.'

Pat's right hand went to his throat. 'All you have to do is give them what they want. No police stuff, nothing. What could go wrong? A cab driver could do it, not so? And blame? Yes. We'll blame ourselves, blame you, blame the bloody stars above. Graham will give you ten thousand dollars tonight. Cash. An advance on your fee.'

He looked at Noyce. Noyce looked at Tom, still languid before the fireplace. Something passed between them. Tom's consent? Did Graham need Tom's permission to follow Pat's instructions?

'Of course,' Noyce said. 'It'll take an hour or so, Frank.'

In my mind, I sighed a deep sigh. 'A few things first,' I said. 'I want to talk to the driver. I'm not even being the bagman here unless I'm happy about him.'

They all looked to Pat. He nodded.

'Tom, your office line, it's diverted?'

He nodded.

'Recording device?'

'All incoming calls are recorded automatically,' Noyce said.

'Other family children. I'd bring them here till this is over.'

'I think everyone at risk lives here,' Noyce said. 'That would be right, wouldn't it, Tom?'

'There are five houses in the compound,' Tom said to me. 'We're the fucking Kennedys of Australia. The kids who aren't here are overseas. We can't bring them back.'

'OK. Which phone will ring?'

'Next door. Diverted calls will ring next door.'

'The girl's parents, where are they?'

A glance between Tom and Barry, between Tom and his father. 'Mark's in Europe,' said Tom. 'We'll speak to him in the morning. Her mother's not well. It's better that we don't alarm her.'

'I'll need to bring someone else in,' I said. 'And I'll have to stay here, so I'll need clothes.'

Tom looked me over like a bloodstock agent. 'Mark's clothes should fit you. There's a room full of them upstairs. Have some put out, Graham.'

Graham didn't like that command. His mouth twitched and he tested the fit of his collar, glanced at Barry. Barry was still engaged elsewhere, not flexing his fingers now but holding their tips to his lips.

Silence, one man standing, four seated, an interlude between something concluding and the future. Into it, Pat said, 'Never thought it would happen twice.' His chin was on his chest, his eyes on the desk. 'And the sinners walk free.'

I couldn't resist it. 'What sinners would those be?'

'What?'

'What sinners walk free?'

Pat raised his head and looked at me, blinked. 'Figure of speech, son,' he said. 'No shortage of sinners walkin' free. Cop, you'd know that.'

'Former cop,' I said. 'Yes.'

THE ROOM next door explained why there weren't any books in Pat Carson's study. It was a library, a striking room, mellow parquet floor, four walls of floor-to-ceiling books, ladders on wheels, armchairs covered in faded fabrics, a long, narrow library table surrounded by upright chairs, stern chairs.

I sat at the table, ran my fingertips over the green leather inlay, unhappy at being bought, tempted to find Noyce and tell him I'd changed my mind. These people were capitulating in the hope that it would save a girl's life. It probably wouldn't. And I was complicit, not abetting them, no, but certainly aiding them, taking money to carry their money. Why? Broke and prospectless, that was a good enough reason. If not me, then someone else.

I got out my book and found the number of Corin McCall, garden designer and lecturer in horticulture, my date after class. It had taken me five months to find the courage to ask her out, five months of doing all my homework, spending hours formulating intelligent questions, shaving before my night class.

'McCall.' She had a deep voice for such a lean and wiry person. A little electric jolt went through me the first time she spoke to the class.

'Corin, Frank Calder.' It occurred to me that I'd never said her name. I coughed. 'Listen, I couldn't get to class . . .'

'I noticed,' she said. 'And you can't make it tonight.'

'Called out for an urgent job. I'm really sorry, I'd turn it down, but . . .'

She said, 'That's fine, Frank, happens to me all the time. I mean, I do this to people.' Pause. 'Anyhow, I'm exhausted, wouldn't have been good company.'

'Can we make another time? Next week? Any night.'

'I'm in the bush on Monday and Tuesday, possibly Wednesday. You could give me a call mid-week.'

'I will. I'll call you.'

'Yes, call me. I await your call.'

'I await calling you. I'm sorry I spoiled your evening. You could've taken up another offer.'

Corin laughed. 'It's early, I may still.'

'Goodnight. See you next week.'

'Goodnight. Call me.'

'Mid-week. Goodnight.'

Repeating myself, breathing too shallowly. What kind of teenage nonsense was this?

A sallow man in a white jacket was at the open door pushing a small serving trolley. Supper was grilled fish, tiny tomatoes and roasted eggplant. I had just finished it when there was a knock: a big handsome man in a dark suit, fortyish, fat coming on, neat short hair. Dennis Whitton, Pat Carson's driver, the girls' driver. I'd questioned Noyce about him. Ex-cop, excellent credentials, four years in the job.

'Mr Noyce said . . .'

I got up and shook hands, closed the door, sat him at the library table, sat opposite him.

'Bad luck, this,' I said.

He nodded, rolled his head ruefully, scratched the back of it. He had pale blue eyes, wary. 'Let 'em talk me into it,' he said. 'Went in the first coupla times, hung around, pretend I'm lookin at the CDs. You feel like a perv, no one more than sixteen in the place. Second time, a bloke come up to me, he's about twenty. He says, "I'm the manager, we'd be happier if you looked at CDs somewhere else." After that . . .'

'How long's this been going on?' I said.

'This term, that's all.'

'Every day?'

'No.' He was indignant. 'Only on sport days. Tuesday and Thursday. It'd be six, seven times.'

'Who talked you into it?'

'They did, the girls.'

'Both of them?'

'Yeah. They worked on me. I gave in, I'm an idiot, what can I say?'

'Who suggested it? Whose idea?'

He shrugged, put up his big hands. 'Jeez, I can't remember. They talk all the time, they tease me, shave your head Dennis, no, he should grow his hair, Dennis, PE teacher said she thinks you're a spunk, Dennis, how old were you when you did it the first time? They go on like that all the time. You wouldn't think they were fifteen. Not like kids at all.' He sighed. 'I dunno who asked first. Really don't know.'

'The times you went in, they talk to anyone?'

'Sure. There's other kids from the school there.'

'Girls?'

'And boys. That's what it's about. Boys.'

'That's what what's about?'

'Goin' there. The record place. Triple Zero.'

'Triple Zero. That's its name?'

He nodded.

'They went there to meet boys. Any boys in particular?'

'Dunno. I said, only went in twice, didn't really notice.'

'But they were talking to boys.'

'Well, yeah. In a group like, boys and girls.'

'The time. How long were they in the store?'

'Twenty, twenty-five minutes.'

'You tell anyone you were doing this? Taking them to this place?'

'No.' Quick response. 'Who would I tell?'

I got up, put my hands in my pockets, looked at a pen-and-ink drawing on the wall above the writing desk: a cobbled street, shops on either side. Somewhere in Europe. It was signed A. Carson. In the glass, I could see Whitton. He was rubbing his jaw with his right hand, looking at the ceiling.

I turned and walked around the library table, perched close to him so that he had to lean back and look up at me.

'They'd kick your tyres a bit before you got a job like this,' I said. 'Cop in WA, that's right?'

'Right.'

'Quit to be a security man at Argyle. Diamond mine pay better?'

'Lots, yeah.'

'And then the Hanleys. Big move. Perth to Melbourne.'

'Married a Melbourne girl, she wanted to come back. Kept on about the green grass, all that. Never stopped.' He shrugged. 'What can you do?'

'How long in that job?'

'Hanleys? Nine years. Done all the driver courses, done one in England. Brands Hatch. Hanleys sent me. Ten days. Blokes from all over, America, Italy, you name it. Then Mr Clive Hanley died. Mrs Hanley wanted me to go to Sydney with her, she went to live in Sydney. Couldn't go, the wife wouldn't go, her family's all here.'

'England. So you know all the stuff. Unpredictable routes, evasive actions, emergency drills, that sort of thing.'

A slight blush crept up from his collar, tinged his jowls. 'Yeah, all that.'

'Put it into practice, driving the girls?'

'Sure, yeah.'

'So you'd never take the same route from the school to Armadale? Use different cars?'

He hesitated. 'That's right.'

I didn't say anything, sat with my fingers on the table, still, expressionless, looking over his right shoulder.

'Not worth much if they know where you're going,' he said. 'All that stuff.'

I didn't comment. 'Know about the other Carson kidnapping?'

'Yeah.'

'Think about it before you gave in to the girls?'

He sat forward, shoulders hunched, eyes on the table. 'Not enough,' he said. 'Jesus, not enough.'

'So you told no one.'

'That's right.'

'And you're not involved in any way?'

'Christ, no.'

'Mr Whitton,' I said softly, 'you're pretty much finished in this line of work. But things can get much worse. Whatever happens to this girl, even the best result, you are going to be gone over by people who will look into every pore of your skin, stick a probe up your arse and look at your eyes from the inside. If you're involved, they'll find out. Believe that, believe it. And then you'll be finished in all lines of work. Listening?'

His eyes were still on the table.

'Look at me,' I said.

His head came up. His eyes were watering.

'I'm asking you again, Mr Whitton. Tell me the truth. You'll be glad you did. Are you involved in any way?'

'No,' he said. 'No, no, no. No.'

The telephone rang at a writing table between the French windows. It was a flat black high-tech device and its ring was a gentle warbling sound, a sound suitable for a library.

Noyce came in without knocking. 'Wait in your quarters, Dennis,' he said.

Tom Carson was in the doorway, Barry behind

him. They stood back to let Whitton leave. Then, not hurried, Tom went to the writing table. He sat down, took a fountain pen from an inside pocket, removed the top, fitted it to the back. He picked up the receiver.

'Tom Carson.'

We watched him listen and write on the broad white tablet in front of him. He said only one word: 'Yes.'

When he'd put the receiver down, Noyce went over to the table and pushed a button. We listened to the ringing, to Tom saying his name. Then a harsh, grating, high-pitched electronic voice said:

Make sure you've got two hundred thousand dollars in notes by twelve noon tomorrow. Fifties. If you contact the police, we'll know and the girl dies. Straight away. Got that?

Tom's voice: *Yes.*

Wait for a call.

They were all looking at me.

'That's pretty straightforward,' I said to Noyce. 'Purely out of interest, ask your friends at Jahn, Cullinan where the call came from.'

WHEN THEY had gone, I rang Orlovsky on the high-tech library telephone. It was a long time before he answered.

'Frank,' he said.

'How did you know?'

'No one else lets it ring for five minutes.'

I saw the survivors of C Troop irregularly but we never lost touch. We were like people who had come through a death camp, bearers of a guilt that knew no rationality and admitted of no untroubled sleep. In any year, I talked to all of them. Except Lucas, who disappeared at night from a prawn trawler lolling in its reflection on a Torres Strait sea, and the small and lethal Jacoby, who went to Burma to fight for the Karen rebels and never came back. They called from truck stops and brothels, from jails and pubs, from backpackers' hostels and a rich woman's beach house in Byron Bay. I went to see one in the feral, freezing high country, slept in a foul-smelling bark tepee beneath strips of rabbit flesh black from smoke. It wasn't that we liked one another that much. It was that we were like children of the same abusive father: beyond his reach now and scattered, but always joined by our secret knowing.

'Listen,' I said, 'I need help with a job. Tomorrow. You free?'

'Free till next Thursday,' he said. 'Then I'm on the road.'

I didn't know what Orlovsky did for a living now. 'Legal drug distributor,' he'd said when I once asked him. I took that to mean he was running tobacco and I didn't want him to tell me any more. He would have told me because my being a cop did not inhibit him in any way. 'Cops should have a moral sense,' he said one day, back to me, fishing on the greasy bay. 'It should be a calling. Even stupid people can have a calling. You should be able to respect cops. People like you, you're only cops because otherwise they'd have to lock you away. They. We.'

I gave him the address. 'Around eleven. There's an entrance at the back to an underground garage. Tell the voicebox you're Mr Calder's associate.'

'Mr Calder's associate,' he said. 'That's nice. It's like a title.'

I felt someone's presence. Noyce was at the door. He had less hair in front every time I looked.

'Bring clothes,' I said to Orlovsky. 'Could be hours, could be a while. Clean clothes. Least dirty clothes.'

I put the receiver down and stood up. Tiredness was settling into my lower back, the feeling of grip, of compression.

'I don't need to stay now,' I said. 'I'll come back in the morning.'

Noyce put his head to one side. 'I think Pat'd be happier if you slept here,' he said. 'I've arranged clothes. OK?'

'I'll pick up clothes and come back.' I didn't mind the idea of wearing expensive clothes. I minded the idea of wearing clothes I didn't own.

'Pat doesn't show much,' said Noyce, 'but he's shaken by this. He'd like to talk to you.' His hands went to his tie, one at the knot, one below, made a minute adjustment, an unconscious gesture, reassuring himself, like touching a gun under your arm, feeling the cold comfort of the fit in your hand.

Pat Carson was where I'd left him, behind the huge desk, glass of whisky now beside his right hand. He seemed smaller, lower in his chair, his hair less galvanized, less electric.

'Sit,' he said.

I chose the chair directly across from him. Noyce

was moving to sit at my left when Pat said, 'Graham, go home. Eat and sleep like a normal person. Tomorrow, tomorrow is its own bloody day.'

I looked at Noyce. He wasn't happy, spread his hands, long fingers for a stubby person.

'Fine,' he said. 'In the morning. Early. Pat. Frank.' He backed out reluctantly. At the door, eyes on Pat Carson, he said, 'Any development . . .'

'Yes, Graham. Thank you. Goodnight. Sleep well.'

Noyce closed the door behind him, a precise, solid click. 'The more he's paid, the more he worries,' Pat said. He pointed at an open drinks cabinet against the wall to his right. 'Help yourself.'

I went over and poured two fingers from a whisky decanter, water from a beaded silver jug, sat down again.

For a moment, Pat and I sat in silence in the comfortable room, calm yellow light around the table lamps, whisky glowing in the heavy crystal glasses. We looked at each other, the hirer and the hired.

'Two hundred, not much money,' Pat said. 'For the trouble.'

'No.'

'Why, do you think?'

'Could be they're not too clever, don't know what the market will bear. Could be that, could be they just want a quick and easy deal, off they go, spend it on drugs in a few weeks. Two hundred thousand, that's four bundles, briefcase, sports bag, shopping bag, doesn't weigh too much.'

Pat studied me. 'What else?'

'It's just a trial to see how we behave.'

'A trial.' He picked up his glass, swilled the liquid. I could see the high-water mark it left. 'A trial you can do with half a million, more.'

I had concerns about things other than the amount of money but I didn't express them, tasted the whisky, just bathed the gums in the anonymous liquid from the decanter. Single malt. Fire in it, and peat smoke and tears. The Carsons probably owned the distillery, the spring, the heather, the whole freezing spray-blasted gull-screaming granite Scottish outcrop.

'They don't know what your pain threshold is,' I said.

'Pain threshold,' he said. 'That's when we scream, is it?'

'Yes. Two hundred thousand it's not likely to be. If they ask for half a million, you might say, that's too much, get the cops in.'

He thought about this, studying me, eyes just slits, took a sip of whisky, said musingly, 'What is our pain threshold? A million? Two million? Ten million?'

'I wish it were two hundred thousand,' I said. 'It's not too late.'

Pat shook his head. 'No. We give the bastards what they want and we hope. Get Anne back, then we look for them, Frank. To the ends of the bloody earth.'

But I couldn't leave it. 'Anne,' I said. 'She's always lived here?'

'Just about. Since Alice's kidnappin'. That's when we bought up around us, bought four places, made the owners and the bloody real-estate jackals rich.'

'And the whole family came to live here?'

'Tom and his wife and Barry and Kathy and their two. Mark and Christine and the little ones, and Stephanie and her fuckin' husband, don't like to say the bastard's name, Jonathan fuckin' Chadwick.'

'Mark's got other children?'

'Little ones. Michael and Vicky.'

'And their mother's not well?'

'Their mother . . .' Pat hesitated. 'Had a breakdown. She's in . . . a place, some kind of place.'

I said nothing, kept my eyes on him, didn't nod. Sometimes it works.

Pat drank some whisky, took a red handkerchief out of the top pocket of his jacket, wiped his lips. 'Drugs,' he said. 'No point in beatin' around the fuckin' bush. Lovely girl, Christine, but she'll stick anythin' in her body. Christ knows why, had everythin' a woman could want. We sent her to Israel,

Tom's idea. Got this clinic there, they put 'em to sleep and they flush 'em out. Buy a decent house for what they charge. Waste of money, comes home, back on the bloody drugs in six weeks.'

'And Mark's in Europe?'

'A lawyer, Mark,' Pat said. 'He was. Bright spark. First grandchild's cleverest, the wife used to say. Some bloody Hungarian sayin'. That's what she was, Hungarian. Lots of sayin's, the Hungarians. Sayin' for every bloody occasion. Could've used Mark in the business. But, doesn't help to push 'em. Come to it themselves, that's the way. He didn't. Didn't do anythin' anyone bloody wanted. Married at twenty, girl three years older, shotgun, still at the uni. That's Anne, scraped in under the wire. Anyway, Christine's from a decent family, couldn't see what Carol was gettin hysterical about.'

'Carol?'

He didn't understand the question for an instant. 'Carol?'

'Who's Carol?'

'Oh. Forget who you're talkin' to. Carol. Mark's mother. Tom's wife. Carol Wright she was. Fancied themselves, the family, the father anyway. Stockbroker. There's a bloody amazin' job for you, all care and no responsibility, buyin', sellin', makin' or losin', the bastards get a cut. I shoulda gone into that, snowball's bloody chance I'd a had, boy left school at twelve.'

He sipped the malt, went far away.

'So Tom married Carol Wright,' I said. For the moment, he didn't mind talking about the family.

Pat came back, hesitantly. 'That's it. Tom went to school with the brother, name escapes me. Mind you, the fella did a bit of escapin' himself. Director of companies, that was his occupation. I ask you. Barry tells me the bugger's livin' in some banana republic where the warrants can't get to him.'

'And Barry's wife?'

'Married into the English aristocracy, Barry. Katherine, met her on a skiing holiday, that's upper bloody crust for you. Some place in America. Don't know what my old dad would've said. Know he'd a liked the bit where the bloody chinless prick of a father tapped me for six thousand quid to pay for his girl's weddin'. Then Louise, that's my daughter, she goes and marries into the local silver-tails, the Western District mob. They play polo, know that?'

'I've heard that.'

'Horses got more brains than the jockeys. But Stephen's not a bad bloke, good father. She's happy.'

'And Mark became a lawyer.'

'Clever lad, got a job with these Collins Street lawyers. Tom put some business their way, that wasn't a good idea. Bastards probably thought Mark was drivin' the gravy train. Made him a partner. Twenty-five years old, couldn't run a chip shop.'

He fell silent, looked away. He was beginning to regret talking to me about the Carsons. I was just a bagman. 'Anyway,' he said, 'Mark's in Europe, some deal with the Poles, I don't know. The deals change all the time. Poles, Russians, Chinese, Indonesians, bloody South Africans, white ones.'

'Anne,' I said. 'She's happy here?'

'Difficult child.'

'Difficult how?'

'School problems. Other things. In a cage here, it's not natural . . .' He tailed off, looked at his glass, drained it, mind turning elsewhere. 'Dennis?' he said.

I shook my head. 'I'd be surprised. Got slack, careless. Too long in the job without anything happening.'

'I hope so. You can understand. Bloke doesn't have little Alice on his mind like the rest of us.'

I wanted to know more about Alice, but there was a knock at the door.

'Come in,' said Pat.

It was a tall, slim woman in her thirties, late thirties, well-cut dark hair on her shoulders.

I stood up.

'Carmen's mother,' Pat said. 'She manages the place, keeps it tickin' over. Part of the family.'

'Lauren Geary,' said the woman. She was wearing a wine-red high-collared blouse and a long black skirt. Chin up, she had an air of competence, a person who managed things, commanded obedience. She put out a hand. 'You're Mr Calder. Graham told me.'

We shook hands.

'I'm sorry to interrupt, Mr Carson,' she said, 'but Carmen's told me something.'

Pat nodded.

'She remembers seeing a man near the record store two or three times. There's a tram stop but once he was still there when they came out.'

'Yes?'

'Well, trams go by every few minutes. It's peak hour. So he couldn't have been waiting for a tram.'

'Can she describe him?' I said. It was hard to keep in mind that I was only a bagman, not paid to do anything else.

Pat put up his hands. 'Frank, this is not the time. Lauren, they want money, we're givin' the bastards money. Tomorrow, Frank will give 'em the money. Then when Anne's safe we'll find 'em, make sure they don't do this again. The police can ask all the questions then.'

Lauren Geary looked at me, looked at Pat. He smiled at her. It wasn't the smile of an elderly employer, not that kind of smile.

'Fine,' she said, nodding. 'Afterwards. Yes, when we've got her back.' She turned to me. 'I've put you in the Garden House, Mr Calder. I'll send over some clothes for you to try on.'

'I'm going home for clothes,' I said. 'But thank you.'

When she'd gone, Pat, revived, held out his glass. I fetched the decanter and poured a fat finger. He drank, studying me. There was something he wanted to talk about. 'Alice,' he said, 'never stopped botherin' me. When she came back to us, the police questioned her. Over and over. Even hypnotized the little thing. Nothing. Very calm, she was, like a little grownup, but she couldn't tell 'em anythin'. Never saw a face except for a few seconds at the start, in the garage. Where they kept her, the man wore somethin' over his head, a mask.'

He sighed. 'Then, when that was over, we had the psychiatrist. That was the advice we got. From America. A specialist in victims. A week here, talkin' to her every day. Dr Wynn. I reckon that was our mistake. Maybe you should just leave people alone. Maybe she would have gotten over it if we just pretended it never happened. What do you think, Frank?'

What did I think? A man who had nightmares almost every night. 'I think you probably did the best you could,' I said.

43

The old eyes were on me, looking for something. 'Man is born unto trouble,' he said.

I said, 'As the sparks fly upwards.'

Deep lines at the corners of Pat's mouth. 'Know your Job. Soldier. Policeman. Haven't been a bloody priest too, have you?'

'My mother,' I said. 'She had a lot of time for Job.'

'This job,' he said. 'Just a good man to give 'em what they want. Don't want any police stuff, any messin' about with who and why. Clear to you, is it, Frank?'

I said yes, drove home, found the two new shirts, the emergency shirts, packed a small bag. It wasn't hard to leave the cold, unlovely unit, drip hitting the kitchen sink like a finger tapping.

WE SAT in the library, four of us, me, Tom Carson reading a computer printout, Graham Noyce writing in a small leather-bound book, Orlovsky apparently asleep, hands in his lap, palms upward, right cupping left. Barry Carson was next door, talking to his father.

I was looking out of a window, watching the flow of life in the compound, when the call came. It was 12.35.

Tom dropped the printout into his open briefcase, let the phone ring twice, three times, four times, going through the routine with his fountain pen. Barry was in the doorway by the time Tom picked up the receiver.

'Tom Carson.'

He listened, then he turned to Noyce, standing to his right, and said, 'Mobile number.'

Noyce had a business card out in seconds. Tom

read a number from it, slowly. Then he listened again and said, 'Yes.'

Pause.

'Yes. What about the release of Anne?'

He took the receiver away from his ear.

Noyce was at the table, pressed the button. The strange voice said:

Give me a mobile number, quickly.

Tom asking Noyce for a number, reading it off the card.

One *person take the money in a sports bag to the Melbourne Cricket Ground tomorrow. Sit at the* top *of the Great Southern Stand. Be there by half-time and wait for a call on the mobile number.* Understand?

Tom saying, *Yes.*

One person. Any funny *business* or *any sign of the* police, *you will never hear anything about the girl again. Understand?*

Tom saying, *Yes. What about the release of Anne?*

You'll *hear.*

Disconnection.

Silence in the room. Tom got up from the writing table. He was in weekend clothes: lightweight tweed jacket, cream woollen shirt.

'Well,' he said, looking at me. 'Over to you. Why the fuck the MCG?'

'This is Melbourne,' said Orlovsky, a finger moving

in the collar of his shirt, loosening the slippery nylon secondhand-shop tie. He straightened in his chair as if he were about to leave.

Eyes were upon him. Mr Calder's associate.

'Carlton plays Collingwood,' he said. 'Even kidnappers, they want the money but they want to support their team.'

Tom looked at Orlovsky for several seconds, the slate eyes, not a blink. Orlovsky looked back, the startlingly blue eyes, not a blink. Then Tom looked at Noyce, blaming him for Orlovsky. Noyce couldn't hold his gaze, accepted blame. I was sorry, because after Noyce, it was me, and I wasn't going to blink either.

'This is just the beginning,' said Barry.

Everyone looked at him. He was leaning against the doorjamb, not in golf clothes today. Today, it was grey, all grey, like a drug dealer or an architect or someone who owned a smart cafe designed by architects. Different glasses too, more oval than the day before, duck's egg shape, with a black rim.

'That's a fucking useful contribution, Barry,' said Tom. 'Matches your finest insights to date. And what a standard that is to live up to.'

In the air, contempt hung like flyspray.

'Big crowd,' I said. 'Easy to switch bags, lots of exits.'

Noyce said, 'Wouldn't they be scared that we'd

seal the ground, check bags?' He coughed, 'Sorry, silly, we're just paying up. Anxiety drives out common sense.'

'Depleting small reserves,' said Tom. 'Get a sports bag.' It was a bark.

I watched Noyce. He straightened his spine, made small masticating movements, opened his lips, not quite a smile, not quite a grimace. The set of his shoulders changed to favour his right side. Then he drew the back of the index finger of his right hand across his upper lip, put his hand behind his head. You can see these signs any time you care to stay late in the wrong pubs, get down to the hard core, just you and men who love life and beating the shit out of it.

'I'd like to say, Tom,' Noyce said, lawyer's smooth and reasonable voice but with a twang in it, the twang of taut piano wire, a little tremolo, 'that I won't be spoken to like that. Not in private. Or in public.'

Tom turned his body to Noyce, full on, challenge accepted. But he didn't have to fight Noyce, he could sack him on the spot. Or couldn't he? There was a moment of indecision, of calculation, of balancing things. Then Tom made a flicking gesture with his left hand. 'Point taken,' he said, no contrition in his low, throaty voice, in his movement only impatience. 'Let's get on to what has to be done.'

That wasn't enough for Noyce. He breathed out hard, nostrils flaring.

'Point taken? I'm not sure it is. I think I'd be better off walking out now and sending you my . . .'

'Graham,' said Barry Carson, his voice emphatic but entreating. He had come across the room, put his back to his brother, extended a hand to touch the sleeve of Noyce's jacket.

Noyce didn't look at Barry, didn't take his eyes off Tom. He had the look of a bullied schoolboy, scared, but determined to look his tormentor in the face.

Barry moved to block Noyce's view of Tom's face. He didn't want Noyce to leave. 'Don't take Tom so seriously, Graham,' he said. 'It's just that he's a man born to command. Pity they timed the wars so badly.'

'What the hell's goin' on?'

Pat Carson was at the door, leaning on a walking stick. Standing, grey suit loose on him, he looked closer to his age, but not much. He looked at Tom.

'Don't bother to tell the old man what's happenin'? That's the attitude, is it? I have to come to find out?'

He turned back towards his study. 'Frank, come and tell me,' he said over his shoulder.

I waited until he was well away, then I said to the Carson brothers, 'Would you like me to do that?'

Barry said, 'Yes. Thank you, Frank.'

Noyce cleared his throat. 'A sports bag,' he said, pride put aside for the moment. 'There must be a sports bag somewhere.'

'Tell Lauren to find one,' said Tom, tone a little less military this time.

I went down the passage, knocked on the open door. Pat was behind his desk again, chair swivelled sideways. The shutters were open and he was looking out at a paved, walled courtyard, a secret place, with low hedges and lemon trees growing in big pots. Without turning, he gestured for me to enter.

Standing, I told him about the phone call.

'What about lettin' her go?'

'Tom asked. He said: "You'll hear from us."'

Pat swivelled to face me, rubbed his jaw, studied me. Finally, he said, 'Don't be a policeman tomorrow, Frank. No police work. Just give 'em the money.'

I nodded. 'I'm in a giving mood.'

'And on the money subject, the advance on the fee, Graham give you that?'

'Yes.' It was in my jacket pocket: a hundred new hundred-dollar notes in an envelope. I didn't want to but I said, 'Thank you.'

He waved a hand dismissively, a hand like a big plucked wing. 'Mind you do what the bastards tell you. Nothin' more. Then we'll settle with 'em. By God, we will.'

TWO HUNDRED thousand dollars in fifties in a sports bag doesn't weigh much, a few kilos. In the VIP car park under the Great Southern Stand, tense in the stomach, I took the soft-leather Louis Vuitton bag out of the boot of Noyce's Mercedes, felt for his tiny mobile phone in my inside jacket pocket.

'Mr Calder?' A fair-haired young man in a business suit, club tie. He put out a hand. 'I'm Denzil Hobbes. I've been asked to meet you.'

Noyce had arranged the parking and the reception. It seemed a Carson company had a corporate box in the stand. Orlovsky was doing it harder. Not a Mercedes but his old Holden Premier, not a VIP parking spot but a long walk from across the river to a public entrance.

'It's pretty much a full house,' Hobbes said. 'I've got someone holding a seat for you. We can go up in the lift.'

'No,' I said, 'I'll walk. Just show me the stairs.'

'They're ramps actually,' he said. 'One in ten incline, very easy climbing. You haven't been here before?'

'No.'

'I'll show you the one to take. Ramps take eight abreast. In an emergency, we can clear the stand in twelve minutes.'

I nodded approvingly. It would be nice if people behaved that way, serried ranks of the terrified moving steadily downwards, eight abreast.

'I'll give you a card,' said Hobbes. 'Ring me if you need anything. Anything at all. When you get to the top, your seat is to the right. First seat to the right. Not the best view. The aisle seat in the back row. Just tap the man in it on the shoulder and introduce yourself. He's expecting you. Obviously.'

Obviously. This was Carson money talking.

'What about my colleague?' I said.

'He's up there. To your left, also on the aisle.'

Traffic was light on the way up. On the long way up. At the top, I came out into the pale grey afternoon light to a stunning scene, thousands upon thousands of people around the green circle, the stand seemingly leaning over it. Then a huge explosion of sound. Something had happened on the field, some event dramatic enough to cause all mouths to open.

CARLTON 38, COLLINGWOOD 17 said the scoreboard. Ten minutes from half-time.

I found the seat, tapped the occupant on the shoulder. Another young man in a suit, a small galaxy of spots on his broad brow. 'Calder,' I said.

He too wanted to shake hands, gave his name: Sean Rourke. Polite staff, well-groomed, the corporate box tenants would expect that.

When he'd gone, I looked left, looked away. Orlovsky was wearing a filthy anorak and holding a radio to his right ear. The Carsons hadn't been happy about him coming along. I took out the mobile phone, held it in my left hand, made sure I knew which button to press when it vibrated. Then, a girl's life at stake, I tried to concentrate on the game. Collingwood were playing a strange brand of football, going sideways, backwards, kicking to empty spaces, no central nervous system in control.

'Sweet Jesus, convent girls, want it, don't want it, they get it, they don't know where to fucken' put it,' said the man next to me, a Collingwood supporter, lean-faced, mostly unshaven, with scar tissue under his right eye and a nose set askew. He caught my eye. 'What I reckon,' he said to me, blast of raw alcohol in the breath, 'piss-poor coachin', that's what I reckon.'

'Me too,' I said. 'That's what I reckon.' Why did

he assume my support of Collingwood? It dawned on me: there were only two colours on display around us: jumpers, beanies, scarves, huge Mad Hatter's Teaparty hats, all in the sacred black and white, sin and purity, evil and innocence, the colours of certainty. This was Collingwood country.

'Get this inya,' said the skew-nosed man, warmed by our mutual contempt for the coach. He was offering a litre plastic bottle of an orange-brown liquid. I took a swig, felt tears start in my eyes, a prickling in my scalp follicles.

'Bottla Bundy in there,' said the man, not taking his eyes off the game. 'Carn ya fucken sheilas!'

Carlton were all over Collingwood until half-time, kicking another goal and a behind just before the siren.

We all stood up.

'Jesus,' said my new friend, 'just lie down and let the mongrels piss on 'em, that'd be better.' He drank some more from the plastic bottle. 'Speakin' of piss, I kin taste it. Comin?'

'I'm OK,' I said.

He squeezed past me. 'Watch the stuff, mate,' he said, cocking his head at his army-surplus canvas rucksack.

The tiny telephone vibrated in my hand, a sensuous feeling.

I pressed the button.

'Yes,' I said.

'Are you where you should be?' The electronic voice.

'Yes.'

'OK, this is what you do . . .'

You do what you're told to do. Afterwards, the crowd didn't hinder me as I walked up the stand, bent on leaving the stadium as quickly as possible. On the last ramp before the car park, I took off the beanie I'd paid a startled fan fifty dollars for, dropped it in a bin.

I didn't have any plans that included a Collingwood beanie.

'YOU MIGHT'VE hung onto a few thousand,' Orlovsky said, getting into the Mercedes with his briefcase, bringing in cold air, brushing rain off his scalp. 'Honesty's a much overrated virtue.'

'Not when it's the only one you've got,' I said. 'What'd you get?'

I had just finished my call to Noyce. We were on the St Kilda beachfront, near the lifesaving club, rain blowing off the bay. Only a few people out: two men in bright rain gear walking a fat and splay-footed black Labrador; an old woman, scarf tied under her chin above layers of sagging clothing; a small and threatening squad of inline skaters, indifferent to weather and fellow humans and gravity.

'Nothing. Call's from a payphone at Royal Melbourne Hospital.'

I was dispirited, watching the skaters. They were

coming up at speed behind the men with the dog, in formation, two tight ranks of three. Just when it seemed the front rank had to crash into the walkers, it parted, two left, one right, second rank following suit, going around the men and coalescing again like water flowing around a rock.

'One thing worth knowing, though.'

'Which is?'

'Camel,' he said.

'What?' I looked at him, startled. 'What's worth knowing?

'Driver's a secret Camel smoker.'

Orlovsky had opened the glovebox. Packed with packets of cigarettes, it glowed like a Walt Disney cave. With two fingers, he extracted a packet, put it in his inside jacket pocket.

'Yes, honesty's a much overrated virtue,' he said. 'There's something else. My original opinion was this dickhead thinks he can hide his voice with some primitive piece of shit from a mail-order catalogue. Wrong. He's no dickhead. That's worth knowing.'

Orlovsky's thumbs released the briefcase catches. The lid popped up. A laptop computer hidden in a battered leather briefcase.

'I borrowed this,' Orlovsky said. 'Box of tricks.' He switched on, did some key tapping.

Are you where you should be? said the electronic voice from the laptop speakers.

Yes. Me.

OK, this is what you do. If there's wrapping on the money, take it off. Then walk down to the front of the stand and throw the money off. All of it. Understand?

Yes.

Don't talk to anyone. We'll know. Just do it. Now.

My voice: *First tell us when we get the girl back.*

Do as you're told. Or the girl dies. Understand? Just do as you're told.

Mick tapped. Now a different electronic voice said the last words. He tapped again. Yet another eerie non-human voice. Then another one. And another.

'This is smart stuff,' Mick said. 'The boy didn't buy this machine anywhere. The Feds' voice ID software can't crack it.'

'You know that?'

'I know that.'

'You're hacking into the Feds' system. What's the penalty for that?'

'I'm not hacking. This is legitimate access.' He paused. 'Someone else's legitimate access.'

I sighed. 'We'd better get back to the Carsons. Maybe these pricks will let the girl go tonight.' I didn't think that was likely. To put it mildly.

'So they just did it to give the fans a treat?' said Mick, closing his briefcase. 'Wow. Maybe the two supporters' clubs got together and arranged it. Kidnapping. Could become a regular thing for clubs.'

'Get out,' I said.

'Sir.'

In Kooyong Road, in heavy traffic, he blinked his lights at me. I pulled over. He parked behind me and came to my window.

'This Merc's transmitting,' he said. 'Why would that be?'

'How do you know?'

'My box of tricks says so. Playing with it at the last lights.'

A tracking bug in Noyce's car? I looked at Mick. We had the same thought at the same instant. I reached into the back seat and got the empty leather sports bag, gave it to him.

In the rear-view mirror, I saw the interior light go on as he got into the Holden. It went off for a few seconds, went on and off as he got out again.

He gave me the bag back through the window. 'Maybe they're standard in bags like this,' he said. 'Sewn in by hand in Paris by an ancient Frog craftsman. Some cunt lifts your bag at the Hilton gym, you track him down, send your personal trainer over to kick the shit out of his personal trainer.'

All the way back to the Carson compound, cocooned in German steel and leather, wipers treating the drizzle with quiet contempt, I thought about Pat's study the day before, the grim faces, Pat's words:

This time, we're just payin'. What they ask, we're payin'. It's only bloody money, it's nothin'. The child safe. That's what we want. That's all.

A bug in the money bag. Someone hadn't embraced the philosophy of *This time, we're just payin'*. Someone wanted to know where the money went. Someone wanted to do police work.

Noyce was on the terrace. As I opened the car door, he said, 'They rang a few minutes ago. It's a bit frightening.'

THIS EVENING, the Carson boys had been joined in the elegant library by a woman. She was thin, in a loose sweater and jeans, blonde hair on her shoulders, sitting upright in an armchair, arms folded, whisky glass on a drum table. At first glance, she looked like a teenager, but then you saw the lines bracketing her mouth, the little frown pinched between her eyes. She was probably in her early thirties.

'Stephanie, this is Frank Calder,' said Noyce. He frowned as Orlovsky appeared in the doorway. Mick was neatly dressed and clean-shaven but he always managed to give the impression that he'd escaped from somewhere.

'And this is his associate, Michael Orlovsky. Mrs Chadwick is Tom's daughter, Anne's aunt.'

Stephanie Chadwick stood up and shook hands. She was tall, Orlovsky's height, only a head below me. When you knew the relationship, you could see her father in her, in the eyes and the jaw and in a certain arrogance of carriage.

Tom Carson was standing behind his daughter, smoking a panatella, in a dark suit now, his face clean and dry from the second shave of the day, drinking something colourless, rattling the ice in the glass.

Barry was seated at the table, no drink, also in a suit. He nodded at us. He had the look of a man who had undergone an ordeal, didn't trust himself to speak.

'Play it, Graham,' said Tom, no bark in his voice this time.

Noyce played it.

Tom Carson.

Pause.

So you think Carson money can buy anything, don't you? Just money, that's what you thought, isn't it?

Pause.

Tom: *We've followed your instructions.*

Becoming less *stupid.* Learning *to do what you're told and ...*

Tom: *We've done that. Now ...*

Shut up. Don't say NOW to me. I don't take your orders. I don't need your money.

Tom: *All we want ...*

Shut up, I'm talking to you. You're not talking to your tame cops now. You don't have the money to buy your way out of this. You're talking to someone quite different now. Do you hear me? Hear me, cunt?

Tom: *We'll do whatever you want . . .*

I WANT YOU TO SUFFER AS YOU HAVE MADE OTHERS SUFFER. I WANT YOU TO FEEL PAIN AS YOU HAVE MADE OTHERS FEEL PAIN. I WANT YOU TO BLEED TO DEATH.

Click.

No one said anything for a while, the harsh electronic voice reverberating in the room. Then Stephanie took a big drink of whisky. I looked at my watch. It was just on 6 p.m. 'Can we watch the news on Seven somewhere?' I said.

Noyce found a remote control. A section of panelling on the right-hand wall parted, revealing a large television monitor. He clicked twice more. We watched commercials and previews before a woman newsreader with a starched and ironed face appeared. She did the *There were amazing scenes today* preamble. Then we saw a man wearing dark glasses and a Collingwood beanie pulled down to his eyebrows on the top level of the Great Southern Stand. He stood at the parapet, reached into a bag, threw handfuls of paper into the air. Some of the bits of paper blew backwards into the stand behind him, some fluttered down and were sucked into the packed tiers below, others drifted down onto the field, where people jumped the fence and a feeding frenzy developed. After half-a-dozen handfuls, the thrower got bored, tipped the bag over the edge, shook it. Large wads of paper fell out. The camera zoomed in on the paper-thrower but my collar was up and I kept my chin down. Then I turned and walked up the ramp.

The voiceover said:

A police spokesman said it was a miracle that no one was seriously injured in the near-riots that developed as football fans fought over the new fifty-dollar notes. No exact figure is available on the sum of money thrown from the Great Southern Stand by the unknown man, but police put the amount at more than a hundred thousand dollars.

We cut to a Collingwood supporter, a woman wearing a black and white sweater and scarf and holding a fifty-dollar note in each hand for the camera. 'One bloke caught seven fifties, stuck together,' she said. 'They was fallin' like rain.' She had a tooth missing next to her left canine, itself a yellow, endangered outcrop.

Noyce switched off the set, and the panels reunited at the behest of the remote.

'Well,' said Tom, looking at me. 'A fucking novel way to redistribute wealth. What point are we at now?'

'At the point where we phone the cops,' I said. 'You're not dealing with the greedy. The unhinged, that's what you've got here. And this is personal.'

'No,' said Tom. 'The old man says no. I agree.'

'He's heard this person?'

Tom nodded. 'We've shown we're willing to pay, not to bring in the police, we should take the next step.'

'I'm not getting this over to you,' I said. 'Next step? Who says there's a next step? If I understand the message, and it's not in fucking code – excuse me, Ms Chadwick – this isn't about money. It's about causing you pain. You personally possibly, maybe the whole family. Pain. Lots of pain. It's not a commercial transaction. Not buyers and sellers. They want to hurt you and the ultimate hurt is killing the girl.'

I paused. 'Don't you think you should let the girl's parents decide whether to call in the cops?'

Silence.

The Carsons didn't want to look at each other, didn't want to look at me. Finally, Barry said, 'We're having trouble getting hold of Mark. It may be a while before we can reach him.'

I pushed on. 'Her mother, then.'

Tom wasn't going to be pushed. He drew on the panatella, exhaled in a resigned way, said in a level tone, not unpleasant, 'Frank, we're not paying you

67

for that kind of advice. We don't need that kind of advice.'

Tightness in my face, around the eyes, the mouth. I paid attention to the feeling. When you know that the rational part of your brain is no longer in full control, you can do something about that. Or not.

I looked at the carpet, at nothing, took my time, looked up, at Tom, he didn't blink, a hard buyer in a buyer's market, at Barry, who met my gaze, flicked his eyes downwards, away, and at Stephanie, whose expression carried a hint of apology for her father.

'OK,' I said, steady now. 'It's not clear to me what you're paying me for. But, since you are paying, let me say that we may be in for a long wait. And sooner or later, you will call in the police. If they release Anne, if they don't, at some point you have to call the cops. So, things we can do now will save hours, days maybe, when that happens.'

'Such as?'

'Ask the basic questions. Try to get some feeling for who these people might be. I don't think we risk spooking them. Fifty cops around the record store, yes. Two blokes looking around, no. And get Jahn, Cullinan to draw up a list of ex-employees who might have a grudge. Going back five years. That'll save lots of time when the crunch comes.'

There was a moment when Tom was poised to

say no. I could see it in his eyes, in the way he moved his head.

Stephanie had an unlit cigarette in her mouth, tilted her head back to look up at her father. 'Yes,' she said, 'I agree with Frank. We can't just sit here hoping it'll turn out well if we throw bags of money at them. And that voice, my God, that's not someone you can buy off. That's someone . . . I don't know. Hates.'

Tom looked down at her.

'Frank's right, Dad,' she said.

He sighed, put his hand on her shoulder. 'I'll talk to the old man.'

'One more thing,' I said. 'If anyone has even the vaguest suspicion about who these people might be, some personal grudge perhaps, this is the time to tell me.'

Silence. Tom shrugged. Barry shrugged. Stephanie and Noyce shook their heads.

'What about Mark?'

'No,' said Tom. 'Mark's been a fool in business but he doesn't have enemies like that.'

CARMEN GEARY didn't seem to be in shock over the disappearance of her friend. She looked me over as if I were applying for a position for which looks were important. Her own looks put her closer to twenty than any fifteen-year-old should be, a long-legged girl-woman with gleaming dark hair that had continually to be pushed away, theatrically, from her face.

'The man,' I said. 'Can you describe him?'

She blinked her lashes at me. 'Sure. Old. Sort of dirty-looking, glasses with thick lenses . . .'

'Dirty. What, like unshaven?'

'No. Not unshaven, just sort of dirty, y'know.'

'The glasses. Shape?'

'Big old-fashioned ones, squarish, with thick black frames.'

'Thick lenses?'

'No, don't think so.'

'How far away?'

'Close. Over there, sort of.' She pointed at the window wall.

'Anything else about him?'

'The cap. A red cap.'

'A baseball cap?'

She nodded. 'Makita logo on it.'

We were upstairs in Pat Carson's mansion, in a comfortably furnished sitting room with French doors to a balcony. Carmen's mother, Lauren, was next door, in an office with filing cabinets and a computer on a neat desk. 'It's like running a medium-size hotel,' she'd said on the way upstairs. 'I was housekeeper at three Hiltons. This is much the same.'

'Although in hotels even the most troublesome guests eventually leave,' I said.

She laughed. It was a deep, good-natured laugh. 'There is that to look forward to in hotels,' she said.

I asked the question on my mind. 'Does the remuneration here include school fees?'

Lauren laughed again. 'That was Mr Pat Carson's idea. He said, "When you live with the family and look after the family, you're part of the family. And so your child goes to school where the Carsons go."'

Now I said to Carmen, 'You saw him three times and he was there when you went into the store and still there when you came out.'

Hair brushed away, fingers flicking outwards. 'No.

He was still there the first two times. The third time he wasn't. Frank. Trams come all the time, so he wasn't waiting for a tram.'

'When was the last time you saw him?'

'On Thursday.'

'What time was that?'

Carmen shifted in her chair, recrossed her legs in her short skirt. 'Twenty past four, around then.'

'That wouldn't give you much time in the store.'

'No. We're only there twenty-five minutes, something like that.' Hand flicking hair. 'How old are you, Frank?'

I ignored the question. 'What sport do you play at school, Carmen?'

'Sport? Oh, tennis.' She was scratching her head. 'And swimming. We swim. What do you play? Do you work out?'

'Does Anne have anyone special she talks to at the record shop?'

'Special?' She smiled, head on one side, lips well apart showing perfect teeth, a cover-girl smile, asked the mock-naive question. 'You mean, like a boy?'

'Something like that, yes.'

'Not really. Well, boys are always coming on to you. I bet girls come on to you. Do they?'

'Not since I stopped washing ten years ago,' I said, unsmiling. 'So there's no boyfriend?'

She had her right hand at her face. 'Boyfriend? No. No boyfriend.'

'And you'd know, wouldn't you?'

She spoke from behind her fingers, the other hand running up and down her left thigh. 'Wouldn't everyone? This place's a jail. Everyone's paranoid.'

'On Thursday, you came out about 4.50 when you couldn't find Anne.'

'Yes.'

'Crowded, the store?'

'Yes. Lots of kids.' Carmen was moistening her upper lip with a tongue tip, a perfectly pink arrowhead.

'Often get separated when you're in the store?'

'Well, if you're talking to someone else, you don't notice what the person you're with's doing. But quarter to five's when Dennis picks us up, so I looked around, couldn't see her, went all over the place.' She looked down. 'I got a bit scared.'

'That's being paranoid, is it?'

Carmen sniffed. 'Bit, I suppose.'

'Happened before? Couldn't find Anne?'

Wide eyes on me. 'No.'

'What did Dennis do when you went to the car and told him?'

'Double-parked. We went back in and looked again. Then Dennis got the call on his mobile.'

'The call?'

'From Graham. About the kidnap call to Anne's grandpa.'

I sat back, elbows on the chair arms, fingers interlocked, and looked into her eyes.

'That's the chaplain's look,' said Carmen. 'He does that, he's a spunk, a girl in another class saw him in St Kilda at one in the morning with this, like, real tart . . .'

'On a mission of mercy, no doubt,' I said, standing, feeling the pain in my leg. 'Thanks for talking to me, Carmen. Think about Thursday, anything could be important.'

'You're a Capricorn, aren't you?' she said, head on one side again, all front teeth on show. 'Can't be faithful.'

'Can't even be hopeful,' I said. 'There's one other thing I just remembered. The school says neither of you has played any sport this term. On Tuesdays or Thursdays. So you'd have to be doing something else on Tuesdays and Thursdays, wouldn't you.'

I gave her a while to answer, held her eyes, not smiling. Then I said, 'It's what you don't tell me you'll be sorry about.'

Her pink tongue came out again and licked a lower lip as red and full as a late-season plum.

'His name's Craig,' she said. 'That's all I know, I swear.'

THE DRIVER'S quarters were in an overgrown brick cottage ten metres from the stairs leading to the Carsons' basement car park. There was always a driver on call, night and day, said Noyce.

Whitton came to the door with his jacket on, ready for work.

'A few more words,' I said.

'Sure, right, come in.'

We went in. 'This is Michael Orlovsky. He works with me.'

Whitton put out his right hand. Orlovsky kept his hands in his pockets, nodded.

The staff did well in the Carson compound. Whitton's room looked as if it had been done by a decorator, tweeds and checks and a group of architectural prints on a wall.

'Sit down,' I said and I went over to look at the prints, precise drawings of small and elegant buildings, some with domes and pillars and steps, one a tapering tower with a curiously fluted roof. For a time in my early adolescence, I'd had dreams about being an architect, taken books out of the library, tried to copy the illustrations I liked. 'Don't be so pathetic, Frank,' my mother said one day. 'Only babies copy things.' I didn't do any more copying, tore up my drawings, didn't take out any more books on buildings.

Whitton sat on the edge of a sofa, pale eyes uneasy, blinking rapidly. 'So what can I . . .'

'What can you?' I said. 'What can you?' I moved to look at the view from the window. A small vegetable garden, then a wall. There were brick paths between the dormant beds, dark soil mounded like plump graves and, against the wall, a low lean-to glasshouse.

'What I told you on Thursday,' Whitton said, 'that's pretty much it.'

I didn't look at him. Who had lived in this cottage, worked in the kitchen garden? The Carsons had bought up the whole block, all their neighbours and their neighbours' neighbours, consolidated the properties, taken down the fences, encircled the whole with a barrier, only two entries, gates and cameras. That the Carson family might live here free from fear, immune to the envy and resentment of those beyond the walls. But only here. They still had to leave the sanctuary, go into the world, onto the streets, into the city, see the passing world through windows, pale teenagers with chemical eyes, poor people clutching plastic bags holding a gas-ripened tomato and two hundred grams of fatty mince, sad men with mortuary stubble eking out their days. Even sitting in the Merc at the lights, cool in summer, just right in winter, the Carsons had no choice but to hear the crude and throaty menace of bored-out Holdens beside them, feel the redline bass from eight speakers penetrating their German monocoque, vibrating it, violating it.

'Pretty much it,' he said again, voice tight.

I turned and looked at him. His face was tight too, pale, colour gone from the flesh, dying fish colour, blood gone elsewhere, to where it was most needed.

'Fucked her,' I said. 'Fifteen.'

His head was pointed left, he shook it a few times, changed his mind, made a rocking movement with his body, still didn't look at me.

'Fucked her,' I said.

Whitton closed his eyes. He looked much younger that way, spiky eyelashes, spears, a fence of eyelashes. Moisture appeared, a rim of liquid, tears, trembling, a sigh could break the surface tension.

He sniffed, shook his head, the heart's pure waters broke, rolled down his face, met his lips.

79

'Shit,' he said. 'Just once, just once.'

I sat down in a comfortable armchair opposite Whitton, leaned back, stared at him, waited for him.

He kept his gaze down, wiped his cheeks with the back of his right hand. 'Carmen tell you?'

'What kind of jobs you going for after this?' I said.

He put his big hands between his knees, squeezed them with his thighs. 'You don't know her,' he said. 'It's not like she's a little girl. Had two blokes rootin' her in her room at Portsea in January, the one's about thirty, maybe more, rubbish she picked up on the beach, they ring her on her mobile, she let 'em in the gate at two in the morning.'

'I don't want to know her,' I said. 'I want to find her. So let's move on from this What-I-told-you-on-Thursday-that's-pretty-much-it shit.'

I took the tiny tape recorder out of my inside jacket pocket and put it on the coffee table.

'Everything,' I said. 'Don't leave out a fucking thing.'

When he'd finished, I said, 'Draw me a map. Show me exactly where you dropped Anne.'

Whitton was in the kitchen looking for paper when my mobile rang.

'I'm home, got the slippers on, sitting here with a beer, in about twenty minutes we're eating octopus.

Caught today by my cousin. And where the fuck you?'

Detective Senior Sergeant Vella. It was Saturday.

'Is that octopus Italian style?'

'No. This is octopus cooked in the Mongolian style. You sew it up in a goat's bladder, full, and . . .'

'Say no more. Twenty minutes, I'm there.'

Whitton came out and showed me a piece of paper, neatly drawn map. 'Here's the school,' he said.

I looked, folded the paper, put it in my shirt pocket.

He took a pace backwards, exercised his thick neck. 'Me and Anne,' he said, licking his lips. 'You got to understand, she's the one . . .'

I shook my head. 'I don't have to understand. I don't care. I'm not telling anyone. Yet. I might not, depends. Just stay close. I don't want to have to look for you.'

Orlovsky and I walked back to our quarters in the Garden House, through what resembled a small park, gusty night, oak trees shaking, shedding leaves like big flakes of dandruff. Orlovsky said, deeply scornful, 'You like this kind of stuff, don't you? Army, cops, you're cross-trained in arsehole skills.'

I breathed deeply, no smell of pollution here, only wet greenery: the rich have power over the wind. 'Listen, wimp,' I said, 'your kind are the first ones

ring for a cross-trained arsehole when they hear
oise in the night.'

'Ah,' he said, 'but does he come?'

SUNDAY MORNING at 9 a.m. with a hangover is a good time to knock on people's doors and ask them questions without having any identification. But Orlovsky, coming from the other end of the genteel Brighton block, hit the paydirt quickly. He fetched me.

'Mrs Neill, this is my associate, Frank Calder,' said Orlovsky, smiling at me.

I shook her hand. She was in her seventies, at least, straight back, hair whipped into stiff peaks like egg white, two-piece tweed suit suitable for church. Anglican, probably.

'I endured it for two weeks,' she said. 'Tuesdays and Thursdays. Then I adopted my late husband's attitude. Thus far and no farther. He also believed in confronting your fears and mocking them. To the very end, I may say.'

'What did you do?' I said.

83

'I simply marched out there and knocked on the window. His head was leaning against it. Gave him no end of a fright. The Lord knows how they can be in a confined space with noise like that. I swear the whole vehicle was moving.'

'And?'

'Well, he wound down the window, my dear, and the noise was even worse and I said, I shouted, this is a residential street and you are making enough noise to wake the dead. So he switched off the record player, whatever those things are, and he turned out to be a rather nice young man, rings in his ears but rather nice. Very apologetic. Took me aback. I was ready for a fight.'

I took out the photograph of Anne. 'The girl who got into the vehicle, is this her?'

It was a recent photograph, taken by Carmen in January at the Carson house at Portsea. Anne was sitting on a low white wall, laughing, a big piece of dirty-blonde hair falling forward. I could see Whitton's point. In a black one-piece bathing suit cut high in the legs and low in front, there was nothing of the gawky adolescent about her. No barman would have asked her for ID.

Without hesitation. 'Yes. Pretty girl in a raincoat. A yellow raincoat, one of those plastic ones.'

A raincoat to cover her school uniform.

'What did he look like, apart from the rings in his ear?' I said.

'Ears. Both of them, three or four little rings. Well, he was darkish. Mediterranean, I would say. If one's allowed to these days. Hair combed back.'

'About what age, would you say?'

'Oh, I'm hopeless at ages. They all look so young. Twenty-five perhaps.'

'Long hair?'

She thought. 'No, not long, not short, tidy hair, little sideburns.'

'Moustache, beard?'

'No. Has he done something?'

'It's possible.'

'Well, he was a tradesman, I'm sure of that.'

'What makes you sure?'

'Overalls. He was wearing those overalls they wear a tee-shirt under. Winter and summer. Don't seem to feel the cold, tradesmen, have you noticed that?'

'It's their training,' said Orlovsky.

'Also, I could see tools and things in the back.'

'Tools?' I said.

'A sort of saw thing, a power thing. And a cabinet with drawers, a metal cabinet. Against the side.'

'Anything else?'

She paused, moved her head in a birdlike way. 'He must like boxing.'

'Why's that?'

'He had two boxing gloves tattooed on his arm, high up, just peeking out of his sleeve. With a little key under them. And two tiny boxing gloves hanging from the mirror, you know the way some people hang things in their cars? Quite dangerous, I think. Distracting.'

I asked more questions but the well was dry. We said our thanks.

In his car, Orlovsky said, 'Anne the poor little rich girl and Craig the crafty tradesman. Probably rooting while the brother or the cousin makes the phone calls.'

I shook my head. 'I don't think so. It's too stupid. Carmen knows his name, Anne knows Whitton's seen her getting out of a yellow fucktruck. Anyway, the bloke's got a trade.'

'There's that,' said Orlovsky, starting the car. 'Something to fall back on.'

'Boxing gloves.'

'I like those fat pink dice.'

'On his arm. Any decent coffee around here?'

'What do you think these Brighton moneypuppies do on a Sunday morning? Sit in the park with a stubby?'

He was right. The sleek inhabitants of the bayside suburb were in the shopping area eyeing one another, drinking coffee, having breakfast, reading the *Sunday*

Age through dark glasses, talking on their mobiles. We found a table on the pavement outside a place called Zacco, ordered coffee.

'The verb to earn,' said Orlovsky, looking around. 'The very concept of earning.'

'What?' Since he didn't bother with preambles, it was often hard to work out what Orlovsky was talking about.

'Nothing that someone whose entirely non-productive life has been paid for out of the public purse would grasp.'

'Earning? I grasp the concept with ease. They want it, you do it, they pay you, you've earned it.'

He closed his eyes and shook his head in a pitying and dismissive way. 'Stick to killing people, Frank, that's what you're good at.'

A young woman wearing a long white apron such as might be worn on the Left Bank in Paris put our coffees on the table.

Orlovsky put twenty grains of sugar into his short black, stirred it with the stem of his spoon. 'You don't seem to be considering the possibility that this is the second grab by the same people,' he said. 'Can I be privy to your thoughts, master?'

I took a sip, burnt my tongue. 'No point in considering it,' I said. 'Got any idea what the cops would've thrown at the Alice kidnapping? They'd have turned over every last person and dog with a possible grudge against the family. Down to the sacked Carson office boys and the miffed Carson hairdressers. That leaves people just doing it for the money. I'm taking the eccentric view that people like that don't wait seven years and then have another go at the same family. They move on. World's full of rich families.'

Orlovsky thought about this for a while, then he nodded in an unconvinced way and said in a musing tone, 'A tradesman called Craig. How many would there be? Thousands, probably the name of choice for tradesmen.'

'A boxer called Craig,' I said. 'How do you find a boxer called Craig?'

We drank coffee. Orlovsky took on his meditative look, gaze upwards, hands in his lap. There was a quality about the tranquil Orlovsky that made people look away lest he come out of it and catch them looking at him.

I looked away, studied our fellow members of sidewalk society. A table within earshot were behaving as if being filmed, assuming poses, bursting into fake laughter, talking with hands, touching hair and skin. A plump man in an advertising agency's idea of yachting wear was in charge, conducting the ensemble.

A boxer called Craig. There would be a boxing association, a federation, some body that registered boxers. He might not be registered now. About twenty-five, Mrs Neill thought. Get all the Craigs for the past ten years. Would our Craig live on this side of the city? How far would a tradesman drive for a quickie in the back of his van? In the case of Anne Carson, going by the photograph, to the ends of the earth, probably.

'Heraldic,' Orlovsky said, still looking upward.

I paid no attention, had the last sip of black, the last tablespoon.

'Give me that little telephone of yours,' said Orlovsky. 'And a pen.'

I gave them to him.

He pulled out a paper napkin from the dispenser, laid it flat, punched numbers. 'Melbourne,' he said, 'Boxer, that's B-O-X-E-R, business, yes. Boxer something. I don't have an address.'

He waited. I waited.

I shook my head.

'That would be it,' he said. 'Dandenong. Right.' He listened, wrote numbers on the napkin, shut down the mobile, closed the flap, gave it back to me. 'You see gloves, you think boxer, pugilist. A literal mind, best suited to mundane tasks like killing people.'

'Tell me.'

'The key,' he said. 'The heraldic key.'

WE PARKED on the stained tarmac apron of a firm called Dollakeen Kitchens in the light industrial area of Dandenong, a part of Greater Melbourne that doesn't get mentioned in the newspaper suggestions for ten fun places to go on a Sunday. Orlovsky chose Dollakeen because its front gate was open and telephone inquiries had no number for it.

I was reading the paper and Orlovsky was leaning against the driver's door smoking one of his stolen Camels when the vehicle drove in the entrance and pulled up on his side, a few metres away.

The driver got out and walked around, came between the vehicles, a young man in a silky tracksuit, medium height, big shoulders and a bodybuilder's neck. I got out and stretched, walked around and leaned against the driver's door.

'G'day,' the man said. 'My old man tell youse I need some ID before I open anythin'? Like somethin' with the business name on it, somethin like that.'

'Sure,' said Orlovsky, putting his right hand into his jacket. 'And your name is . . . ?'

'Craig Boxer,' said the man. 'Boxer Locks.'

Orlovsky was close to him, side-on, getting closer. 'Craig,' he said, looking into his inside pocket. 'Now what have we here. Wallet . . . ah.'

He brought his right hand out of his jacket, nothing in it, fingers half-closed, punched Craig Boxer under the nose with the heel of his hand. Boxer made a noise, a yelping sound, fell backwards against the yellow Ford van, rocking it. As he was bringing up his hands to the blood pouring from his nose, Orlovsky kicked his legs out from under him. Craig hit the tarmac hard, banging his head against the van. Blood went out from him in an arc.

In the van, I could see the little gloves hanging from the rear-view mirror. They were swinging.

'Fuck,' said Craig, through his hands. He sounded like someone with a bad cold. A bad cold and a bad nosebleed.

'That's a little hello from the Carson family,' I said. 'Anne's family.'

Craig was trying to get up. He took one hand

from his face, put it on the ground, put some weight on it.

Orlovsky kicked him just above the elbow, not very hard. Craig's arm went behind him and he screamed in pain and fell over sideways.

'Don't move,' Orlovsky said. He walked around the body carefully and put his left foot on Craig's head. 'Just answer when you're spoken to.'

'Where's Anne?' I said.

Blood was pooling under Craig's head. 'Dunno,' he said. 'Jesus, fuck.'

'Anne's missing,' I said. 'She's been kidnapped. But you'd know that, Craig.'

'No,' he said, visible eye showing lots of white. 'No, fuck no.'

'Fifteen-year-old schoolgirl. Fucked and kidnapped by you,' I said.

'Christ, fuck, no.' He had good clotting power. The blood flow had stopped.

'No?' said Orlovsky. He ground Craig's face into the tarmac, into his own blood, with his sole. 'No? Did I hear you say no?'

'Said she was seventeen,' Craig said from under Orlovsky's shoe. 'Christ, I'm sorry.'

'Kidnapping,' I said. 'You're going to be in the papers, Craig. On TV. Go to jail for ever. Where's Anne?'

'Don't know,' he said, eye rolling. 'Dropped her

on Thursday, was gonna pick her up Tuesday. Jesus, I don't know, please.'

I didn't say anything for a while. Quiet place on a Sunday, the Dandenong light industrial area, just the even murmur of traffic on the Princes Highway, somewhere a yard dog barking.

'I'm going to ask you once more, Craig,' I said. 'If I don't like the answer, the man standing on you is going to kick your head off. It'll take a coupla kicks but he'll get there.' I cleared my throat. 'Where's Anne?'

'Swear to God my witness don't know. Please. Went around the corner in Armadale, that's . . .'

'She phone you, Craig? Get any calls from her?'

'No, no, no calls, just pick her up Tuesday and Thursday.'

Orlovsky was grinding him again, grinding him, but looking at me and shaking his head in sorrow.

'Nothing, done nothing, no calls, I swear, oh Jesus . . .'

I nodded at Orlovsky. He took his foot off the man, stepped back. 'Sit up, Craig,' I said. 'Lean against the van.'

For a moment, he was too scared to move. Then he raised himself fearfully to his hands and knees, turned his face towards me. The right side and his neck and chest were dark with blood and bits of grit and grime were pressed into his skin.

'Sit back,' I said.

He sat back, torso rigid, hands to his face, looking at Orlovsky in fear.

'Craig,' I said, 'I don't think you kidnapped Anne. I think all you're guilty of is screwing an under-age girl. From a rich family. That's naughty but it's only going to get you two, three years' jail. Sex offender, young, some bloke'll make you his girl. You know what they like to do? After you blow them, they piss in your mouth. It's a power thing. Use your mouth for a toilet. Stand back and aim. Make you swallow, how's that?'

He closed his eyes. 'Seventeen, I swear to almighty God she told me that. Never touched her otherwise, never, never, my old man'd kill me.'

'Where'd you drop her, Craig, on Thursday?'

'Revesdale Street, park in the loading zone outside the florist there. She goes up the street, down the lane.'

'Lane?'

His nose was swelling rapidly. 'Like a lane near the end, service lane? For the shops.'

'Why'd she do that? Go down the lane?'

Craig hawked. I looked away, heard him spit. 'There's a door into the music place, saves goin' round the corner.'

'That day, see anything unusual? Notice anything?'

He shrugged. 'Well, y'know, we were sort of sayin' goodbye . . . kissin', I don't . . .' His eyes flicked to Orlovsky. 'Didn't know she was fifteen, I swear.'

'Anything unusual?'

'No, she got out, come around to my side, she's always lookin' around.'

'Why's that?'

'Reckons she could be watched. Her family. Paranoid, she says. Like she sees this bloke, she goes, second time, that could be a Carson spy only he's not bad-lookin'.'

'She saw someone twice. In Revesdale Street?'

'Yeah. Just a bloke, not even lookin' at us.'

'Where in the street?'

'The other side, further down.'

'Opposite the lane?'

He frowned, hawked again. I closed my eyes.

'Suppose. Yeah.'

'This's on Thursday? The second time?'

'Nah. Tuesday she said that.'

'You didn't see him on Thursday?'

'Nah. Like I was in a hurry Thursday. Job in Noble Park, my old man's on the mobile, we didn't . . .' He stopped. 'Just dropped her, like. Had to get back. I swear . . .'

I straightened up, went over and stood above him. Between fingertips, I took a few hairs on his scalp, a small clump, twisted them, pulled. 'Tell your mates about all this, Craig?'

He winced, shook his head, found that too painful. 'Never said a word, Jesus, never told anyone. I'm engaged, her family'll murder me.'

I didn't say anything, looked around, weighed and measured the quality of the moment: three men on a strip of stained concrete, mournful wind worrying at the tin buildings around us, making them creak and whine and croon and speak of failure and loneliness, and this one man so scared that he could evacuate his bowels at any moment.

All these things reminded me of why I'd thought I would be happier growing things.

I let go of the twist of hair, put my hand under the man's chin, cupped it. 'Craig,' I said, 'don't go away, don't say a word to anyone about today.'

Relief in his eyes.

'Look at me.'

He couldn't look up at me, just sniffed and said, 'Not a word, I swear, I promise you.'

'Do that, your lovely bride-to-be's family won't have to murder you. Why's that?'

He nodded, eyes closed.

On the way back, in the sluggish highway traffic, I said, not looking at Orlovsky, 'Arsehole skills. Not too rusty, are they?'

He took a long time to answer, lit another stolen Camel, one of the last. 'The difference between us,' he said, 'is that I'm just doing this for the money. You're another matter entirely.'

'ONE OF those things with sliding doors,' said the tweed-jacketed Malcolm Cherry of Hayes & Cherry, a narrow shop in Revesdale Street that sold bathroom fittings. 'A pretty battered one with curtained windows. Tarango? Durango? A name like that. People movers, I understand they're called. What does that make your ordinary car?'

I looked at the price tag on an impressive piece of plumbing, chrome-plated pipes forming a sort of shower cage. Showering once a day, roughly a dollar a shower for twenty years. 'This is not your ordinary shower,' I said.

'Nice, isn't it? Prince Philip has one.'

'He always looks clean. This vehicle?'

'Parked in our loading zone. People do it all the time. Run off to get something, back in minutes. There's a marvellous deli two doors down. Some of them are coming in here, God forbid you'd complain.'

'But the people mover?'

'Repeat offender. Not the vehicle, the people in it. Before they were in an old station wagon. White.'

'The same people. You're sure? How many?'

'Absolutely. Two. The vehicle pulls up, passenger gets out, well, falls out is closer. He could use a shower. He's always in a tracksuit. A garment not too familiar with the Surf, I can tell you. And a baseball cap. Red.'

'Anything on the cap? A logo, anything?'

'Makita. And he wears these huge runners. Big plastic things. Like boats. Grotesque. And off he goes. Then the driver has the effrontery to think he can lounge around until the other creature comes back.'

'Did you get a look at him, the driver?'

'Not a good look. Too much facial hair. And dark glasses and some kind of headgear. It looked like a back-to-front cap with the peak cut off. Strange.'

'The passenger. Wear glasses?'

'Those ghastly black frames like Buddy Holly. Or is that Roy Orbison?'

'How old?'

'Hard to say. Fifties. More.'

'And this happened again on Thursday with a different vehicle?'

'Again, only worse.' Malcolm Cherry flicked a finger at something on his tie. 'This Tangelo thing pulls up and, lo and behold, the older dero-type gets out. Wearing the cap. I thought, bugger this, this time I'm ringing the council, get the bloody parking inspector around here from wherever he's hiding. I'm at the back, on the phone, waiting for someone to answer, when the vehicle leaves.'

'What time was this?'

'Just before five, I suppose. But hold on, hold on. A minute later, the young fellow who works part-time here goes out and what does he find?'

I could feel the tiny pulse in my throat. I shook my head.

'The bloody vehicle's in the lane. Someone's reversed it into the lane. That's private property. Only three businesses are entitled to use the lane. Us, the record store and the florist. I said to James, that's it, and I'm out the front door.'

He paused. 'And at that moment, out comes the Tarango or whatever and off it goes.'

'Didn't get the rego, did you?'

'No. Didn't really think about it. Get it next time.'

'What was he doing in the lane? Young fellow see anything?'

'James says the driver was just closing the sliding door when he walked by. Wasn't picking up anything from the shops, checked straight away. Business vehicles only, that's the agreement.'

'James,' I said, 'I wouldn't mind a word with him.'

Malcolm looked at his watch, a big chrome-plated deep-sea diver's instrument, the sort of thing you wouldn't be scared to wear in the Prince Philip shower cage. 'He went off for a coffee just before you came in. Be back any minute.'

I went for a walk down the street, around the corner, in the glass side door of TRIPLE ZERO!, the record store. I was in a small vestibule, pulsating music audible, facing another door. I opened it and the sound was like a blow to the whole upper body. It hit you, then it invaded you, stuck probes up your nose, into your mouth. My fillings seemed to be transmitting sound and I could taste them. I subdued the impulse to flee, stood my ground. When my brain accepted that it could function in these conditions, I went around the bend into the long leg of the store. It didn't look like a place that sold recorded music. It looked like a series of minimalist lounges separated by Art Deco pillars, teenagers sitting around, standing, in groups, in pairs, alone. Near the entrance was what looked like a bar from some fifties film. It was all so casual, not a store, a hangout. But when you walked around, you could see there were clear lines of sight from the bar and from a glass window in a partition wall and there were camera pinholes everywhere. Management didn't want their radical store to also serve as a shootin' and rootin' gallery.

I walked around. No one paid any attention to me. With a bigger crowd, you could lose sight of another person in here, no doubt about that. But Carmen hadn't lost sight of Anne because on Thursday she wasn't with Anne. She was waiting for Anne to arrive from trucking with Craig. Then they would step out the front entrance and into Whitton's double-parked car and get home at the expected sports day time. Conspirators all.

There was no point in looking for Anne on Thursday's security video because she was never in the store. Anne didn't get to the end of the laneway, to the delivery door into TRIPLE ZERO! There was a vehicle in the lane. To reach the door, she had to pass between it and the wall. Perhaps the vehicle's sliding side door was open. Perhaps someone came around the back as she was abreast of the door. Perhaps the person took her by the shoulders and pushed her into the vehicle. Perhaps there was someone else inside, someone who dragged her in, put something over her face, prevented her screaming . . .

I went back to Hayes & Cherry. Malcolm introduced me to James, a fair-haired teenager so clean and so dapper that he appeared to be genetically destined to sell aids to cleanliness and grooming.

'Tall,' he said. 'And thin. Wearing a beanie and dark glasses.'

'Beard? Moustache?'

'Moustache, quite a big moustache. Dark.'

I said to Malcolm, 'You said the driver had a beard, didn't you?'

'The one on the other days did. On Thursday, I didn't get a good look at him. I was too enraged at the sight of the other one coming out of the vehicle.'

'Moustache, definitely,' said James. 'Not a beard. He had a weak chin. It sloped back.'

'How old?'

'Thirty, perhaps a bit older.'

In the car, driving back to the Carsons', I said to Orlovsky, 'We may have to rethink this. They may have smart technology but these people are not A-list kidnappers, they would be lucky to get onto any list. Not without expanding the alphabet.'

'Is that good or bad?'

'Bad, very bad. The stupid are capable of anything.'

'Unlike the clever, who are generally capable of nothing.'

'Nothing this clumsy,' I said.

'On the other hand,' Orlovsky said, 'they may not be stupid. Perhaps they just don't care very much.'

I didn't want to hear that. I said, 'Don't say that. Not caring is much worse than stupid.'

The Express Post envelope arrived just after 10 a.m. the next morning, addressed to Tom Carson. The writing had been done with a ruler and the sender was a B. Ellis, who lived at 11 Cromie Street, North Melbourne.

There was nothing in the envelope except a Smartie box, a cheerful package, aglow with the colours of the sweet flat beans.

But it didn't contain chocolate pills. It contained something wrapped in aluminium foil.

Two joints of a little finger, clean, odourless, fresh as chicken from the best butcher in Toorak.

LEANING FORWARD, elbows on the desk, chin in his hands, Pat Carson looked gaunt, shrunken, every minute of his age. He was breathing deeply but he seemed to sigh out more air than he took in.

With me in the study were Noyce and Orlovsky and Stephanie Chadwick. Noyce was clasping and unclasping his hands, swallowing a lot.

'I've told Tom and Barry,' he said. 'They called Tom out of a meeting with the institutions.'

I looked at him. 'Institutions?'

'The big investors, super funds, that kind of thing. For the float. To sell the CarsonCorp float.'

Orlovsky was in his trance again, unwavering gaze on Pat Carson's courtyard garden.

'It's the police now,' said Pat Carson. 'You were

right, Frank. Should've bloody listened. Pigheaded-
ness's done a lot for this family, startin' from the top.'

Noyce nodded rapidly. 'I think that's the course
of action to follow, yes,' he said. 'We had no way of
knowing this sort of thing would happen. And we
let Alice's kidnapping weigh too heavily on us.' He
looked at pale Stephanie, who was sitting near her
grandfather. He coughed. 'I'll speak directly to the
Chief Commissioner. Ensure they pull out all the
stops.'

I didn't say anything. I was scared about what I
had to say, ashamed that my instinct was to go far
away, and so I was thinking about waking in the
Garden House, showering in the huge slate-floored
shower room, putting on the towelling dressing gown,
thick and soft and smelling faintly of cinnamon.
Thinking about the three newspapers on the table in
the hall and how somehow the kitchen knew you
were up and breakfast came under cover on a trolley
pushed by a kitchenhand in white: today, fresh orange
juice in a tall, cold glass beaker, cereals, creamy scrambled eggs and thick-sliced smoked ham with grilled
tomato. The server made sourdough toast in the
kitchen.

'The butter's from Normandy,' he'd said. 'It's very
good.' He went away and came back with coffee in
a stainless-steel vacuum flask.

Orlovsky had come to the table wearing only his own towel, a sad threadbare thing, drank a glass of water and made himself a grilled tomato sandwich. 'It starts with food,' he said darkly.

'And ends as food,' I'd said, having no idea what he meant. 'Live a little.'

'Frank?' Pat was eyeing me. 'When Graham's talked to this fella, whoever he is, you deal with the cops on behalf of the family. OK? No offence, Graham, Frank knows the set-up, knows how the buggers work.'

'Fine,' said Noyce, nodding vigorously, not happy, 'that's fine, that's a good way to do it. Right, Frank? No time to lose either.' He started to rise.

'If that's what you want to do,' I said.

Orlovsky came out of his state, turned his cropped head slowly. Noyce sat down.

'That's what we should do, not so?' Pat Carson said. He was on to me, his chin was out of his hands, up, his head tilted, twenty years off his age.

I tried to work out the best way to do this, to be truthful and to escape. I couldn't. 'It's your decision,' I said.

Noyce said, 'On Saturday evening, you said . . .'

Time to say it.

'And on Thursday and on Friday,' I said. 'Today's Monday, Graham.'

'Don't understand,' said Pat, eyes crinkled. 'What's all this? We shoulda done it, we didn't, now we do it.'

'It's too late,' I said.

Orlovsky was studying me like some strange object in a gallery, a curious piece of sculpture perhaps, judgement held in check only by fear of not quite getting the point.

Pat sat back, put his hands on the desk, spread the fingers on the silken mahogany, lowered his chin. I hadn't done him any good. In his eyes and his hands and his shoulders and his chin, you could see the resentment. I heard the round snick into the breech, waited for the bullet, wanted the bullet.

Stephanie leaned across and put her left hand on her grandfather's right hand, kept it there.

Sack me. I willed him to say the words. I wanted to be away from this grand house, back in my own life, such as it was.

Anne Carson's face in the Portsea photograph came into my mind. The schoolgirl screwed by her driver. The girl who opened the holiday-house gate for grown men, drunk men with breath as pungent as woodsmoke. The girl in the back of the yellow van with the cocky locksmith.

There was something in her face, something in the eyes, the look of a child wanting praise, wary of displeasure.

A girl with only a stub for a little finger. It would be bandaged now. By what crude hands? Perhaps they had given her a painkiller. Perhaps they had given her a shot of something before. Before and later. Heroin was as easy to buy as aspirin, easier in some places, an excellent painkiller. And they could keep doing that, she'd do a bit of projectile vomiting, then she'd be relaxed, she wouldn't feel too bad about the whole thing.

'Tell me, Frank, tell me.' Pat Carson's voice was soft. He was still sitting back, chin almost touching his chest, shaggy eyebrows raised.

The old man didn't want to fire me. He wanted me to tell him what to do. He didn't know that I didn't want the responsibility, that I was scared of having it, that the idea of telling this family what was best for the safety of the girl made me feel sick at the stomach. To carry the bag for them was one thing. I was just an expensive courier. But to shoulder the weight of a girl's life, a girl lying somewhere, probably in the dark, terrified, in pain ...

'They've had her for more than seventy-two hours,' I said. 'Keeping someone hidden, it doesn't get easier. These people are sweating, they're under the gun. And they've lifted the stakes, they're trying to pump us up to something. It's too late for the cops.'

Pat was moving his jaw. He still wasn't sure what I was saying.

'They told you not to bring in the police and you didn't,' I said. 'If you had, the newspapers, television, the radio, they'd have co-operated with the cops for a while. Media blackout. But the media won't keep quiet for long. Seventy-two hours, that's about it. Then it's just a question of who goes first. I'm assuming that the kidnappers know this, that they've read about other kidnappings.' I paused. 'In particular, about your other kidnapping. They may be those kidnappers. I doubt it very much, but it's possible.'

I looked at Orlovsky. He was interested in his hands. I looked at Noyce. He'd got the point, didn't necessarily agree with it. So had Stephanie, who recrossed her legs at the ankles and bit her lower lip. She looked like someone who slept badly, never felt rested, feared the small hours. I knew that feeling.

'Mr Carson,' I said. 'My fear is that the police won't even get a ten-minute media blackout now. It's too long after the event. And the force leaks. Too many people are involved. You can't keep it secret. That's why they have to go to the media and beg them not to print stories like this.'

'Yes? That means?'

'It means the kidnappers will assume that you went to the police straight away and the police arranged a media blackout. On Thursday. That you disobeyed instructions from the start. Like Alice again, Mr Carson.'

Noyce held up a hand, like a schoolboy in class. 'Mr Carson,' he said, a pressing tone of voice, 'I think we need to talk to Tom about this.'

Pat looked up, looking at me not at Noyce. He blew out breath, a sad sound, half sigh, half whistle. He leaned forward, put his forehead on his clasped hands, closed his eyes.

We sat there, not looking at one another, for a long time. Finally, Pat spoke, voice barely audible.

'In your hands, Frank. We're in your hands.'

Hands.

Without thought, dread making a ball rise in my stomach, press against the solar plexus, I looked at my hands lying between my thighs, palms upward. My mother's voice was in my head, the sharp intonation, the pauses:

We will fall into the hands of the Lord, and not into the hands of men. For as his majesty is, so is his mercy.

I didn't have the hands for this kind of thing any more, not the hands, not the heart. The ability to take responsibility for the lives of others had gone from me in a few horrible moments, left my being and floated away. I hadn't known that then. Learning it took time. Much too much time.

Weak at heart, I said, 'I want to talk to the girl's mother. And to take the calls from now on. I want them diverted to me.'

That done, that leaden step taken, Orlovsky and I walked back to the Garden House in silence. Inside, hands in pockets, he stood looking out at the garden, patches of sunlight falling on it, drifting like memories, not warming anything.

'I know the money's nice,' he said, 'but are you out of your fucking skull?'

I was sitting in an armchair, an armchair stuffed with horsehair, firm. 'I didn't walk when I should have,' I said. 'I wanted the money. They call the cops now, it's on the radio this afternoon, TV tonight. She's dead. Dead today. I had to tell them that.'

Silence. He didn't look at me. The phone beside me rang.

'Calder.'

'What's this crap about talking to Christine? Whose idea is this?' Tom Carson, gruff voice.

I waited a few seconds. 'You don't want me to? That's fine with me. I'm happy to take leave of the Carsons now. This second.'

Tom's turn to pause. Then he said, no change in

tone, 'What I'm saying is, isn't there anything more useful you could be doing?'

Orlovsky was looking at me, a little cock of the stubbled head.

'In these matters,' I said, 'what's useful is pretty much a matter of judgement, usually retrospective judgement. I'd be pleased to leave the judgement to you. And to give you a partial refund.'

Another pause, just a second, then Tom said, 'You sound like a lawyer. Except for the refund. Tell Noyce to arrange the chopper.'

THE HELICOPTER landed on an expanse of mown grass a hundred metres from the complex of modern buildings. Its rotors blew away grass cuttings in all directions, a violent cuttings storm that caused the two people waiting to turn their backs and put their hands to their faces.

I waited until the noise stopped and the blades stopped before I got out, walked out from under the drooping swords and shook hands with the tall middle-aged woman and the younger and shorter man. She was wearing a white polo-neck shirt and black pants. He was in a dark suit, white shirt, striped tie.

'We haven't seen anyone from the family for quite a while,' the woman said. She was English, could talk while exposing horse teeth and pink gums.

The man looked at her, their eyes met. 'No criticism intended, of course,' she said. 'We understand how busy people are these days.'

I didn't say anything, nodded at them.

The man smiled at me like a doorman at a five-star hotel. 'We absolutely do,' he said. 'Do understand. Now Mrs Carson's not in a terribly receptive mood, Mr Calder. Her doctor will give you a full briefing.'

'Is she violent?'

The man was taken aback, tilted his head, raised his eyebrows, little downturning of the mouth. 'Well, she can be that way inclined. It's the price one pays. A trade-off. The alternative . . .' He let the alternative hang, float off.

'Forget about the briefing,' I said.

'It would be advisable, Mr Calder.' A serious tone.

'No. I don't have the time.' There wasn't any pleasure in working for the Carsons unless you could behave like one.

They looked at each other, assigning responsibility.

'You'll have someone with you,' the man said. 'That is our policy.'

We walked across to the building, down a wide verandah with groups of plastic outdoor furniture, through a glass door into a reception area done in 7me and grey commercial chairs. It was empty, no one behind the counter.

'Quiet around here,' I said.

'Generally, visits are by appointment,' the woman

said. I wasn't looking at her but, at the edge of my vision, I saw the wet teeth and gums. She went to the counter and picked up a handset, said a few words.

We went down corridors lit by slit windows, passed doors with numbers, went through a gravelled court-yard with a square of grass and a drought-stricken birdbath, and came to a door at a dead end.

A woman in her twenties was waiting for us in front of the door, facing us, another short woman wearing the same white poloneck and black jacket and pants uniform. Jaggedly cut hair, a home job, dyed blonde, dark roots, no neck to speak of. Martial arts, said the balanced stance, the level shoulders, the loose arms. The cockiness.

'This is Jude,' the man said. 'She'll be with you while you talk to Mrs Carson.'

Jude moved her lips, some attempt at communication.

The man opened the door with a key. Jude went in first. Then her handler. I followed him in. It was a small square room, lit from a skylight. There was a door in the far wall and beside it a low window, one pane of thick security glass. In the wall beneath the window was a stainless-steel drawer front. A chrome and grey chair stood in front of it.

'With other patients, we would ask you to visit from this room,' the man said. 'However, Mrs Carson won't come near the window.' He flicked a switch beside the window and a monitor above the door lit up.

It showed a grey view of a room, rectangular items of furniture, a figure slumped on one of them.

'Your visitor's here, Mrs Carson,' the man said.

The woman didn't respond. He unlocked the door and opened it. Jude went in first. The man ushered me in after her, closed the door behind us.

'A visitor, Christine,' said Jude.

Christine Carson was lolling on her spine in a chair carved from a cube of dense grey foam rubber, no cover on it. There were three more foam chairs in the room. That was it. No other furnishings, no pictures. A television set was behind security glass in the wall to my right, controlled by big soft rubber buttons below it. To my left was another room reached through an archway. I could see the end of a low grey foam rectangle, presumably a bed. Light came through slit windows, panes of security glass set in the masonry, behind Christine.

'Don't call me Christine,' said Christine. 'You've never been asked to, never will be.' She looked at me. 'I don't know you. Have you been sent to kill me?'

She was about forty, thin, big eyes in a long face made longer by close-cropped hair. She was wearing a shift of some stretch fabric, high neck, long sleeves, only her bare feet showing. I couldn't see Anne in her.

'No, not to kill you, Mrs Carson,' I said. 'I gather that's a job you'd rather do yourself.'

She looked at me for a while, cold grey eyes, a few shades lighter than the furniture, straightened up in her chair. 'Well,' she said, 'you don't pussyfoot around, do you? Get this bitch out of here and we can fuck. Or she can stay and watch.'

'Christine, don't –' said Jude sternly.

'Shut up, I won't have servants speak to me in that tone. What's your name?' Christine was looking at me.

'Frank Calder.'

Christine stood up. She was tall. 'Well, Frank Calder,' she said. 'You look like a man who's seen a bit of the world.' In one movement, she put her hands to her garment and pulled it over her head, threw it at Jude, stood there, naked, pelvis thrust forward, smiling.

I didn't look away. There were scars on her wrists, her stomach, on one of her breasts, on her neck. She'd inflicted a lot of pain on herself.

'Mrs Carson,' I said, 'this is entertaining but I'm here to ask you a serious question. Do you know of anyone who would kidnap your daughter Anne?'

The smile went, her eyes widened, she held out a hand for her dress, pulled it on as efficiently as she'd taken it off. 'No,' she said. 'Please God, no.'

'Let's sit down,' I said.

We sat down. She was shaking her head, looking down, breathing quickly and shallowly. 'Poor baby,' she said. 'Poor, poor baby.' Then she looked up slowly, eyes narrowed, smiled. 'Just a trick, isn't it? They sent you to play this trick on me. They want me to go completely out of my mind.'

'Who would want that?'

'Tom and Barry. Who fucking else? They used to put a tape recorder next to my bed when I was asleep. Telling me what a bad mother I was, telling me I should kill myself, how that was what was best for the children. Of course, Carol was behind it all. She hated me from the start. Detested me. She told Mark I'd trapped him, that I should've been on the Pill.'

She was moving her head from side to side now, her right hand at her throat inside the shift collar, feeling the scar tissue.

'They sent you, didn't they? Didn't they?'

I took a chance. 'Pat sent me,' I said. 'He sends you his love.'

She was startled. Her head stopped moving. 'Pat? Did he? Why doesn't he come and see me?' Her voice had taken on a sad, whining tone. 'I love Pat. Like a father. Pat doesn't know what the others are doing. He'd never let them do anything to me . . .'

'Anne hasn't been kidnapped,' I said, tasting the lie on my tongue. 'I'm the new person in charge of the children's safety. I'm trying to identify any possible threats to them. So that we can act in advance, keep them safe.'

She nodded, thoughts now somewhere else. 'My father doesn't want anything to do with me,' she said. 'He married his secretary six months after Mum's death. They killed her. Murdered her.'

This was not the person to be asking questions about possible kidnappers of her daughter. I should have accepted the briefing, accepted it and flown back to town afterwards. I could have had the briefing on the telephone, never flown here at all.

'They destroyed Jonty too, you know. And Mark, their own flesh and blood,' Christine said. 'Although he's the sick one, he's the one who's sick.'

'Jonty. Who's Jonty?'

'Stephanie's husband.'

I remembered Pat's words on the first night, in his study sipping malt whisky:

. . . *and Stephanie and her fuckin' husband, don't like to say the bastard's name, Jonathan fuckin' Chadwick.*

'How did they destroy Jonty?'

Christine sighed, scratched her scalp, put her hands into her sleeves, scratched, took them out. 'Isn't it time?' she said to Jude, standing behind me. 'Jude, isn't it time? Darling?'

'In a while,' said Jude, power in her voice. 'When your visitor is finished.'

I repeated the question.

Christine got up, began to walk back and forth in front of me. 'Jonty? Oh, they have their ways. They got his licence taken away. Tom and Barry. They've got the power. Just pick up the phone.'

'What licence was that?'

'Licence to be a doctor, I don't know what they call it.'

'On what grounds was his licence to practise suspended?'

'They're so fucking self-righteous. Stephanie found her father screwing her school friend in the tennis pavilion at Portsea, did you know that?' Her shoulder twitched, moved again.

'Tell me about Jonty.'

'Jude, it must be time, why can't I have a fucking watch, what fucking harm can that possibly do? How do I fucking kill myself with a watch? Please, Jude . . .'

'Your visitor's not finished,' said Jude curtly. 'Pay attention.'

Christine looked at me, jerked her head from side to side. 'Jesus. What?'

'Tell me about Jonty.'

'Shit, he's no saint. The guy was dealing in his office, right, he was shooting up junkies in his office. The far gones. Including me. He used to shoot me up, shoot up too, then I'd leave and he'd go back to seeing patients. Old ladies.'

'And after he was suspended?'

'Kicked him out. Expelled him from the family. Like me. Started dealing in clubs, in the street. He owed huge fucking sums to the suppliers, they were going to kill him . . . Can you go now, please, please.'

'Just one last thing. How did they destroy Mark?'

'Wouldn't have him in the business. Barry wouldn't have him. Barry hates him. I don't know why. Won't be in a room with him. He got Mark's law firm to fire him. Then his own father wouldn't give him a cent.'

She was rubbing her hands together, scratched her face. 'Can you go now. Please?'

I stood up. 'Thank you, Mrs Carson,' I said. 'I appreciate your talking to me.'

'Yes. Goodbye.' She wasn't looking at me, she was looking at Jude. 'Jude, darling, he's going . . .'

The man was waiting for me in the anteroom, presumably had watched us on the monitor.

'As you've seen,' he said as we walked down the corridor, 'Mrs Carson is not the easiest of patients.'

'She's not a patient,' I said, 'she's an inmate.'

We flew home over the lush hills, beneath us the fields, the settlements, the roads, the cars, they looked like the perfect countrysides model railway enthusiasts build: one of each thing and everything in its place. I thought that there had probably been a time when the Carsons imagined they had built a perfect landscape, shaped the world with their money. Then strangers came and took Alice away from them and suddenly their money was as shells and flints and sharks' teeth and Reichsmarks; a basketful would not preserve a hair on the girl's head.

The pilot was looking at me. 'Ex-military?' he said. In his dark glasses I could see my reflection, bulbous.

'Why?'

'Dunno. Something. I had ten years.'

'Ex all kinds of things,' I said. 'Ex-everything, basically.'

He looked away, flash of glasses.

We were over the Dandenongs and ahead, choking on its own foul breath, lay the imperfect city. Many of each thing and nothing in its place.

FROM ORLOVSKY'S car, coming in on the hideous tollway, I rang a cop called Vince Hartnett in Drugs and didn't say my name.

'Give me a number, call you in a minute.'

He'd be going outside to talk on a stolen mobile newly liberated from a dealer.

'Got two private sales of Taragos to check,' said Orlovsky. 'And that's it. The market in old Taragos is sluggish.'

'The auctions,' I said. 'Could've been bought at auction.'

'Could've been bought in 1988.'

I nodded, thinking about Dr Jonty Chadwick shooting up Christine in his consulting room, shooting up himself. Putting the blood pressure cuff on shaking junkies, pumping it up tight and giving them the needle. Not an old-fashioned family doctor but a doctor for the new family, the family of addicts. Still, even junkie doctors would have much experience of performing small procedures: extracting splinters, lancing boils, carving out plantar warts.

Cutting off two joints of a little finger. His niece's little finger.

That would be a minor procedure. Hygienically done.

Was that likely? The son-in-law kicked out, expelled from the Carson family, struck off the medical roll. It was possible.

My phone rang. Vince Hartnett.

'A doctor called Jonathan Chadwick. Mean anything?'

'Jonty baby. Dr Happy. Added a new depth to general practice. Yes, I know Jonty.' He had a quick, streetwise way of talking.

'What happened to him?'

'Inside. Got five years in, let me see, '96, '97. Trying for the big time. Hopeless case. Sadly missed by the street life.'

I thanked Vince, went back to thinking about the Carsons. I knew something about one of them: Pat Carson junior, Alice's brother. A few weeks after I'd ended the little hostage drama in the underwear store, Graham Noyce invited me for a drink at a small and horrendously smart hotel called The Hotel Off Collins. The Carson family owned it, he told me. They wanted to show their gratitude for the handling of the lingerie incident. He put an envelope on the table. I said thanks but life had taught me that whatever joy the contents of envelopes brought, accepting them was a step on the way to sadness.

He didn't press it, put the envelope away, gave me his card. Then, when I was out of the force and desperate, I sent him my card. This claimed that I was a Mediator and Negotiator. About a month later, he gave me a job to do for Barry Carson. Barry's nineteen-year-old boy, Pat Junior, was getting some life experience from a thirty-four-year-old table dancer called Sam Stark, formerly Janelle Hopper. Sam was professing undying love for the young Carson, and he was lavishing gifts on her and talking about marriage when he turned twenty-one and got his trust money from his maternal grandfather. I had a word with Sam and found her to be sincere in her love for Pat. At least until we got to fifty thousand dollars and a one-way ticket to Brisbane, business class.

At that point, before my eyes, her love for the youth withered. Noyce rang the next day to say thanks, Sam Stark had broken off with Pat Junior, booked a flight to Brisbane.

Had Sam told Pat that she'd been bought off? How would he take that? He was a wild young man by Noyce's account. Dropped out of university. In with bad company. Casino lizards, Noyce said. Pat had already sold the car his mother gave him when he left school to pay off gambling debts. Would he be part of the kidnapping of his cousin's child? Angry, in debt, in the company of fast people. Someone might have suggested it, made a joke of it.

I rang Graham Noyce's mobile. 'It's Frank,' I said. 'Anything happening?'

'Nothing. How'd you go with Christine?'

'An unwell person.'

'Yes, a variety of problems, including, would you believe it, narcissism.'

'Anything with a narc in it I'd believe.'

'So not a useful trip?'

'No. What's Pat Junior doing these days?'

There was a short silence. I could see his worried face, more hairs jumping scalp. 'That's not a, a casual question, is it?' he said.

'No.'

'He's a worry for Barry. And for Katherine. They got his grandmother, she's in her eighties, to change the terms of the trust. I told you about the trust, did I?'

'You did.'

'Pat won't be getting his three-quarter million till he turns thirty now. His mother told him on the phone from England. I understand he went berserk, grabbed some antique glass thing, smashed a mirror dating from Napoleon's day. Security had to be called in.'

'Who says money can't buy happiness?' I said. 'Like the Kennedys.'

'I won't say I haven't dreamt of a man in a window with a rifle.' A pause. 'Pat . . . you don't think . . .'

'What do you know about Pat's reaction to Alice's kidnapping? And his mother taking her to England?'

In my mind, I could see the shrug. 'Only what Barry's said. He thinks Pat's got some kind of emotion-deficit disorder. Doesn't seem to have any attachment to Barry or Katherine or Alice. Anyone, for that matter. Well, perhaps that whore you bought off. He took that badly.'

'How did he find out?'

'Wouldn't have to be Einstein. Eternal love one minute, the next she's gone. Plus . . .'

'Plus?'

'He knows what the family money can do. We had to solve a pregnancy matter when he was sixteen. Quite expensive, it turned out to be. The girl's father saw an opportunity to get a unit in Byron Bay.'

'Pat's been told about Anne?'

'No.'

'Where would he be at this time of day?'

'Wherever he is, he'll be asleep, building up his reserves for another assault on the casino. He's got an apartment in South Melbourne, behind the Malthouse. Courtesy of Grandma. The block's called, odd name, hold on a sec, it's called . . . Anvil Square. In Anvil Square East, I think it is.'

Noyce paused. 'He's a weird kid, Frank, cold as stone, bit out of control, bit of a smartarse, too much stuff up the nose, but . . .'

'But is probably right,' I said. 'Talk to you later.'

They rip his girlfriend off him, they keep his money from him. Dangerous people squeezing him to pay his debts. Coke habit. He could get others to help him, to make the kidnap seem to be about something other than money.

Orlovsky was looking at me, an inquiry in his left eyebrow. 'Pat Junior?'

'Barry's boy. Twenty-one this year.'

'Ah. Generation X. Wants to finance an Internet start-up, perhaps? He's looking for venture capital. Kidnap a relative. Cut off a big bit of finger, that'll show them we're totally full on.' He sniffed. 'Feeling in full control of whatever it is we're doing, Frank? Pardon, you're doing. I'm just driving the car and kicking fellow human beings on demand.'

I sighed. 'Rich kids have done worse things. Like killing their parents to speed up the inheritance. Go to the orphans' picnic. Kidnapping a cousin is nothing. We need a bit of surveillance.'

'We need something. I'm on the road on Thursday, bear that in mind.'

I rang Vella. 'I liked that Mongolian octopus. You Vellas, you're across so many cultures.'

'We come across easy. Marco's bookkeeper's looking for you. Some rent matter.'

'Trivial. Give him my love. Listen, let's say you want your girlfriend watched, you're insane with jealousy, you have to know. But if she spots the prick, she phones your wife to complain. Who's your man?'

'Woman, my woman. You sleep through the gender-sensitivity workshop?'

'I was sick that day. My mother wrote a note. Name and number?'

ANGELA CAIRNCROSS was an in-between person: between clothing styles, between ages, possibly even between genders. She pushed over a set of photographs. 'That's me,' she said.

I looked through them. She was good. A bag lady on a bench, a plump man walking two small dogs, a tired-looking nurse going home, a man in overalls next to vans with Telstra and Optus written on the sides.

'Don't get a chance to go out any more, the business's got so big,' said Angela. 'Once it was just Bert, my late husband, and Harry Chalmers and me. Now it's ten full-timers, thirty temps on call, part-timers, they do a shift. Works well, you never see the same person, same vehicle, twice. Variety, that's the key. Variety. The police have trouble getting that part right.'

I didn't demur. The jacks didn't get lots of things right. I'd tried very hard to point some of them out. In a manner that was held to be extreme. Murderous in fact.

'Yes,' said Angela. 'You can't run a business like this on trade union lines. Flexibility, that's what you need.'

We were in the cheerful offices of Cairncross & Associates above a printery off York Street in South Melbourne. There were prints and posters on the yellow walls, flowers on the desks. Down below, the presses were running: you could feel the vibrations in the soles of your feet, coming up your chair legs.

'Pat's a rich kid, may be out of his depth,' I said. 'Bad company, gambling, that kind of thing. We're worried he might be doing something stupid.'

Angela scratched an eyebrow, just a pale line, with a middle finger. 'Stupid? Illegal?'

'Might be involved in a kidnapping.'

She turned down her lips and nodded. 'That is stupid. Reported, is it?'

'No. Not yet. We need twenty-four hours on him, more if anything shows. You'll understand, there's a fear the victim will be in danger if they get even a wrong feeling.'

'It's more than him?'

'There would have to be. A courier's on the way

with a photograph of Pat and a rego number but that's it.'

'Anvil Square. I know it.' Angela looked at the ceiling. 'All new buildings that area, apartments. It'll be hard. There's no street life. Got a budget in mind?'

'If you need an airship, hire one.'

'So that will be stills and video.' She wrote on the form, looked up.

'We don't do interceptions, bugs, without a warrant, you know that? We can get some sound. Outside, public places. Not guaranteed, of course.'

'It has to start soonest.'

'Starts as soon as the picture gets here. I've got two people free, can bring in others. Is Pat one of those Carsons?'

There wasn't any point in telling lies. Her business was lies. 'Yes. They're not keen on publicity.'

'Won't get any out of this office. We've done all kinds of people, I can tell you. And that's all I'll tell you. Bert used to say we live or die by confidentiality. Any sensitivity about where the bill goes?'

'No.' I gave her Graham Noyce's address and my mobile number. 'How do you report?'

'Office is staffed twenty-four hours. In a case like this, operatives call in every hour or whenever something happens.' She wrote a number on a card and handed it over. 'I've written the case number there.

You can ring this office at any time for an update. Just give the case number. It's like your PIN. Any important development, we'll be in touch with you immediately.'

I got up. 'This sounds businesslike, Angela.'

She smiled, pleased. 'We're in the business of service, Mr Calder. That's what Bert used to say. The McDonald's of the industry, I like to think. Many of our competitors are more like fish and chip shops.'

Orlovsky was leaning on the car, talking on the mobile. He finished as I approached, eyed me, half-smiling.

'Could have the vehicle. A youngish bloke and an older one, driving an old station wagon. Paid cash. Sounds like the two in Revesdale Street, beard on the younger one.'

'Jesus. Show ID?'

'No. The seller didn't ask.'

I closed my eyes, sagged. 'Station wagon rego?'

'No.'

'Then we have exactly fuck all.'

I WAS asleep in the Garden House, in a big bed in the middle of a large room, dreaming a dream of childhood, when the call came. My unconscious tried to work the mad-bird sound into its story but quickly gave up, let the noise wake me.

'Mr Calder?' A woman.

'Yes.' I was sitting upright, swung my legs out of the bed, put my feet on the floor, the warm floor, heated from inside.

'It's 12.14 a.m. The subject left the dwelling a few minutes ago, alone, in his vehicle.'

'The casino.'

'No. Travelling south-west on Sturt Street. The operative has him in view but the traffic isn't heavy so there is some risk. Not great. We have two vehicles. Do you wish them to continue?'

'Yes. Can I speak directly to your people?'

'Certainly. I'll instruct them to call you direct.'

I took the phone into the bathroom, wet my face, brushed my teeth, admired the stained-marble appearance of the whites of my eyes. Then I went back to the bedroom, opened a curtain and stood in the dark looking across the garden, misty rain around dozens of concealed ground lights. No lights showed in the main house, but, above the walls of what I thought was Pat Carson's study courtyard, a faint glow coloured the wet air. A security light or perhaps Pat was sitting there, drinking the single malt and thinking dark thoughts. Thoughts of Anne, of little Alice, who saved herself from slaughter but could not be healed; of Christine, who loved him like a father and heard voices, slashed her wrists, her throat, plunged sharp objects into her concave belly; of Jonty Chadwick, who must once have looked like an ornament to the family and ended up as Dr Happy, running a shooting gallery.

The dark thoughts. And those were only the ones I knew about. There was a lot of darkness inside this family.

Mad-bird ring.

'Calder.'

'Mr Calder, time's 12.36 a.m., subject's driven into premises in Port Melbourne, a converted factory, the old Bonza Toys factory on Conrad Street.' A male voice, hoarse, the voice of someone who sat in parked cars smoking cigarettes, breathing shallowly. 'Opened roller doors from the vehicle. Either that or someone inside opened them. Door to the house in back right-hand corner. There's another vehicle in the garage.'

I was still looking at the main house, the glow where the old man might be sitting.

Please God, a people mover, a Tarago.

'Any idea what kind of vehicle?'

'Guessing. New. Squarish back, I'd say Alfa Romeo, maybe Honda. Red, so maybe Alfa.'

'The building, what can you see?'

'The renovated part of the factory's on the corner of Conrad and Castle, front door's on Castle. There's three lights in that, one's a bathroom, toilet. The garage entrance is on Conrad. I've given the office the address, they'll give you some ratepayers' info pretty quick.'

'Any way to get a look?'

'There's a building going up across the road, four floors, might be vision from there. We risk trespass.'

'Risk it.'

'I'll have to have that authorized, I'm afraid. Be back to you.'

The waiting. You have to learn how to wait, how to let time drift by without nagging at it. I sat in the chair beside the window, steepled my fingers in front of my chin, closed my eyes. No Tarago in the garage. Why should it be there? How did the voice of hate on the phone fit in? Scripted?

The phone.

'Mr Calder, the address in Port Melbourne, it's in the name of a company, Tragopan Nominees. I have the directors' names. Mr and Mrs E. J. Lamond of 27 Kandara Crescent, Rockhampton. Mrs Cairncross asks me to say that she has authorized the request from our operative on the understanding that the financial liability is yours. Are you agreeable to that?'

Call waiting pips.

'Yes. Thank you.'

I ended the call and the mad bird warbled.

'Calder.'

'We have vision of two windows.' Urgent voice. 'Subject's gone into curtained room with female. She appears to be handcuffed or hands tied behind back with something metallic.'

My heart filled my chest cavity, I felt the thumping pulse in my head, my arms. 'Description?'

'Blonde, shortish hair, youngish, he says.'

'On my way. Where in Conrad Street?'

'Park in Otway between Conrad and Jessup. I'm in a Yellow cab just before Conrad.'

I got dressed, dark clothes, went across the hall to Orlovsky's room, opened the door.

'What?' said Orlovsky, wide awake.

'I think we've got her. Dark clothes, quick.'

THE AGENT was a large, balding man in his fifties called Andrew. His cab smelt faintly of fish and chips. Angela Cairncross would not be pleased. McDonald's yes, fish and chips no.

'Young fella's up the building,' he said. 'Call me if he sees anything more.'

I was in the front, looking at the quiet street, not a light on. Volvos, Saabs, BMWs, hard to believe that dock workers once lived here. The light from a street-lamp came dimly to us.

'We need to go in,' I said. 'What do you reckon?'

'Place's like a jail,' Andrew said. 'They left all the factory bars on the windows, front door's solid as a brick shithouse. That's on Deacon Place.'

'How many entrances?'

'Just the front door and through the garage. They bricked in the big door on Castle Street.'

'We could just wait,' said Orlovsky from the back seat, speaking in his voice of reason. 'Nail him when he opens the garage door.'

'The thought occurred to me,' I said. 'Could open it in three or four days' time. I'd prefer a speedier end to this shit.'

Andrew pointed to the gloomy two-storey brick building across the intersection. 'That one, the other bit of the factory, that's empty. Haven't tarted that up yet. Knock it down, probably. Might be able to get from that into the back. Dunno what you do then.'

'No,' I said. 'We might just drive by, have a look. Andrew, hang around, could want you keeping an eye on the place for a while.'

'Can't go beyond surveillance. Policy.' He held my gaze, telling me something.

'Of course.'

In his car, Orlovsky said, 'Drive by?'

I nodded. 'Take it slow.'

We drove around the corner. The old double-storeyed toy factory occupied the width of the block on our right, built on the boundary line. Once it was in two parts, probably a yard in between where a double garage now stood. Over its roof I could see the two upstairs lights.

'Park in the garage,' I said. 'Reverse park.'

'In the garage?'

'This thing's built like a tank.'

Orlovsky looked at me. 'Jesus, you're subtle. Hang on.'

We went up Conrad Street, beyond the garage doors, a good fifty metres beyond, slowed, stopped for a second, and then went backwards in a sweeping curve, not fast. At the last second, Orlovsky put his foot down.

We hit the electronic roll-up garage door full on, maximum bumper contact, knocked the door out of its tracks, went in under it so that it lay on us like a crumpled tin blanket. There was a small impact as we touched a parked car.

I was out, ran around the front of our car. Orlovsky was already trying the door into the house.

'Locked,' he said, stood back.

I kept running, hit the door with my left shoulder, painful impact against the torsion-box door, cheap but strong, splintered the lock out of the jamb, was in a short passage, kept going, two strides to open the door at the end.

Kitchen, light from the street shining off stainless steel countertops, huge copper range hood.

Double doors, to the right, open.

Into a huge room, a sitting and dining room, stairs to the right, the original broad staircase, a landing halfway up, dim light coming from the floor above.

We ran up the stairs abreast, Orlovsky on my right, reached the landing, looked up.

Nothing.

Up the stairs. At the top a broad corridor, ahead a door open, light on tiles, mirrors, a bathroom. Door to the left, another one to the right, against the back wall, window in the centre of the wall.

Perhaps twenty seconds since we'd smashed open the garage door.

Orlovsky reached the door first, turned the handle.

Locked. Heavy four-panel door, break your shoulder first.

I looked around. A copper bowl was standing on a low table, thick crude top, stout turned legs, a stool not a table, a piece of poor farm furniture migrated to an ultra-smart house in the city.

I picked it up by a leg, bowl hitting the polished wooden boards with a hollow gong-like sound, tossed it to Orlovsky.

He caught a leg in each hand.

'Panel above the handle,' I said without needing to, he was already swinging.

The panel was solid oak, raised, hard as iron, resisted the first blow, the second. Orlovsky changed hands, swung a corner of the stool at the bottom right-hand corner of the panel, knocked the whole thing out, sent it flying into the bedroom, a dimly lit room.

I reached through the opening, found a double-bolt deadlock, opened it, turned the knob, butted the door open with my sore left shoulder.

The light in the large room was from two brass lamps with heavy shades standing on tables on either side of a massive four-poster bed, a modern version of a four-poster, designed to be curtained, made of heavy-gauge black steel with brass fittings.

Pat Carson junior was between us and the bed, walking backwards, naked except for a broad leather belt. He was tall, built like a swimmer, big pectorals and rounded shoulders, with an immature face, now frozen in fright. His erection was dying, his scrotum had contracted to nothing.

The girl was on the bed, her thin back to us, naked. Her head hung down, her upper body was in the air, suspended from the bed's steel curtain rails by ropes attached to leather cuffs around her wrists. Under her belly were cushions, her rump was elevated and her legs were spread, drawn apart by ropes from leather ankle cuffs tied to the bed's foot posts. Even in the weak light, I could see the welts across her back, her buttocks, the backs of her upper thighs.

'Lie on the floor, face down,' I said to Pat. 'If you want to live through this.'

He didn't hesitate, went down on the carpet.

'Anne,' I said.

The girl didn't reply, didn't raise her head, didn't turn her head.

I went across to the bed, the right of the bed, took her face gently in my right hand and half-turned it towards me.

Not Anne.

Not a fifteen-year-old girl.

Stephanie Carson/Chadwick, aged a girlish thirty-eight, last seen clasping her grandfather's hand in the study.

A mature woman, a mother, engaged in sado-masochistic practices with her cousin, a cousin young enough to be her son.

I let go of her face. 'Oh Jesus,' I said. 'Oh, sweet Jesus.'

I looked at Orlovsky standing in the doorway, still holding the stool, shook my head, looked back at Stephanie.

'You won't be needing me any longer, then,' Orlovsky said, the expressionless voice of a butler.

'No.'

Stephanie turned her head, chunk of hair fallen over her face like Anne's in the photograph. She was very fetching and she met my gaze. 'You won't tell anyone?' she said. Her tone was pleading.

'No,' I said, 'I wouldn't be able to find the words. You need some new doors, starting with the garage.'

I walked out, flicked a glance at Pat Carson, face hidden in the thick woollen carpet, buttocks palely gleaming. 'Don't adjust the set, Pat,' I said. 'Normal transmission is resuming.'

We didn't speak on the way back until Orlovsky said, 'Calling off the surveillance?'

'No. That didn't tell us anything. Bright young fella like that can turn his hand to many tasks.'

'His whip hand. What now? Tomorrow?'

Tomorrow? I didn't want to think about tomorrow, which had already arrived. I closed my eyes, put my hand under my jacket and rubbed my sore shoulder and said, 'Sufficient unto the day is the evil thereof.'

'I love it when you quote Elvis,' said Orlovsky.

BACK IN the Garden House, too wound up to sleep, I slumped into an armchair in the downstairs room housing the television. Orlovsky came in, opened the liquor cabinet and found a bottle of Black Label, two heavy crystal whisky glasses and a bottle of mineral water. Without asking, he poured three fingers in each glass, splashed in water.

I took my glass, sipped the healing liquid. It went straight to the base of my spine and the tension began to lose its grip. 'That kid's getting one hell of a sex education,' I said. 'Impregnating at sixteen, Sam Stark, now this.'

Orlovsky was channel-hopping with the remote. 'And learning the most interesting bits inside the family,' he said. 'That's really old-fashioned.'

He settled on CNN, a casually dressed man speaking earnestly against the backdrop of a rubble-littered and smoking street. 'Ah, Serbia,' said Orlovsky. *'Wie viele Todesmeister kann Europa ertragen?* My father won't be watching.'

Orlovsky's father was a Polish Hungarian, a teenage veteran of the Hungarian uprising against the Russians. He came to Australia alone and penniless, worked in the steel mills in Newcastle, saved money, learned English. He went to night school, went to university and did an electrical engineering degree, married a girl of Irish convict descent from Dubbo, fathered Michael and his sister, made lots of money. Then he packed them all up and went back to Europe to become a Cold Warrior, working for Central Intelligence Agency fronts and disappearing into Communist Eastern Europe for long periods. Orlovsky spent ten years in a German village outside Cologne, grew up to speak accentless German. Then they came back to Australia. He once told me that he'd accused his father of turning him and his sister into immigrants in their country of birth.

'Can't bear the news from *Mitteleuropa,* my old man,' said Orlovsky. 'Makes him feel his whole life's been wasted. I was watching with him one day and this Serbian woman said she prayed every night for the old Communist days to come back. My dad went out and chopped wood for two hours.'

We watched pictures of military convoys passing

through shattered villages, of sad-eyed and ragged women and children standing in hopeless queues, of strutting young men armed with the best the death merchants had to sell.

'Ever think about Afghanistan?' said Orlovsky, not looking at me. He had never raised the subject before, not once in the years since.

'Yes. And I dream about it, pieces of it. The worst pieces.'

'I never thought about it, never dreamed about it,' he said. 'Then this Defence bloke arrived at work one day, asked me if I'd talk to Cowper's father, tell him about, y'know . . . He was going nuts with not knowing, the father. They didn't tell them much.' He drank some whisky. 'I said sure, I'll tell him. And I did. Nice bloke. He cried. Seemed to make him feel better. And then I went home and that's when it started. Like I'd pulled a trigger.'

Orlovsky had been the one to come out of Afghanistan in the best shape. Like the rest of us, his military career was over. But he seemed undamaged, cheerful even. He started a new life immediately, did a four-year electronic engineering course in two, married a fellow-student, went to work as a civilian for a technical branch of the Defence Intelligence Organization in Canberra. We spoke on the phone at least twice a month, late-night conversations, drinks in hand, laughing a lot, never mentioning the past that bound us, two men whose parachutes had once become entangled in pitch darkness and who had plummeted earthwards in a terrified embrace.

Then he stopped calling me. And when I called him, he was abrupt, terse, keen to end the contact. Then the phone wasn't answered, his daytime number only took messages, all ignored. I rang his wife at work. She was reserved, said she'd left him, couldn't live with him, he seemed to have had some sort of breakdown but he wouldn't seek help, wouldn't even talk to her. She thought he'd left his job.

On a Thursday in July, a doctor from a psychiatric ward in Brisbane rang me. Orlovsky was under observation, committed by a court. He'd walked onto a rich people's beach at Noosa, thin, bearded, long-haired, filthy, and naked except for a belt. A concerned beachfront property owner suggested that he leave, tried to force him to depart. Orlovsky rendered the man unconscious. When two police arrived, Orlovsky was paddling in the shallows. They didn't take any chances, the larger one showing Orlovsky his revolver. Orlovsky disarmed him, threw the weapon into the sea, did the same for the partner. More police were called, all the police in Noosa. Orlovsky suggested they shoot him, held out his arms like Christ inviting the cross. With a large crowd watching, the police declined. Instead, they netted him like an animal and beat him with batons.

I took two days off, flew to Brisbane, talked to him for half an hour in a scented tropical garden. He was clean shaven, short-haired, clothed in a towelling outfit with matching slippers. I rang people, all the people I could think of. That afternoon, a pale Defence shrink who ceaselessly rotated a gold wedding ring, and a Defence lawyer, a major in uniform, arrived by military aircraft from Canberra. The major insisted on calling me Captain. The shrink talked to Orlovsky's shrink, to Orlovsky, then the major went to see the Public Prosecutor's office. Just after 6 p.m., we went to an out-of-session court hearing where the charges against Orlovsky were formally withdrawn. The two of us were on the 8.10 flight to Sydney.

On the plane, drinking whisky in business class, I'd said to him, 'We're quits, sunshine.'

He'd looked at me, thought about it. 'You're getting off bloody lightly,' he said.

Now we sat in silence. I sensed that he wasn't finished with the subject of Afghanistan.

'What do you feel about it now?' he said.

'Guilt.'

'For what?'

'For not being able to save them.'

'Inquiry didn't think you could've done anything.'

'Inquiry wasn't there. I could always have done something.'

'That's bullshit.'

'Yes. But it's my bullshit. What's your problem?'

He sniffed his whisky, drank half the glass. 'I haven't got a problem. I had a problem, a minor problem.' He opened the old briefcase on the coffee table and fiddled with the laptop. 'Been thinking about something else,' he said. He put a speaker plug in his left ear, tapped keys.

The electronic voice from Saturday:

Becoming less *stupid*. Learning *to do what you're told and* ...

'What's that mean?' he said. 'Less stupid than when? Nothing done before that.'

'Probably just a way of speaking.'

'You don't think he means less stupid than the last time? The first kidnap?'

'I've said this before. I don't see people waiting seven years for another try.'

'Maybe they would if it's for revenge. People who want to punish the Carsons, make them suffer, they might wait.'

He tapped again, listened, tapped:

I WANT YOU TO SUFFER *AS YOU HAVE MADE OTHERS SUFFER. I WANT YOU TO FEEL* PAIN *AS YOU HAVE MADE* OTHERS

FEEL PAIN. I WANT YOU TO BLEED TO DEATH.

'Aimed at Tom or the family?' said Orlovsky.

'At Tom, but he might simply stand for something. The bastards. The rich. People hate the President, hate the Queen, hate the Pope, but it's not personal.'

CNN had moved on to an explosion in Egypt, ambulances, sirens, police and soldiers everywhere, people comforting each other. A dog, just a skeleton covered in thin stretch-cloth, was licking a dark patch on the hard-packed dirt.

'So do they want money or revenge?'

The thought had been on my mind since the phone call on Saturday. How long ago was that? Early Tuesday. Saturday seemed far away. Was the girl alive? Two joints of a finger will keep in the fridge. Her body could be in the ground somewhere, not far down, waiting for a pet dog to snuffle at the wet soft earth like a trufflehound one evening, a happy dog digging frantically, rolling in the find, the owner calling it away, fearing the stench of dead possum, of having to wash off the smell of something rotten.

The smell of Anne Carson, age fifteen.

'Maybe both,' I said. 'Lots of both. Then again, maybe they're just crazy. Think it's fun to see people throw money into a crowd. We've got to get them to show us she's alive.'

'And then?'

'If she is, we try to find them before they kill her.'

Orlovsky picked up the bottle by the base and tipped whisky into our glasses. 'Not we,' he said. 'You. You're the sad case, you think you're doing this for the money but you're not. You're the guilty person who wants to make amends, save people.'

'Just one would be nice,' I said. I finished the drink and went to bed and on the slide into sleep I thought about Alice and came awake as if plunged into cold water.

BARRY CARSON had a surprisingly modest office on the fourth floor of Carson House: two wood and leather chairs for visitors, old desk, desk chair just like the ones in the office outside, faded Persian rug on a parquet floor, a nondescript view of the building opposite. On the dull cream wall hung black and white photographs of bulldozer-gouged building sites, concrete pours and tree-raising ceremonies on the windswept tops of buildings, construction workers and men in suits wearing hard hats and raising cans of beer. Only the construction workers' hard hats fitted and only they looked as if they planned to drink the beer.

'Two or three months with Katherine's family in England,' said Barry in his boyish voice. His hands were locked behind his head, he was being open, unguarded. 'We all thought it was a good idea. Get away, somewhere different. But they've never come back.'

His phone rang.

'Excuse me, Frank.' He looked at me as he listened, studied me as he spoke into the old-fashioned handset. It wasn't the unseeing look. He was looking at me.

'Miranda, forgive me,' he said, 'I should have made more of this, made sure everyone understood.' He had a gentle delivery. 'All media inquiries about the float and the company go to Tom's people.' Pause. 'Yes, I know some people may wish to talk to me or to other senior staff but this is a Tom affair. He has a regiment of unemployable ex-journalists waiting to handle it. Yes. Thank you, Miranda.'

He put the receiver down. 'This couldn't have come at a worse time for Tom,' he said. 'It's taken all the shine off going public, emerging from my father's shadow.'

I detected no sympathy in his voice. 'It's a long shadow,' I said.

'Yes, these generational changeovers should happen when you're in your forties, I suppose. In some families, the children take over in their thirties, earlier. But.'

Not so much a smile as a lip signal of resignation and acceptance.

'Alice,' I said.

'Yes. The kidnap shook us, changed our whole world. We've never been the same again. The whole family. We went from being pretty carefree to verging on the paranoid. My wife in particular. She seemed more disturbed than Alice. Visibly, that is. Alice was just quiet. Not that she'd ever been all that vocal.' He looked away. 'Well, perhaps I didn't notice. Always busy, travelling a lot. Pretty standard confession that, I suppose. The absentee father.'

He brought his arms down and folded his hands on the desk, long-fingered hands, square-clipped nails. 'Katherine almost took our son Pat to England too but the old man talked her out of it. Good at that kind of thing, the master manipulator. I think he had some premonition that Katherine was going for good.'

'Can Alice talk about the subject?'

'I don't know. I've never raised it with her, never wanted to. She may have talked to her mother about it, I don't know. Katherine wouldn't tell me if she did.'

I followed his eyes out of the window. We could see two men in an office in the building across the street, one seated, the other standing at a whiteboard. The seated one's chair was quarter-turned away from the whiteboard; he didn't want a lecture.

'They're in trouble,' said Barry. 'Someone's been selling them down for weeks.' He looked back at me.

'I might as well say it. Katherine blames me for what happened. She never said it at the time but when I went to England to see them the first time, she spat it out.'

'Blames you for the kidnapping?'

'No. For calling in the police. She believes that if we'd waited for the ransom instructions and paid the money, Alice would have suffered less.'

'She was assaulted?'

He looked away again. 'Yes, but apparently not until the story broke in the media. It may be that that was when they decided to kill her. So I suppose the logic is that if we, I, hadn't called in the police, we wouldn't have had the media exposure, and the kidnappers wouldn't have decided to kill Alice and wouldn't have done anything to her.'

'That's pure conjecture,' I said. 'To kill her may always have been their intention. If it had happened, you would be blamed for not calling the police.'

Barry nodded, still looking out of the window. 'I try to look at it that way. Katherine sees a reluctance to part with money as being involved. Nothing in my life has ever hurt me more than that accusation.' He sniffed, a delicate intake, moved his head. 'But there you are. It may be clearer now why we didn't want the police this time.'

'Yes. What does Alice do?'

He looked more cheerful now, making eye contact

again. 'She works with children, with autistic children. In a public clinic in London. She started as a volunteer, then they offered her a job. We give the clinic some money, which we earmark for salaries, an annual grant, quite generous. Alice doesn't know about that and it doesn't matter. She's very good at what she does and the clinic values her.'

'Will you ask her today if she'll talk to me?'

'Why?'

I felt uneasy, shrugged. 'It's remotely possible that the abductions are connected. Remotely.'

'The same people? Seven years apart? What suggests that?'

'Something the voice said on Saturday. About becoming less stupid, learning.'

'Just a way of being threatening, I thought. Anyway, if the police couldn't track them down then, what chance do you have now?'

'Something may have come back to Alice. It's worth trying.'

Barry hesitated. 'I'll ask her. Have to catch her early. Do you want a video link up?'

'If possible.'

Barry nodded, sighed. 'Her mother will come back and kill me if you upset Alice.' Pause. 'There's something we should've said. Tom didn't raise it and his presence made me reluctant. In his relentless pursuit of the deal, Mark's been involved with some extremely dodgy people.'

I waited, nodded.

'About three weeks ago, Tom had a call from Poland. A man with an American-accented voice, but not an American. He said Mark owed his syndicate two million dollars American and if he didn't come up with the money, they would hold his family responsible for the debt.'

'Responsible? What did Tom understand that to mean?'

'Financially responsible. They expected us to pay Mark's debt.'

'What did Tom say?'

'He says he told the man to take it up with our lawyers.'

'And?'

'The man said they didn't deal with lawyers and the family should ensure that Mark paid up. He said a polite goodbye.'

'What's Mark say about that?'

'We should've been more open about that too. Can't get hold of Mark. That's not unusual, let me say quickly. He's got a secrecy mania, everything's terribly hush-hush, he talks behind his hand.'

'But not to you. I gather you won't be in the same room with him.'

Barry put his right elbow on the desk, rested his chin on his palm, his index finger rubbing the side of his nose. 'Where'd you hear that?'

'From Christine.'

Barry closed his eyes. 'Ah, from Christine.' He opened them. 'A singular woman, Christine, but not someone directly connected with reality.' He was smiling without a trace of humour. 'Or did you form a contrary view?'

'Will you be in the same room with Mark?'

For a moment I thought I'd gone too far. Then Barry's smile warmed and he laughed, the first time I'd heard him laugh, a pleasant sound.

'Only if I have to,' he said. 'And then I keep as far away as possible. There's something about Mark that chills me, always has.'

I smiled back. 'And Tom's heard nothing from the American-accented man since the phone call?'

He put his head to one side, smile gone, gave me a long look. 'Not unless the Polish syndicate is using an electronic voice.'

The statement floated in the air between us as I sat there thinking that I was totally inadequate to the task I'd taken on. I gathered myself.

'Does Tom think that?'

'No. He thinks Mark would tell him about any threat to the family. Particularly to children.'

'You could ask Interpol to look for Mark,' I said. 'There's no need to mention Anne. Graham can go to the Chief Commissioner, tell him the family's worried about Mark.'

Silence. Then Barry said, 'I suppose we should. I'll have to ask Tom. He won't like the idea. Not with the float coming up. I can see it now: Interpol Hunt For Missing Carson Millionaire.'

'Is he a millionaire?'

'In reverse. Owes about that. Doesn't have a cent more than Tom will give him. But to the media all Carsons are millionaires.'

'Tell Graham to stress confidentiality. I think you've got the clout to have the inquiry kept secret.'

He snorted, a genteel snort. 'Clout? I couldn't keep my daughter's kidnap out of the media. That's clout.'

'The police took the decision. This is just a person missing overseas. It's different.'

'I'll see if I can get Tom to believe that. Leave your number with Belinda outside and she'll call you about the video link up arrangements. If Alice agrees, that is.'

I was getting up when he said, 'You haven't got anywhere, have you, Frank?'

'All I'm doing is trying to rule out possibilities,' I said. 'For the real detectives to come.'

'Tom seems to think I suggested you talk to Christine. Disabuse him of the notion if you get a chance, will you?'

'Why would he think that?'

A shrug. 'Tom's got a paranoid streak. Not even his family are above suspicion. No, particularly his family.'

'In the matter of my seeing Christine, what are you suspected of?'

'Who knows? Encouraging you to go down fruitless avenues, I suppose.'

I didn't understand. 'What about Mark? Is he above suspicion?'

'I think it's crossed Tom's mind that Anne's kidnapping may be – how shall we put it – related to Mark's activities.'

I wanted this spelled out. 'Are you saying Tom thinks Anne's kidnappers might be people Mark has had dealings with? But not the current deal?'

'Not thinks that. Crossed his mind. And not the current deal, no.'

In the cold street, I hesitated, walked several blocks to the shoeshine stand and had my disreputable shoes polished. 'Frank,' said the Chilean, 'you don' have the right attitude to shoes. You got contempt for shoes.'

'Contempt?' I said. I was looking at four office

workers out of their building for a smoke, all facing outwards, not dressed for the street, pulling at their cigarettes quickly, not talking, just addicts. 'Contempt's too strong, Ramon. I just don't look down often enough.'

I GOT on at Museum Station, sat in the second row from the doors. Just before Flagstaff, Vella sat down opposite me. He put a Myer carrier bag between his feet, looked at his reflection in the train window, fiddled with his tie. I looked at his reflection too, examined his long-nosed face, eyes and hair and suit too black to show up against the underground darkness outside.

'What the fuck's this you're doing?' he said, barely audible.

'Making ends meet, that kind of thing.'

'Out of ten-year-old kidnaps? Someone's paying?'

'Not the kidnappers. I've taken a decision not to work for kidnappers.'

'You should be inclusive,' he said. 'They've got their rights.'

We were cruising into Flagstaff, a soft hand on

the brake. A young woman sitting opposite us got up and hung on the bar, hips canted. She was wearing high heels, a red suit with a short skirt, and pantyhose that gleamed like the skin of a fresh flesh-coloured fish. Vella looked at her, lechery betrayed only by long fingers stroking the hair on the back of his right hand. Her eyes flicked to him, held, she tossed her head, if a movement so minute could be a toss. Then she concentrated on the door.

The train stopped, the doors opened and she got out. But, on the platform, she turned her head and looked at Vella, lifted her chin, winked at him, a wink an audience would be able to see on a stage. It was an audacious wink, sexy. Then she was gone.

'See that?' said Vella.

I nodded.

'What's it mean? I jump off, go up to her, what?'

The doors closed, train shrugged and moved, gained speed. I said, 'You tell her you've got a loving wife, two lovely kids, but, hey, what about a drink or something, we can just talk. That's one possibility. Or . . .'

'One's enough,' Vella said. He looked around. There was no one close, mid-morning lull, the commuter frenzy far away. He pushed the carrier bag over to my side with a foot, leaned forward, put his head down. His shoulders came up like a big black bird roosting.

'Frank, getting this, offence number one, is taking my life in my fucking helpless hands. Giving it to you, number two. They will blow me away. There won't be a foreskin to bury.'

I was grateful, but an unbeliever. 'That bad? Shit, just the other day any prick could buy a file in a pub in St Kilda.'

He shook his head and pulled a face, looked around. 'A file? A file? You think this is a file? There's no file to get. There's no paper. Files like this are history. I had to get you the whole SeineNet.'

'The what?'

'SeineNet. It's what used to be ZygoNet.'

'I thought they scrapped that.'

'They did. Threw money at it and it couldn't do half of what it was supposed to, so they canned it. Then it turns out they've been reinventing sex. Some secret Defence outfit in Canberra's already done something much better for the Feds, version of a military logistics program.'

'That's not a promising pedigree,' I said. 'So now ZygoNet's SeineNet. What does it do?'

The train was easing into Spencer Street.

'Organizes this massive abduction and missing persons database. Brought together after the Chee girl and the other one, forget the name. Took fifty million man, woman and person hours. Everything's in it, known offenders, statements, interviews, door-knock sheets, every warrant, every suspect's bio, all known addresses, bank statements, phone records, gas bills, electricity, you name it.'

He leaned closer. 'But the bad news is it doesn't come with a manual. So this may be of limited use to you. Whatever the fuck it is you're doing.'

'I've got better than a manual,' I said.

Vella got off at Flinders Street. I went all the way back to Museum, rode the almost empty escalators up, everyone going the other way, black- and grey-clad people, faces pale in the hard underground light, people taken ill at work, going home early, going down towards home, an aspirin and a good lie-down.

'JESUS CHRIST,' said Orlovsky, staring at the large computer monitor. 'I know this software.'

We were on the sixth floor of Carson House in Exhibition Street, in a huge work area, alone except for two women and a man looking at three-dimensional views of a tower building on a wall-mounted computer monitor.

'My contact says it's based on an army program for keeping track of how much the cooks, the clerks and the storepersons are stealing. The Feds are using it.'

Orlovsky made a noise of contempt. 'Correction, the Feds would be using it if they could work out how to.'

'Does that mean you know how to?'

He shook his head in pity. 'Frank, it's my software. I worked on it for fucking Defence. Two years of my life. This is what I was doing when . . . anyway, it's mine. Partly. Largely.'

He concentrated on the screen, loaded and unloaded CDs. 'Christ there's a lot of data here,' he said. 'Text, program files, image files. Compressed to buggery.'

'All we want is the Carson kidnap,' I said.

'Got the grunt here to run the whole thing.' He hummed. 'There's a lot of sweat gone into this.'

'It's a sex substitute for people like you, isn't it?' I said. 'Caress the keyboard, instant response, feelings of power and dominance.'

He didn't look at me, tapped. 'Sex add-on,' he said. 'For people like you, it could be a healthy substitute. But there's nothing like real power and dominance is there, Frank? You should talk to Stephanie Chadwick. She'd understand you, your special needs.'

'Sometimes,' I said, 'I think I should've left you snivelling in that tropical swamp, wearing your little blue towelling pyjamas and those nice slippers.'

'Tropical paradise,' he said. 'Pure paternalism, Daddy knows best. I was happy there. Free drugs and some intelligent people to talk to. You ripped me away.' He tapped. 'We can do this. Yes.'

He looked happier than I'd seen him in years. 'So what do you want to know? Captain.'

'What can it tell me?'

'Depends. Try something.'

I said, 'See what it's got under Carson.'

Orlovsky looked at me and shook his head. He tapped and the heading CARSON, ALICE and a date in 1990 came up, followed by menu boxes, dozens of them. 'Be a bit more specific.'

I was reading the menu over his shoulder. 'Crime scene.'

He tapped. 'Stills or video?'

'Video.'

More tapping. Almost instantly, we were watching film shot by a police camera inside a brightly lit four-car garage, two cars in it. The camera panned around the space, walls, the floor, went up to the nearest car, a BMW with driver and front passenger doors open, circled it, looked into the driver's side, into the footwells, along the dashboard, everywhere, came back to the passenger side and did the same. Then the camera left the garage through an open door and went slowly, painfully slowly, down a driveway, filming the brick paving, the verges, around a bend to a gateway with open spear-pointed steel gates. It filmed every square centimetre of the entrance and the pavement and gutter outside.

'That'll do,' I said. 'Records of interview.'

'Who do you want?'

'Alice. And the witnesses. I assume the driver of the car was a witness.'

He tapped again, produced a sketch, a view from behind the BMW, both front doors open. A man wearing a balaclava was pulling a small schoolgirl out of the passenger side. On the other side, another man, short, also hooded, was pointing an automatic pistol at the driver.

'Only witness,' said Mick. 'Dawn Yates. The nanny.'

He typed in her name. Her driver's licence picture appeared, a woman in her late twenties, thirtyish, short fair hair, square jaw. She looked like a tennis coach or a gym instructor. Mick scrolled and her biographical details came up, her work history. She had been a nurse and a part-time karate instructor before taking the Carson job. Then a diagram appeared, a complex relationship diagram: Dawn's family, family friends, their friends, Dawn's friends, their families, their friends, all annotated with ages and jobs. Of the dozens of names, three were starred.

'What's that mean?' I pointed at a star.

Mick tapped the asterisk on the keyboard. Three drivers' licence pictures appeared, two men and a woman, names, biographical details.

The woman was Dawn's cousin's wife. She had worked for an arm of the Carson empire in 1985–86.

The men were both Carson employees, one an architect in Sydney, the other an office manager in Brisbane.

'What about that bloke with the key next to his name?'

Tap, tap. Another face. 'Did eighteen months in New South Wales for fraud. Her father's cousin.'

'Jesus, they shook Dawn's tree,' I said. 'Can you print this stuff?'

'Gee, that's a hard one.'

'Print Alice's interviews, will you?'

When he'd issued the command, Orlovsky said, 'That's it? That's all you want? They give you a banquet and all you want is a fucking cocktail sausage roll?'

'I'm tired, Mick. Brilliant inquiries will come to me. Can you get into the system from outside?'

He gave me the kind of look I'd once given him, the look that said, shape up, Sunshine, the day's just beginning, it can only get worse from here, looked away, started fiddling with the computer. Happy now, in charge, happy as he could be. Who could know how happy that was?

'First I've got to make it hard for anyone else to get into,' he said.

I went over to the printer, watched the paper being spat into the collating trays, felt the ache growing in my back, the point men of pain advancing down my legs.

IN ORLOVSKY'S car, just after 9 p.m., the long night before and the whole of Tuesday felt in the spine, crossing the Yarra bridge, smart Southbank glowing on the right, people eating and drinking there, lots of other people about, the city alive, the water not its daytime mud-grey, now a surface that reflected and glittered. The city's Arno, romantic. Behind us, Flinders Street station, the first of the night people on the steps: prey, predators, and the guardians, young cops from nice families in the suburbs, from the country towns, getting their taste of the real, their eyes getting harder every night.

The studio was in South Melbourne, not too far from the premises of Cairncross & Associates, whose operative had reported both Pat Carson and a woman in a red Alfa leaving Conrad Street not long after we did. Pat had gone home and hadn't moved today. I'd called them off.

I closed my eyes and tried to concentrate, opened them to see the technician behind the glass saying things I couldn't hear into the black stalk in front of his mouth. He looked down at the console in front of him, then his voice was startling in my ear.

'They're ready if we are, Mr Calder. Try not to look away to right or left or down for too long. It's disconcerting for the other party. Ready, are we?'

I nodded at him. He wasn't looking at me, he was looking at something else. 'Ready,' I said.

A young woman appeared on the big monitor on the wall, her right hand at her right ear. She was looking straight at me, a thin, intelligent face, no make-up that I could see, short dark hair in no style, just combed back, straight line of eyebrows, almost meeting, ungroomed.

It was just after 9.30 a.m. for her and Alice Carson, kidnap victim, almost a murder victim, was looking at me on her studio monitor somewhere in London. She looked fresh for someone who had been woken by a telephone call from her father at 5.30 a.m.

'Good morning, Ms Carson,' I said. 'I'm Frank Calder. Your father's told you who I am and the reason for this. May I call you Alice?'

She seemed startled by the question, nodded. 'Yes, yes, of course. Good . . . evening.' She was nervous, you could see it in her mouth.

'I know this is difficult for you,' I said. 'I wouldn't think about asking you to do it if it could be avoided.'

She nodded again. 'That's all right.' She paused. 'I'm in a bit of shock at . . . at the news. I don't really know Anne well, but . . .' She tailed off, blinking rapidly, said, 'I don't know what I can tell you that . . . it's so long ago. I try not to think about it.'

Across half the world, we were looking at each other as though we had eye contact. We did have eye contact. I could see her swallow, see the cords in her neck move. I smiled, she responded, smiled back, a tight smile.

I said, 'We'll get this over with quickly so that you can get on with your day. Alice, I've read the police interviews with you and I've only got a few questions. I know you never saw anyone and that you only heard voices from a distance, through walls.'

'Yes.' An uncomfortable look, her head moving left.

'Voices are strange things, aren't they? We read so much into them.'

She didn't give any sign of agreement. Suspicious eyes. Waiting.

'In the interviews, they kept asking you about what you heard. Noises, the voices.'

'Yes.'

'They asked you what you heard. Over and over.'

'Yes. Over and over.' She lifted a glass of water and drank some. 'I felt so tired, all I remember is, I felt so tired, I wanted to go to sleep in my own bed. Forever.'

I drank some water from my glass. 'A precious thing, your own bed. You're never really home till you're in your own bed.'

What did I know about the preciousness of own beds, a good part of my life spent in institutional beds I hated or didn't give a shit about?

Alice smiled, half a smile, a smile. I smiled. We nodded at each other across the world, images bounced off a satellite.

'I feel ridiculous asking you questions all these years later,' I said.

I waited, looking at her, trying to keep the full smile in my eyes, in my face. Thinking about smiling.

A nod, not an unhappy nod now.

I said, 'Alice, if you can bring yourself to think about the voices, a last time.'

She looked uncertain, lowered her chin.

'You told the police that you heard two voices and they sounded the same to you. Is that right?'

A nod. 'Yes. That's right.'

'The people who talked to you didn't follow this up. You heard two people with similar voices?'

'Not similar, the same. At first, I thought it was

someone talking to himself, having a conversation with himself.'

'You didn't tell the police that.'

'I don't know. Didn't I?'

'It's not in the transcript. In the transcript, they move on to asking you about noises outside. But that doesn't matter. You thought it was one person but it wasn't?'

'No. I could hear they were apart.'

'You could tell them apart?'

'No, but the voices were apart, coming from different places. It was two people.'

'Two people with identical voices.'

She frowned. 'Well, I couldn't hear what they were saying. I suppose the wall was too thick. So I can't say identical, but the voices went up and down in the same places. I . . .' She hesitated.

'Yes?'

'I've got quite a good ear for music, so I suppose . . .'

'Yes. I'm sure you've got it right. Now the other thing I want to ask you is whether you've remembered anything else. In the years since. It's not uncommon. You were in shock when the police talked to you, I could see that in your responses. Is there anything else, anything at all that's come back to you?'

We looked at each other. Alice moved her shoulders, her head, apologizing with her body.

'This is rather silly,' she said, 'but two things . . . I'm not sure if it's just my mind playing tricks. I'm always reading something into nothing. Harmless strangers, parked cars.'

I smiled. 'I'm constantly reading something into nothing. It's a way of life for me. Go ahead, it doesn't matter whether it sounds silly. What's rather silly?'

She seemed reassured. 'The one thing is, we use the television and computers a lot at work. I work with autistic children.'

I nodded. 'Yes, I know that.'

'Well, about a year after I started working there, one of the other people put on a computer game for a child and it had this music, this simple tune repeated over and over . . .'

She was distressed by the story. Her hands had moved from the arms of her chair into her lap. She was clenching one hand with the other, I could see the tension in her neck and shoulders.

'Yes,' I said.

'I felt sick. And scared. I couldn't bear it, it's impossible to describe, I had to go out of the room, out of the building. I went to a toilet and . . . and I was physically sick.'

'You couldn't recall hearing it before?'

'No, never.'

Time to leave the subject. 'The second thing. There's another thing.'

She was feeling even more tense now, tried to smile, just a baring of teeth, nice small teeth.

'I went to Sardinia for a holiday last winter. With my mother and my grandparents, we were staying at this new hotel, a resort sort of place, they showed us to our cottages and I thought they were lovely, adobe, sort of Moorish-style and we unpacked and I went to have a shower and I got out all wet, water in my eyes and I had to steady myself and I touched the wall . . .'

She stopped. In her rushing speech, words tumbling over rocks, no still water in sight, I could hear the horror she was trying to keep out of her mind. And I could see white all the way around her pupils.

Find the words. Find a form of words.

'Sardinia must be a nice change from London in winter,' I said. 'I spent a winter on the English moors one year. Very moorish winter. All I can remember is the way my fillings tasted in the cold. Normally, you don't notice your fillings. If you're unlucky enough to have fillings, that is. I've got five fillings. Sweets in childhood. But when your nose is blocked by a terrible cold, you breathe through your mouth, you suck in that freezing moorish air, and it gets to your fillings. They get colder than your teeth. And then you can taste them, it's some chemical thing or something to do with metals. The most unbelievably awful taste, like sucking lead filings.' Pause. 'I often suck lead filings, so I know.'

I stopped. As I'd drivelled on with this boring rubbish, she'd looked less likely to bolt, more likely to make a polite excuse and leave.

'The message is this,' I said. 'Only have ceramic fillings.'

'Ceramic? Can you have ceramic fillings?' She was smiling, not going to bolt, not going to leave.

'You can have fillings made from anything you like. Titanium, Kevlar, old-fashioned stainless steel. They say you should go for the tusks of departed walruses. Not killed for their tusks, of course. Washed-up walruses. Peacefully departed. Recycled.'

Alice laughed, not a big laugh, but on her mouth and in her eyes there was a laugh. I laughed with her, celebrated my own stupid ability to amuse her. In her face, I now saw the resemblance to her father. They were handsome people, the Carsons, and they selected for handsome genes, even if that sometimes meant ending up with handsome people missing the warmth chromosome.

But they could laugh. It was possible. I'd seen two of them laugh. As a sub-species, they had the capacity to laugh. The single-minded pursuit of money, the worship of it, the fear of losing it, these had made redundant, vestigial, almost everything that had once made them social animals. But the ability to laugh, that had some value and it lingered.

Time. Time to speak of the things that the mind does not want spoken of.

I said, 'So, you touched the wall. And . . .'

She was more relaxed, she closed her eyes. 'Repulsive, revolting, the feel of it . . . I ran out, I didn't have anything on, I think I was screaming, I gave my mother a terrible fright . . .'

She opened her eyes.

I was nodding, as if I understood.

She swallowed, swallowed again, looked at me, her face coming to me in brilliant clarity, grey eyes, a sad person, sad forever, nothing could subtract from what had happened to her, nothing could bring her back into the world of people who hadn't endured what she had.

'I couldn't stay there,' she said, 'so they moved us, put us in another part of the hotel, the main building.'

'Adobe,' I said.

She nodded, looked down.

'Thank you, Alice,' I said. 'You've been brave and I admire you.'

She looked up and there were tears in her eyes.

*

On the way to the Carson compound, waiting to turn, Orlovsky said, 'Mr Compassion. That's another side. Sorry I didn't get to see that side.'

I was looking at the couple in the Mercedes next to us. A woman with a long, pale face was driving, the man next to her was fat and angry, gesticulating. He had rings on all his fingers.

'You didn't qualify for compassion,' I said. 'You only qualified for a kick up the arse. And that was too late, anyway.'

We were in the underground garage when he said, 'And now?'

I needed a drink badly, my back needed it. 'Mark,' I said. 'There's nowhere else.'

MARTIE HARMON worked for Hayes, Harmon, Calero, a firm of solicitors in South Yarra with an office next to a Thai restaurant.

'Mark's been involved with him in a couple of interesting ventures, his so-called associate,' said Barry, speaking briskly from his car at 7.15 a.m. 'One was importing caviar from the Caspian, a container load. I gather they paid half in advance, some fabulous sum, and the Russians sent them a container of fish meal. Hold on, I've got another call.'

Music, trippling piano music. I ate sourdough toast spread with Normandy butter and bitter Scottish marmalade and watched a gardener, a slim woman dressed for wet weather, choosing flowers from the cutting garden in front of the Garden House. She felt my eyes, turned and nodded a greeting.

Barry came back. 'Frank, yes, Martie Harmon.

Mark and Martie also combined to sell the Indonesians a South African crowd-control device. I don't know how that went. I'd have thought the Indonesians already had shotguns. I'm indebted to Stephanie for this information. Tom ends up paying and he confides in her.'

'And she in you,' I said, not a clever thing to say.

I could hear the music on his car stereo: a symphony.

'Something tells me,' he said, 'that you may end up knowing more about this family than we would have wanted. Perhaps we should have had you sign a confidentiality agreement.'

'Take it as signed,' I said, to make amends.

I was Martie Harmon's first of the day, no waiting. He was fortyish, short, plump, red-lipped, had opted to confront baldness by shaving his head.

'Sit down, Mr Calder. How can I be of help?' He had a warm, welcoming smile.

'Mark Carson. I'm engaged by the family. They're worried.'

The smile went and he made a scornful laughing noise. 'Mark. They're worried? Believe me, Mark worries lots of people. I no longer have anything to do with Mark. There is nothing I have to say about Mark. I don't want to discuss Mark. Full stop.'

I looked around the office, at the framed things on the walls: a degree certificate, something with a Rotary cog on it, a graduating class photograph.

'That's it,' he said. 'Now if you'll excuse me, this is a working office.'

I sat absolutely still, hands below the desk, looked him in the eyes, looked down, looked at him again, focusing on the inside back of his skull, didn't blink.

He couldn't bear it.

'What are you, some kind of intimidation? Fuck that, buddy. Fuck the Carsons. I'll get security in here in thirty seconds flat.' He picked up his phone.

'How'd that crowd-control device go?' I said. 'I reckon the best way to control crowds is to spray them with Russian fish meal. From the Caspian.'

Martie Harmon replaced the receiver, held both his hands up, pinkies facing me. 'That's not funny. That's why Mark and I are no longer in any way associated. I have believed the lies and I have paid the price. Also I have done nothing wrong or unethical. So, will you go?'

I shook my head. 'We've got off on the wrong footing, Mr Harmon. No one's accusing you of anything. It's Mark the family's concerned about. They can't contact him in Europe.'

Martie Harmon made a chewing movement and his shoulders relaxed a little. 'Just as long as it's understood,' he said. 'I have no involvement with the bastard, nil, zip.'

'Understood,' I said. 'His father's had a threatening phone call. From Poland.'

Martie closed his eyes, shook his head. 'Mark and the fucking Poles,' he said. 'And they're not even Poles, they're Russians. The Poles are the frontmen. They're the ones you meet, the ones that went to college in America.'

'You know about this Polish business?'

'Oh yes. Mark came to me with this crap about building a film studio in Warsaw. I told him, Mark, are you mad? This is the fucking Russian Mafia, they kill people they don't like by putting a helium hose up their arse and blowing them up till they float away and pop.'

'What was the deal?'

He jiggled his hands at me, like someone with palsy. 'The Russians wanted a two-million-dollar, that's U.S., line of credit. They don't intend to draw on it, what it's for is to bring in the other investors, sucker them in. It's for show. Then when they invest and the fucking studio's built, Mark owns twenty per cent of it, plus he gets twenty per cent interest on the two million no one's ever had to put up. Fucking dream deal, right?'

'Why would you build a film studio in Poland?'

'Porn. The Russian Mafia wants to take over the world porn industry. They can supply women by the planeload. Ukrainians, Chechens, Tartars. All colours, shapes and sizes. They'll do anything, all the things the girls in the West won't do. And you can forget about your fucking safe sex. Anything goes. Mark was really taken with the idea. There's a weird side to him, I don't know. He can give you the creeps.'

'How'd you get involved with him?'

Martie sighed. 'I fucking ask myself that. Daily. Hourly. I met him about ten years ago when he was with Ross, Archer & Stegley. We used to have them on the other side every now and then. He was Mr Hotshot Young Lawyer. And compassionate, night a week at the Altona Legal Centre. Out there in the chemical smog. Then he resigned at Ross's, gave up a partnership.'

'Why?'

'Well, the prick says it's because he wanted to get out of the law, make some real money. That'll be the fucking day. Anyway, I ran into him again, we got talking, he had this terrific-sounding proposition.'

He made a gesture of despair. 'In short, I was a boof-head. It's the Carson name. He trades on it to the max. He comes on like he's fully underwritten by CarsonCorp, like he's the entrepreneurial arm of the company. Entrepreneurial arsehole'd be more like it.'

'This Polish deal, what could have gone wrong?'

Martie laughed. He had big teeth, capped teeth. 'How about everything?' he said. 'Every last fucking thing. A, they're bullshitting you from the word go. B, they don't have a highly developed respect for the contract as a document binding both parties. They think a contract is like where you write down how much you're going to give them. And C, if they find out they can't screw you, they get really pissed off. You know the way these junkie streetkids tell you to fuck off if you won't give them a dollar? Magnify that by a million and you've got an idea about dealing with the old evil empire's new capitalists. Bring back fucking Stalin, that's what I say.'

Orlovsky's father wouldn't approve of that view, I thought. 'In this particular case, what would you say went wrong?'

He shrugged extravagantly. 'I'd be guessing, right? But what I'd say is Mark found some fuckhead American to fall for this not-to-be-drawn-on two-million-buck-line-of-credit shit. Then the Mafia says, listen, we need some of the money for a little while, the investors want to see the gold. So maybe the prick actually forks over some cash. Then the Ivans want a bit more. Mark's sucker sees the light and says no, sue me. What's this, says the Mafia to Mark, we've got a fucking deal with you? Give us the rest of the money. Or else. And since the bastard's been handing out CarsonCorp business cards, the Mafia feels entitled to come after the family too.'

'Martie,' I said, 'as someone who knows a bit about how these ex-Communists work, would you say they'd be capable of operating here?'

'Operating? How d'you mean?'

'Carrying out threats, that sort of thing.'

Martie's phone rang. He had a short non-committal conversation, not a definite word in it. 'Get back to you on that,' he told the caller. 'But keep breathing.'

He looked at me, frowned. 'Oh yes, operate here. I'll tell you a story. There's a bloke in Sydney, a stock-broker, he decided he'll broker other things. So he gets involved with these Russians in selling crop-dusting planes to the Philippines. Big deal, about six million bucks involved. A couple of planes arrive, tiptop. Some money paid. The buyers' rep, he's also an Aussie, he goes to Russia to see the rest of the planes loaded, put on the ship. No problem. Goods as described loaded. The buyers hand over the rest of the money. But when the buyers open the crates in Manila, they find they've bought the biggest fucking collection of aeronautical junk ever assembled, much of it dating from World War Two and not airworthy then.'

Martie had a good laugh, he liked this story, took

out a spotted handkerchief and wiped his eyes and his mouth.

'Anyway,' he said, 'for various reasons, the stock-broker hasn't paid the Russians yet when the shit intersects with the fan. You'll understand, they expected to have the money by then. And he tells them he's got these Filipino feudal lords on his back, he's not handing over anything until they get the right planes.' He paused. 'Well, the Russians made a few threats. He told them to piss off, this is Australia.'

Martie was nodding at me. I waited.

'The bloke lives in an apartment block, just a small block for millionaires, on the harbour. North shore. The Russians ring up. They tell him, watch your boat. He can see his sixty-foot motor yacht from the balcony. Before his eyes, it explodes, they find yacht fittings a kilometre away, the blast takes out three other boats.'

He laughed again. 'But there's more. The explosion's still ringing in his ears, the alarms in the under-ground car park go off. The place has had about half a tanker of petrol poured into it and now a few million bucks worth of cars are burning. A miracle the whole building wasn't blown into the harbour.'

'What'd he do?'

'Sent them the money. In the Swiss bank inside an hour. He thought he'd rather take his chances with the Filipino land barons. That answer your question about can they operate here?'

'Comprehensively. Martie, I'm grateful for your time. Can I ask you just one more thing?'

'Sure.'

'When you say Mark's got a weird side, that he can give you the creeps . . .'

Martie was less happy about this line of inquiry. 'I don't know, something in the eyes. My wife saw it, my ex-wife. And she normally likes good-looking blokes, believe me. Does something about it, too.'

'Just something in his eyes?'

He fiddled with his tie. It had little yellow ducks on it.

'He's got a way of talking about women, I can't describe it, it's like a contempt, like they exist for his benefit, like they're dolls or something.'

'He liked the porn studio idea.'

'Excited by it. We were on the plane . . . Well, he loved it.'

'You were on the plane.'

Martie checked his watch. 'I've got a 9.30,' he said, 'some preparation required, so if . . .'

'The plane from Europe? Is that after you'd talked to the Poles?'

A show of palms, a frown. 'I never said I didn't check out this deal. I never said that.'

'No, you never said that.'

'No, I didn't.'

'So you went to Poland with Mark?'

Nods. 'I had other business in Europe, so I went, yes. Not in Poland. The other business.'

'And you checked out the deal?'

'Yes. We went to fucking Poland and got the spiel and I came back and talked to some people and I told him, I told him, no way am I dealing with these animals. And I was out. Out. Haven't seen him since, don't want to, never will. You can tell the Carsons that. Don't know where he is, what he's doing. He doesn't call and I wouldn't know how to call him.'

Swallow, the bobbing of the throat apple. 'Mark Carson is not in my life any more.'

'I'll tell them,' I said. 'Martie, what excited Mark about the deal?'

Martie opened his eyes wide, then closed them for a while. Long curving eyelashes, noticed for the first time. He ran both hands over his naked head, penitent's head in other times, clasped the back of it, pointed his elbows at me. A man trying to tell me he was comfortable.

'Couldn't stop talking about the women in the films,' he said. 'They showed us some films. Blonde Ukrainian women. These Russians, three of them, they talk about the girls like . . . like, I don't know, cattle, sheep. Here's a good one. Do you like that? There are many more like her, we can deliver a dozen, easy, that is easy.'

He was anxious now, anxious about what he'd been involved in, seen.

Done.

Done on his trip to Poland. Perhaps.

I said, 'Martie, I'm very grateful that you're talking to me at all. So anything about Mark, the family will be grateful. The women in the films, is that what excited him?'

'Young girls,' said Martie. 'With these massive blokes, never seen anything like it. Dicks, fists, dogs, anything. Violent. I closed my eyes, I can say that honestly. That's not my idea of fun.'

'Mark enjoyed it?'

He said nothing for a while, biting his ruby bottom lip, making small hand movements.

'On the plane,' he said, 'he was pissed. He kept saying things like, the little bitch really got it, didn't she, did you see the look in that fat cow's eyes, that wasn't acting, that was live, she didn't know what hit her . . .'

Martie tailed off. 'That kind of talk. He couldn't stop talking about it. I had to pretend to go to sleep. Listen, I've got a client in about five minutes, I really . . .'

'One thing. Apart from these Poles, would Mark have any special enemies? People who'd really want to hurt him? Really hurt him. Do anything? Hurt his family? Kids, anything?'

He looked at me for a while, working out the meaning of the question, held up his hands. 'No idea,' he said. 'Just business between us. Personal. I know nothing. Tell them.'

I said my thank you. He came to the door with me.

'Mark'll turn up,' he said. 'He'll talk the Poles into something. And I'm clean. Clean.'

'MARK SOUNDS nice,' said Orlovsky. 'In fact, I feel the whole family really growing on me.'

We were drinking coffee down the road from Martie Harmon's office. 'Mark's a concern,' I said. 'But my heart says this thing isn't masterminded by Russian pornographers. The stunt at the football, why waste the money?'

'And why bother with the girl in the first place?' said Orlovsky. 'Presumably they've got Mark. They could ransom him.'

'That might backfire. Barry for one wouldn't be chipping in unless it was to have them keep him.' I drank black coffee. 'The vehicle, the Tarago. How long have they got to register it in a new name?'

'Fourteen days.'

'Too long.' All the rivers ran dry. You knew more about the Carsons than you wanted to but that didn't help you find the girl. Was that something to feel bad about? You could have all the resources of the force on this and still not find her. Anyway, I had no hope of finding her. I needed to keep telling myself that. I was just asking the basic questions, clearing the underbrush for the real investigators to come. If she was dead, that would be Vella and his gang of cropped-haired Homicide plodders.

I should not have stopped the Carsons calling in the cops. My chance to get out from under this mess thrown away, the perfect opportunity missed. I urged them to tell the cops, then, through sheer force of argument, I convinced them not to.

'What makes you think she's alive?' said Orlovsky. He was watching a young woman in grey inserting wine bottles into an overhead rack. Every time she reached up, she exposed milky skin and vertebrae as prominent as the knuckles of a clenched fist.

'Nothing.' I had the last inky drop. 'I just think they're not finished. If I'm wrong and it's not crazy people having fun or simple payback, something else, she may well be dead.'

'What would something else be?'

'I might have another one. You?'

Orlovsky nodded. I stared at the espresso machine jockey for a while, caught his eye, made the snail sign. His face said he didn't like signals, he might or he might not respond.

'Coffee's like horse,' Orlovsky said. 'Millions of coffee junkies, that's perfectly OK. They can't get through the day without it, they'd rather drink it than eat. About something else? Like what?'

'Who the fuck knows. What worries me is the silence. There's nothing been done that could spook them. This is a very confident silence.'

'The voice,' Orlovsky said. His gaze was now on the street. 'I should have thought of this earlier. That's something to think about. It's got intonation.'

'What?'

'Stresses words. As in saying "I don't *screw* for money" and "I don't screw for *money*". The intonation makes all the difference.'

'So?'

'Well, what the guy is doing is speaking into a device. I said it before, it's not a cheap voice-disguiser. If it was, we could get his real voice in seconds. It's a voice-recognition program that's producing an electronic version of what he's saying and it's mimicking his intonation. It's not just volume, it's the actual way he's saying words. Like when he says *bleed*. He says it with about five es in it. *BLEEEEED*. Capturing that, that's a very complicated thing to do.'

The coffees came, brought by the wine stacker.

'Thank you,' said Orlovsky. 'And may I say that you have beautiful lower vertebrae.'

She smiled. 'Thank you for saying that. You don't know the work I've put into those bits of cartilage.'

We watched her go.

I cleared my throat, got his attention. 'What does it mean if it's complicated?'

'He didn't buy it. He developed it or he got it from the developer. I can't see the developer lending it, though.'

'Let's say he developed it.'

'There's probably only a couple of dozen people in the country working on stuff like that.'

'How many here?'

'Not many.'

'Could you find out?'

'I could ask the obvious places, sure. If it's a bloke in a garage, that's a problem.'

'Would a bloke in a garage develop something like this without ever talking to other people in the field? How would he know it hadn't already been done? What would he be planning to do with it? Presumably he didn't do all this work just to disguise his voice for a kidnap.'

'There's no knowing what blokes in garages will do. But those are certainly interesting questions.'

'Interesting questions?' I said. 'You know, I liked your personality more when you didn't have this air of running a special tutorial for the dim-witted, when you were just a scared prick trying to prove he was as hard as the next man. And failing. Remember that?'

Orlovsky gave me a smile that conveyed enjoyment, drank some coffee. 'Can't bear it, can you?' he said. 'Other people move on, develop, grow. You were snap-frozen at fifteen, thereabouts. Know what they do with these huge tuna they catch to sell to the Japanese? First, they hook them, then they shoot them, in the water, in the head, get them close to the boat and shoot them in the head with a .22. But that doesn't kill them, that isn't what you want to do. You want to get them on board, very gently, they're upset, they've been hooked and shot, then you core their brains while they're alive, like you'd core an apple, with that thing you force in, push down, twist, pull out the core. Then they stick a wire down the spine. Now the fish is brain-dead, automatic nervous system gone, no more alarm signals being sent out to the flesh, and in top-class condition for slicing and eating. Raw.'

I finished my coffee, wished I hadn't had a second one. 'You're saying I'm like that?' I said. 'Like a tuna?'

'No, you're the guy with the .22 and the piece of wire.'

'That's better. So you're the tuna?'

'I could have been,' said Orlovsky. 'I could have been. But I resisted.'

'Swam away with a bullet in your brain. See if you can find out who's working on this voice stuff,' I said. 'Start now. About tomorrow, you're going on the road.'

'Before dawn,' he said.

'How much do you make?'

Orlovsky eyed me suspiciously. 'It's a commitment,' he said. 'It's an obligation.'

'Far be it from me to come between you and your commitments. Can you get a stand-in?'

He rubbed his jaw, an imperfectly shaved jaw, a shave in progress. 'The boss might do it himself. Can't just bring in a temp for work like this, you know. There's trust involved, I'm dealing with people . . .'

'Don't tell me,' I said. 'I'm not a cop any more and I still don't want to know. Tell the boss your temporary employer has urgent need of your services and he'll pay, what, five hundred? For inconveniencing the man, the person. How much do you make?'

'For the three days, six-fifty a day.'

'OK, two grand to you for lost earnings, five hundred to the boss. He saves the two grand you get, he's up two-and-a-half on the deal.'

'If he wanted to save two grand, he'd always do it himself. He doesn't like going out there. That's why he pays me.'

'A thousand.'

'This is Carson money you're spending. You're acting as if it's yours.'

I shook my head at him. 'The concept of honest stewardship of other people's money means nothing to you, does it?'

Orlovsky smiled, stroked a patch of stubble. 'Nothing that I can think of, no.'

We drove back to the Carson compound. No one was waiting in the underground car park, no messages.

Walking though the garden, I listened to the voice in my head saying: It's not too late, it's not too late. Call Noyce now. Tell him you think you were wrong. They must call in the cops now. But I knew I couldn't, wouldn't.

FROM THE Garden House, with nothing else to do, in deep dread, unable to simply wait, I rang Graham Noyce.

'Two things. First, if and when they ring, I want proof that she's alive. I'm giving them a deadline to produce it. I've got a bad feeling.'

'I'll clear it with Tom,' he said. 'I think he'll agree. What else?'

'I'd like to ask Mark's old firm some questions. Ross, Archer & Stegley.'

A moment's silence. 'Why's that?'

I gave him a moment's silence back. 'Idle curiosity.'

A sniff. 'It's a reasonable question, Frank.'

'You didn't tell me about Mark and the Poles. The Polish Russians.'

'Jesus, what else haven't I told you about? Let's set aside a week or two, I'll give you a background briefing on the Carson family, close and extended, near and far. In the meantime, I don't think these shonks Mark gets mixed up with would actually get around to abducting his daughter, cutting off her finger. Do you?'

I gave him another measured silence.

'For Christ's sake, Frank,' he said wearily, 'Mark is the one who gets ripped off in these insane deals.'

'Is Mark out of bounds? Just say the word.'

'Fuck. I'd like to kick the cunt out of bounds. Listen, the reason it's not a good time to be asking around about Mark is simply that the float's two weeks off. People are sniffing around. Journos, the fucking stockbrokers' analysts. And someone's putting out the word that the institutions think Tom should stand down as chief executive, that he's too old, lacks vision, he's a drag on the company's future. With me?'

'Just vaguely.'

'So this is a really tense time. Anything can have a spin put on it, we can see five years' work, fifty years' work you might say, all go down the tubes.' Pause. 'Anyway, who told you about Mark and the Poles?'

'Pat. And Martie Harmon.'

'Who put you onto Martie Harmon?'

'Barry.'

'To what end, may I ask?'

'He thought I should have been told about the phone call from the person with the American accent. Should I have been, do you think? And another question: who do you work for?'

'I work for the company. I'm a servant of the company.'

'You work for Tom?'

'It's not that clear-cut.' Another sniff. 'I work for the Carsons. All the Carsons. I steer my frail craft among the Carson shoals and reefs. Tom is now formally the head of the company but until recently I reported directly to the old man, to Pat. And I was hired by Barry.'

Only the questions are simple. Who said that? I felt sand in my eyes, grit, and I blinked and blinked.

'Tom was at the first meeting,' said Noyce. 'He had ample opportunity to tell you about Mark and the threat from the Poles, whoever. He didn't. I took my cue from that.'

A moment's silence. Then he said, 'Is Barry suggesting Mark's Poles are relevant?'

'No. I mentioned Mark and he told me about the phone call.'

Now Noyce sighed, a sigh felt deeply. 'Frank, a month ago a newspaper wanted to do a two-part feature on the Carsons. On the family. Life and times and empire. I cannot tell you what I had to do to get that project shelved. Things that make me shudder now, in the clear light of day. And I am not a shudderer. And the reason was Mark. All we need is the media getting onto the story of the family fucking idiot and his loony deals and his scummy associates. Not to mention his totally crazed wife.'

'It's his daughter I'm worried about.'

Breath expelled loudly. 'Obviously. We have to do whatever we can to get Anne back. But essentially we are waiting for instructions on how to ransom her. Not so?'

Two people were coming down the brick path beside the cutting garden, a tall woman and a man, shoulder height to her. They were smiling at each other.

'Tom's wife,' I said. 'Is she around?'

'Carol? Sometimes. She travels a lot. Shopping trips. Why?'

'There's a woman in the garden with a much younger man. Tall blonde woman.'

'That's her. He's probably the latest plaything.'

'She'd be concerned about her granddaughter.'

'Carol's not exactly your doting grandmother. I gather she can't stand Anne. About Mark . . .'

'Yes.' Outside, Carol Carson raised her right hand and brushed her fingertips across the young man's full mouth.

'Poking around Mark's life, that's not going to help. All you'll do is create a danger of someone tipping off the media that the Carsons are paying an ex-cop to dig into Mark's life. Frank, we can't run that risk. Not now. Are you with me?'

I said I was. Carol Carson and her friend were walking back the way they had come, close together, touching. Clearly, the man had no fear of meeting an angry spouse.

I went to the kitchen to make a pot of tea, had to choose from five teas, imported from France. France? What did the French know about tea? I chose one at random, looked out of the window while I waited for the kettle to boil. The day had turned fine, weak lemon sunlight bathing the garden, turning the rain lying on the evergreen leaves into drops of mercury.

He was Mr Hotshot Young Lawyer. And compassionate, night a week at the Altona Legal Centre. Out there in the chemical smog.

Compassionate Mark, Mark drooling over violent porn films. Incompatible emotions? Perhaps not. Humans were dealt all the cards. Life and a bit of choice decided which ones they'd play.

Mark's wife had said something, something about him being the sick one. But not a reliable informant was Christine.

I made a pot of tea, in a bone-china pot, kept in a cupboard with teacups thin as parchment, and left it to draw.

Mark would have been a volunteer at the Altona Community Legal Centre around 1988. I rang Enquiries, got the number, was put through to the centre's solicitor, told her a lie.

'In 1988? Wow. I've only been here since 1998. Hold on, I'll ask someone.'

She was gone only a minute or two.

'That was easy,' she said. 'Our secretary had a stint here from '85 to '90 but she's gone out for a bit. I looked up the records, the solicitor then was Jeremy Fisher. He's a big-deal corporate lawyer now. I think he's with Stone, Boyle, Carides – they're takeover specialists, takeovers, mergers, company stuff like that. He'd know your person. I don't think they had many volunteer solicitors then, too far from the bright lights.'

I poured a cup of tea through a silver strainer, squeezed in a drop of lemon juice. Excellent French tea. Was this what your Bordeaux vigneron drank after a hard morning's work doctoring the fermented grape juice with battery acid and Algerian plonk?

I got the number and rang Stone, Boyle, Carides.

It was easy to get to Jeremy Fisher's second secretary. Then I moved on to a full secretary. They were both bright-voiced, both infected with the superiority of working for a first-tier law firm. They wanted to know my business and not in vague terms. I didn't want to tell them my business even in non-vague terms. At length, I was put on to someone who was apparently an actual solicitor, not Jeremy Fisher but someone I imagined as a work-experience person operating out of the basement car park.

'Jeremy's tremendously busy,' he said, another cheerful person. 'Can't I help you?'

'Listen, son,' I said, 'I've had it with the runaround. I represent Carson Corporation. I'm going to give you my number. I expect Jeremy to ring me inside five minutes.'

'I'll take that number,' the man said. 'And get back to you soonest. ASAP.'

The phone rang inside the limit.

'Mr Calder, Jeremy Fisher. Forgive me, my people should've put you straight through. Bit over-protective, I'm afraid.'

It was a smooth voice, a competent voice, an unflappable voice that would be balm to a troubled corporate ear. It said: *You are in good hands.*

'I understand you represent Carson Corporation,' Jeremy said. 'We obviously haven't met. In what capacity would you be representing the company?'

I was getting a feeling, not a good feeling. 'Not

Carson Corporation, the family. Check that with Graham Noyce, if you like, he's the in-house counsel. Would you like the number?'

'No. I talk to Graham quite enough as it is. The float's taken its toll of both of us. How can I help you?'

Takeovers, mergers, company stuff like that.

Like companies going public? Like CarsonCorp?

My instinct was to make an excuse and leave.

But.

If Graham was scared that bad publicity could harm the float, the leak that brought the publicity certainly wasn't going to come from the law firm handling it.

So, what the hell.

'In the strictest confidence,' I said, 'and without giving any reasons, I'd like to ask you a few questions about the time when you were the solicitor at the Altona Legal Centre and Mark Carson was a volunteer.'

'Yes?'

He said *Yeees?* An intonation conveying extreme caution. The kidnappers' electronic device could convey that intonation. I was beginning to see that it might be a technical achievement.

'It was about that time that Mark left Ross, Archer & Stegley. I wondered if you knew anything about the circumstances of his leaving the firm?'

'The circumstances?' A musing tone. 'As far as I can remember, Mark was with Ross's all the time that he was helping out at Altona. So that must have been later. But I really can't say, it's so long ago.'

Pause. A pause for thought.

'Mr Calder, I've got an overseas call on the line,' he said. 'I'll get back to you soonest. Sorry about this, these people won't wait. Talk to you again.'

Not in this life, I thought. I didn't know why, but I knew. I took my time finishing the very fine French tea, held the cup to the light, extended a finger behind it. Through the pale, translucent, expensive shell, I could see its shape, like a boat's shadow on the seabed.

The phone rang.

'What the fuck is this about?' Graham Noyce, equal stress on each word, not the affable, careworn, reasonable Graham Noyce. 'Frank, exactly what the fucking hell is this about?'

I didn't have the remotest idea what it was about. And every hour that passed left me more ignorant.

Mid-week. It was mid-week.

CORIN McCALL answered her phone from what sounded like a building site, brute machines roaring in the background.

'Back from the bush, yes,' she said. 'Came back last night, had to. My earthmoving man found he had a day free, you don't let that get away.'

'That's him in the background?'

'Rearranging nature. Socrates Kyriakos. No one can play an earthmover like Soc.'

'The earth moves for him.'

A laugh, not big, but a laugh. The laugh when I'd called off our date, that hadn't been a laugh.

'I'm in a bad position,' I said. 'Sort of a twenty-four-hour-a-day job, open-ended, no end in sight.'

'Well,' she said, 'thanks for calling. Anyway.'

'No,' I said, nervous. 'Lunch. What about lunch? Eat lunch?'

'Eat my sandwiches. My sandwich.'

'Where are you?'

'In Hampton. My client's flattened two houses and he wants to get the landscaping done before he builds some appalling structure.'

'I can get to Hampton in fifteen, twenty minutes, we can have lunch in Hampton. Many good places to have lunch, I'm sure.'

She thought about this incredibly appealing proposal for a long time.

'I'll give you the address, but I'm not dressed for eating out,' she said. 'Bring your own sandwich. We'll eat in my vehicle.' Pause. 'Buggered old Land Cruiser with bags of compost in the back. How's that suit your style?'

'To perfection. How do you like your coffee?'

Another pause. 'Black. Long black.'

'The address?'

I took a Carson car, an Audi, the high life coming easily to me now, stopped at a smart coffee place, ordered bagels with smoked salmon and other exotic ingredients, long black coffees.

At the address, the Land Cruiser was parked in what would once have been the driveway of a house. Twenty metres away, a small earthmover was triumphant on a heap of sandy earth. On the street frontage of the two suburban quarter-acre blocks, a large rectangle had been pegged out where the building would go.

Corin McCall got out of the Land Cruiser as I parked. She was dressed like a workman: check shirt, sleeveless oilskin jerkin with many pockets, jeans, lace-up boots. I'd never seen her in work gear, only in lecturing gear, which was suits and high-collared blouses. It was hard to say which outfit made the more favourable impression on me.

We met on the pavement, dishwater sky, the wind off the bay blowing right through me. She put out her right hand and we shook.

'Welcome to the glamorous world of landscape design,' she said, running her left hand through her short dark hair.

'What's happened to Socrates?'

'Soc's got another job going in Sandringham. He's gone over to check on Soc junior in his lunch hour, get on the machine and redo everything the boy's done today.'

'Ah, the family firm,' I said. 'I'm learning about the family firm.'

'In your twenty-four-hour-a-day, open-ended job?'

I nodded. 'I'll get the supplies.' I went back to the car and got out the box with the bagels and coffee.

'I hope this vehicle doesn't smell of manure,' Corin said. 'I'm beyond being able to detect it.'

The Land Cruiser didn't smell of manure, it smelled

of nothing except a suspicion of perfume, such as might come to you in a memory.

'This is nice,' she said. 'Like an urban picnic.'

I opened the box, offered her a bagel. 'I thought you could save your sandwich for afternoon tea.'

She looked at me, eyes narrowed. 'How did you know I'd prefer smoked salmon and cream cheese on a bagel to Vegemite on last week's bread?'

'Call it intuition, call it a shot in the dark.'

We settled down to eat. After her first bite, Corin said, 'Good filling, proper boiled bagel too. Do you mind me asking what you do for a living?'

'I'm a mediator.'

She was looking at her bagel, gave me a sideways glance. 'Someone at the college said you used to be a cop.'

I nodded. 'It scares people off, ex-cop. I usually say I used to be a soldier, that's more acceptable somehow.'

'Were you?'

'A soldier, yes. Much longer than I was a cop.'

'Why'd you stop being a soldier?'

'I got hurt.'

I paused. That was what I always said, all I said. Today, I added, 'Other people got hurt at the same time. And afterwards I didn't think I had what it took any more.'

We chewed in silence. Then she wiped her lips with a napkin, no lipstick, and said, 'What does it take?'

'A certain indifference to personal safety. How'd you get into landscape design?'

She wasn't easily deterred. 'Why'd you stop being a cop?'

'That was a matter of someone else getting hurt. A fellow officer.'

'You were blamed?'

'Not unreasonably. I was trying to strangle him.'

We sat in silence for a while. I knew I should not have said that. She had turned away from me slightly; she would have formed the view that I was a psycho.

'So,' she said, 'you showed a certain indifference to his personal safety?'

'Total indifference. And no, I'm not a psycho. Do it again tomorrow, though.'

Corin shook her head. 'The accused shows no remorse,' she said.

'Well, you know enough about me now to stop taking my calls,' I said. 'How'd you get into landscape design?'

She turned her upper body towards me. She wasn't rejecting me.

'Total indifference to personal solvency,' she said. 'I was an architect and all I did was work on tower blocks and shopping malls and ablution blocks. No one ever asked me to join their smart little practices, do restaurants and things. So I said, I don't think I have what it takes to be an architect, to hell with this, and I went back to uni and starved while I did landscape design.'

'And became an ornament to the profession,' I said. 'To the landscape, for that matter.'

Our eyes met. Grey with light flecks, hers. I looked away first, swallowed, balled up my bagel wrapping. 'Trying to flirt with the teacher,' I said. 'That's probably not done.'

'It's flirting with students that's frowned on,' she said. 'I'll have to be careful. While we're asking questions, what's a person of your, um, varied background doing at horticultural college?'

'I like gardens,' I said. 'I had a garden when I was a kid, a veggie and flower garden. The lady next door marked off this plot for me in her back yard, gave me the seeds, showed me how to plant them. I used to go there every day with my little watering can, water the ground. Sit there and watch. I didn't want to miss the moment . . .'

I tailed off. It wasn't a story I wanted to tell. I'd already said things I didn't want to out of some need to explain myself to this woman, have her like me.

'When they came up.' She finished the sentence

for me. 'I know. You only have to look away and up the bastards come.'

We were smiling at each other when one of my phones, Noyce's vibrating phone, fluttered against my ribs.

'Phone,' I said, taking it out. 'I'll just get out. Coffee's getting cold.'

I got out, closed the door, stood in the cold wind, felt it on my scalp, felt the fear in me, and pressed the button.

'Yes,' I said.

'Who's that?'

The voice.

'Frank Calder. I work for the Carson family. Who's that?'

Silence.

'Put Tom Carson on.'

'No,' I said, 'from now on you talk to me. And don't start shouting, I don't give a shit about shouting, I don't give a shit about the Carson family either, I'm just someone paid to do this and shouting is a waste of time. You talk to me or you don't talk.'

Silence.

The voice.

'OK, listen, this is what you do . . .'

'No,' I said. 'We don't do anything until we know the girl is alive. Don't like that, fuck off.'

Silence. I waited, then I said, 'Send us a photograph, Express Post, same as your last letter. A Polaroid, any picture. We want to see the girl, see her properly. She's got to be holding today's newspaper, any paper, the front page. Today's paper. Close up. And we want to see her pinkie, the little finger, see that it's properly bandaged. You with me?'

Silence.

'Then you ring at 11.30 a.m. tomorrow. We're convinced she's OK, you can tell me what to do and we'll do it. No argument. To the letter. Failing that, fuck you and we'll find you if it takes fifty years.'

Silence.

A click.

Dear God, what had I done? Condemned the girl to death?

Not if she was already dead.

Corin was looking at me from inside the vehicle, styrofoam cup under her lips, a faintly quizzical look. She had nice eyebrows, I registered for the first time.

I opened the door and got back in, felt the body warmth.

'A client,' I said. 'How's the coffee?'

I took the cap off mine, had a sip, a thrumming in my body, in my chest. A new feeling. A sign of weakness, thrumming.

'Good coffee. You've got the kind of client I'd like.'

She'd watched me speaking.

'What kind of client is that?'

'Someone you can give orders to. Instead of the reverse.'

'You lipread?'

'I wish. You were doing all the talking.'

I drank more coffee, half the lukewarm cup. 'I've got to go,' I said, hesitated. 'I'm hopeless at this kind of thing. Can I see you again? Is that possible?'

Corin had some coffee, touched her short hair.

'That's possible,' she said. 'That should be probable. From my point of view.'

'I'll call you tonight,' I said. 'Is calling you always OK?'

She gave me her slow smile, put a hand out and touched my sleeve, plucked something off it. 'A leaf. You won't get anyone else, if that's what you mean.'

'That's what I mean,' I said.

'What about you? Are you safe to call?'

I got out a card with the mobile number. 'I don't know whether it's safe to call me,' I said. 'But I'm on my own, if that's what you mean.'

'That's what I mean,' she said.

I RANG Graham Noyce and told him about the call.

'What if they don't come through?' he said.

'Call the cops. It's over then.'

'I'll tell the Carsons.'

Aware of the pointlessness of what I was doing, I drove to Altona, over the Westgate Bridge and along the freeway to Millers Road, down towards the bay past the carbon black factory and the refinery with its chimneys that flamed day and night.

The Altona Community Legal Centre didn't spend any money on front. It was housed in an ugly yellow-brick building that still carried faint fancy signwriting saying it had once been the premises of the Modern Bakery.

A young woman with two children was sitting in the reception room, the children fighting for her attention like small but vicious animals attacking a much larger and wounded creature. Behind a counter bearing neat stacks of pamphlets on subjects such as rape counselling, domestic violence and the legal rights of teenagers, a woman in middle age, good-humoured face, was on the phone. She eyed me warily, ended her conversation.

'Yes?' she said.

I introduced myself, said I'd spoken to Sue Torvalds, the solicitor, earlier in the day about someone who had been a volunteer solicitor in the late 1980s.

She smiled. 'Yes, Sue told me. I'm Ellen Khoury, I'm the only worker who was here then.'

'Can you spare a few minutes?'

'Sue's not here. I can't leave the phone really. We can talk here if you like.'

'You had a volunteer solicitor around that time. Mark Carson. I represent his family. They're a bit worried about him and I'm trying to get some idea of the kind of person he is, the people he knew then, just scratching around really.'

She bit her lower lip. 'You're some kind of investigator?'

'No. It's a favour really. To the family.'

Ellen wasn't happy about something. 'That's a long time ago,' she said. 'You should talk to Jeremy Fisher, he was . . .'

'I know. I'd like to talk to him but he's a big-shot lawyer now. You have to make an appointment three months ahead to see him. Did you know Mark then?'

She nodded, didn't want to look me in the eye. 'Yes, there were only a few solicitors came in then. And now.'

'I suppose it would have been unusual for someone from a big city firm to find the time to come out here at night.'

One of the predator children let out a piercing scream. I turned in time to see it strike its fellow predator a full blow in the face, instant retaliation for some wrong. The victim stumbled, fell over backwards and hit its head on the brown nylon carpet, screamed too.

Without venom or force, the mother backhanded the striker, leaned forward and pulled the victim upright by the bib of his tiny overalls, dragged him into the moulded plastic chair next to her. 'Don't bloody go near each other,' she said. She looked at us. 'Kids, Christ, I'm up to here.'

I turned back to Ellen Khoury. 'Mark would have been an unusual volunteer, would he?'

'I suppose so. Most of those we get work for the labour firms or small firms around here.'

'And he did a good job?'

'Well, I was just the front-office worker, you'd

have to ask Jeremy Fisher.' She was drumming the fingers of her right hand on the desk, fast.

This looked like having even less point than I'd expected. With nothing to lose, I said, 'And after the incident, he didn't come any more?'

Ellen stopped drumming, scratched her head at the hairline. She looked relieved. 'No,' she said. 'Well, he could have. Jeremy told the police Mark was here until after she would have been picked up or whatever. So he was in the clear.'

'Yes. In the clear. The police came here when . . .'

'The next day. They didn't know she'd been here until they talked to a friend of hers early in the morning.' She was talking easily now. 'I was here and they came in and gave me the name and I couldn't find the book. Never found the book, it vanished. So we couldn't help them. Anyway, they showed her picture to Moira Rickard, she was the vol on the desk that night, and she remembered her, remembered she'd seen Mark. Last client of the night. She was still with him when Moira went home. We never did that again, go before the last client's gone.'

I nodded. 'And Jeremy was here?'

'Yes.' Ellen's face was expressionless. 'He resigned a few months later, went to some big firm.'

'I can't remember the woman's name,' I said. 'I've gone blank.'

'Anthea Wyllie. She was a nurse at the hospital. You still hear people around here talking about it. They say her parents blame us. That's a bit rough.'

'Certainly is,' I said. 'Well, thanks for talking to me, Ellen. I'll have to make an appointment to see Jeremy.'

'Yes,' she said. 'Jeremy's the one to talk to.'

Back over the bridge, sun behind me like a poisonous fireball heading for earth, to the left Docklands, ahead the shining towers of the city.

Anthea Wyllie. A missing woman, a woman missing after seeing Mark Carson, never seen again. What sort of curse lay on this family, rich beyond greed, cradled in luxury, that their children were stolen from them, that those they touched they marked with crosses of ash?

MR PAT CARSON would like to see me if it was convenient, said the security man in the underground car park, taking the Audi keys from my hand.

It was convenient.

'Frank, get a drink,' Pat said, a glass on the desk at his right hand, his knuckles touching it.

I poured a finger of the peaty liquid, dusted it with water, sat down opposite the old man. There was something about the room, the panelling, the armchairs, the soft lights. At the end of a long and fruitless day, my lunch engagement excepted, it brought a little peace to the soul.

I had a sip. Pat had a sip.

'Jesus,' he said. 'What'd a man do without a drop of the nerve tonic?'

I nodded. He'd had a good few drops. My gaze fell for the first time on a photograph on the wall behind Pat, a photograph lit by a brass picture lamp, of a big gathering, outdoors, everyone standing: Pat and a woman, dark eyes, grey hair pulled back, severe-looking; Tom and Barry with their wives; a woman about Barry's age, probably their sister, Louise, smiling at a tall man who had his arms around three girls, one a teenager. Next to him was Christine, carrying a baby, that would be Anne. In front was a small boy, tennis racket in hand: Pat junior. The dark-haired child with the serious face next to him was Alice, her ordeal still to come. On the left of the crowd, I identified Stephanie, long and lithe in a bikini, her hand on the shoulder of a handsome blond man, probably Dr Jonty. She wasn't looking at the camera, she was looking at someone in bathers on the oppo-site fringe, someone who looked as if he had arrived late, got out of the pool just in time for the photo-graph. It was a young man who looked like Tom Carson with thirty years removed, softly muscular, with thick wet hair fallen across his forehead like a spray, dark and handsome and with a sardonic look. Mark Carson, I had no doubt.

'Graham says you told the bastard to give us proof Anne's alive,' said Pat.

'Yes.'

'No risk there? Not normal people these. Could do anythin'.' His voice was hesitant, he had a look in his eyes that said: tell me good news. Not the Pat Carson of a few days before, but that Pat Carson had been sober.

'Mr Carson,' I said, 'I think Anne's dead.'

He looked into my eyes, sniffed twice, had a sip of whisky, didn't put the glass down, touched it to his lips again, moistened them with whisky.

'I thought, the finger,' he said, 'I thought that meant she was alive.'

'It's a feeling,' I said. 'I've spent a lot of time with people who want to hurt other people, to punish them.'

'Punish? Who? Mark?'

'Perhaps the family or Tom, perhaps Mark.'

Pat shook his head. 'Don't understand. Punish? For what?'

I said nothing, looked away, looked at the photograph behind him. This was what a dynasty looked like. The builders' labourer who ended up owning the building. All the buildings. The boys, who transcended their unschooled father's violent past, his lack of education, who went to private schools and ended up with handicaps of six or eight at Royal Melbourne, were members of a city club that would never have admitted their father, a club whose older members, close to death now, in the home straight, still muttered 'bog Irish' and sprayed spittle at the mention of names like Carson. The boys, who married the daughters of stockbrokers and minor English aristocracy. And the girl, who married into a family of Western District graziers, polo players with city homes in Toorak.

In the crowded photograph, people close together, the eye went first to Pat because he had space around him. His nearest and dearest did not press upon him. He remained at a small distance, his chin up, a rich and powerful self-made man surrounded by his handsome family, a man who had undoubtedly bought and paid for many members of clubs that would not admit him.

'I don't know for what,' I said. 'I just hope I'm wrong. But there wasn't any other way. We have to have proof that Anne's alive.'

'You know what you're doin',' he said, resigned but not convinced. 'What's the proof?'

'Photograph of Anne holding today's newspaper.'

Pat nodded. 'That'll do.'

'Stone, Boyle, Carides, do they do much of the company's legal work?'

He coughed, coughed again, seemed to have trouble coping with the change of topic. 'All of it far's I know. Watterson's used to be our lawyers. Got rich on us. Mark's firm got a fair bit while he was there. Then Tom shifted all the business over to Stone's. Big fight with Barry about that. Lawyers used to be Barry's business, I left it to him, didn't want anythin' to do with 'em. Put your dog in a hole with the other fella's dog, you don't expect 'em both to come out in better shape than they went in. That's lawyers.'

'Why did Tom change firms?'

'Dunno. I stayed out of it. Gettin' too old to worry about stuff like that.' He made a throwing-away gesture. 'Pour me a bit there.'

I got up and poured, put the glass in his hand.

'After Alice,' I said, 'the police put together a list of people who might have had a grudge against the family, the company.'

He nodded again, smiled, pushed his head forward. He was ancient and ageless and reptilian when he did that. 'Like a phone book. Bloody hundreds of names. Still, that's business, that's life.'

'People hating you enough to want to harm your children?'

The smile went away and he had a careful look at me, a long and judgemental look from under eyelids without lashes.

'You sound like that Royal Commission lawyer, Frank,' he said. 'Know about that? The commission?'

'Yes.'

'He asked questions like that. Bit of a question, bit of a comment. He was a smartarse. Mr Ashley

Tolliver, Queen's fuckin Counsel. You answer the question, mainly pretty bloody stupid question, then the bastard asks it again, only he's addin somethin from your answer, makes it all sound different.'

I felt his tone of voice on my face, like a cold-room door opening, old, dead, chilled air coming out, and I said, 'I wasn't making any comment. It was just a question.'

Pat Carson shook his head, nodded, shook his head. 'Mr Ashley Tolliver, counsel of the fuckin' Queen. Her fuckin' Majesty. Two days of the sneerin' bastard, never done a day's work, talked like he knew the buildin' business, wouldn't know a concrete pour from a fuckin' wet dream. Talked to me like I was some piece of shit, no respect, bit of dogshit on his shoe.'

He drank some whisky. A drop rolled down his chin, caught the light and glowed like a tear of gold. 'Had a bad accident later, Mr Ashley Tolliver, Q fuckin' C, two years later, a good time later. Just lost control of the car. Mercedes, mark you. Into the sea. Down there other side of Lorne, the cliff's steep, go off the edge ... Never walked again, they say.' He looked at me. 'No respect. He had no respect.'

I finished my drink. 'I'll come over in the morning. Wait for the post.'

As I neared the library door, I heard Tom saying

loudly, '. . . sources close to the company, that means a source *inside* the fucking company, now who the fuck could that be, I ask you?'

Barry's voice, stiff: 'You're becoming paranoid, Tom, do you know that? They make this stuff up, they don't need a source.'

'Bullshit. It's not the first time. Someone's feeding this bastard. You know that, don't you?'

I couldn't linger. I very much wanted to.

'PROVING TRICKIER than I thought,' said Orlovsky. 'There's lots of people doing bits and pieces of voice work. Most of it's for talking to computers, asking them questions, that sort of thing.'

We were in the kitchen of the Garden House, leaning against opposite counters. I'd told him about the day: the kidnapper's call, my conversations with Jeremy Fisher and Graham Noyce, my visit to the Altona Community Legal Centre.

'Where'd this beer come from?' I said.

Orlovsky drank some of his Dortmunder Pils out of the bottle. 'A rather nice woman came in to check on the stocks and she asked if there was anything we needed. So I told her.'

'So suddenly you're not above eating the rich's cream. Surprised you limited yourself to beer. Anyway, what's wrong with typing in your questions to computers, why do you have to talk?'

He drank some more beer, all the while giving me his pitying look. 'Say you're being operated on, you're hooked up to the computer, the surgeon's got both hands inside you, he's worried and he wants to know your vital signs. He can't look up, so what does he do?'

'He says: "This one's a goner. What are you doing later, nurse?"'

'This is post-nurse, I'm talking about the future. He asks the computer. And it answers in a way that he can't possibly misunderstand. Same for pilots, air controllers, cops, fucking soldiers.' He smiled his sinister smile. 'Of course, soldiers already have robots answering their questions. Robots asking, robots answering.'

'The dignity of the profession of arms. That escaped you, didn't it?'

'Must have. I didn't notice much of your actual dignity, that could be why. Any, now that I think of it. Noticed plenty of your actual indignity.'

'A literal mind. Best suited to buggering around with computers. So that's the best you can do on this intonation stuff?'

'Basically, yes. Feelers out, I stressed the urgency. There's something, it won't help. The voice, it's a mixture of old Hollywood voices, John Wayne and James Stewart and Alan Ladd, actors like that. From Westerns.'

I had difficulty with this. I closed my eyes and drank some beer. 'Tell me about it,' I said.

'I played a little compilation, carefully chosen, to this extremely advanced woman at RMIT. She did a linguistic and acoustic analysis, don't worry about it, it's beyond you. They've got a huge voice bank, the test shows the intonation of some dead Western stars. It's all based on a mark-up language called Tone and Break Indices. She was excited, never heard it done that well before.'

'Well, I'm excited too,' I said. 'I may have to leave you and go to sleep, I'm so excited. I hope you found a way to handle her excitement, channel it into something productive.'

Orlovsky smiled and shook his head.

'And this Teutonic beer's got an old-sock element to it,' I said. 'Old Prussian sock. Research at the cutting edge of technology all day and still we know sweet fanny. Correct me if I'm wrong.'

He sighed. 'Right. But you probably don't even know where Prussia is, never mind the taste of an old Prussian sock.'

I said, 'Son, I've done my time with Prussian socks, I've night-jumped over the German plain, at a certain level, you get the feeling you're falling into a cabbage, that's the smell. Then you land on the plain the Russian tanks were supposed to come charging over to get what they didn't get in World War Two.'

I drained the bottle. 'But you wouldn't know about World War Two, Mick. You're an eighties boy. What kind of people would have a use for a voiceshake of old Western actors?'

'Well, anyone who needs voices. I'll show you.'

He went into the sitting room and came back with his briefcase, put it on the counter, opened it and fiddled with the computer.

The voice said:

So you think Carson money can buy anything, don't you? Just money, that's what you thought, isn't it? . . . Don't say NOW to me. I don't take your orders. I don't need your money. . . . Shut up, I'm talking to you. You don't have the money to buy your way out of this. You're talking to someone quite different now.

'OK, that's the voice we heard,' said Orlovsky. 'Now listen to this.'

The voice was deep and sonorous now and the speech slower.

'And this.'

Now the voice was feminine, light, a woman speaking quickly.

'And so it goes on.' He was shutting down the machine.

'Modulate the basic voice, you can get any number of voices, male, female, young, old. Once you'd done the work, it would be the cheapest way to put a multi-voice track on anything. All it needs is one person to speak with the intonation you want.'

'And you can't buy it?'

'No one's ever heard of a commercial product like this. Or anyone working on one. This woman at RMIT, Kim Reid, Dr Reid, she says a bloke came wandering into the place a few years ago and asked a lot of intelligent questions about linguistic and acoustic patterns, about Tone and Break. Said he was working on games. But she doesn't know his name, not sure he gave it, can't really remember what he looked like.'

'Anyone can just wander in? You just wandered in?'

'No. I rang her, she invited me over, came to the office to meet me. But it's a uni, people wandering everywhere.'

'Why did this person pick on her?'

'He'd read something she published about the voice bank.'

Orlovsky opened the drinks fridge, a full-size refrigerator, took out another Dortmunder, offered it to me.

'No thanks. Was that a Miller's I saw in there? Published where?'

'Christ, I don't know. I didn't ask. What does it

matter? We've got Miller's in the longneck bottle, yes, imported from a country that doesn't know good beer from fermented horse piss.'

'Can you ring her? Got a home number?'

He closed the fridge, put the beers on the counter, studied me with his head tilted, his eyes expressing a complete lack of confidence in my state of mind. 'To ask her what?'

'Where the stuff was published.'

'Jesus, Frank.' He took a bloated wallet out of an inside pocket of his jacket, rejected half a dozen bits of paper before he found what he wanted, a business card. 'There's no home, there's a mobile.'

'Try it.'

He shook his head, left the room. I went over and uncapped the beers, rinsed my mouth with Miller's, thinking about old Pat Carson and the crippled QC, the Carson brothers arguing in the library. Then the mind sideslipped without warning to Corin McCall, to the little garden I'd had when I was a child, to the day my mother told me I was forbidden to go next door, could not go next door ever again, could not water my garden. But everything I'd planted came up. I knew because I climbed onto the garage roof and from up there I could see my little garden, saw the peas and the pumpkins like bombs, the tops of carrots. And I saw the flowers.

Orlovsky came in, pleased, took his beer in his long-fingered hand, drank. 'She was in a pub, very friendly. Enjoyed our encounter, she said. Mostly these balloon heads go home and eat cereal in front of the computer. I might ring her again some time.'

'Published where?'

'Something called *JIVS*. Stands for *Journal of Intelligent Voice Systems,* it's published at some university in the States. To help nerds get tenure, I would think. A minimum of so many thousand words published in a refereed journal, that's a condition of getting a permanent job. So there's thousands of refereed journals. Six nerds get together and put out a journal and they referee each other's stuff.'

'Sounds like the police force. How would you get the list of subscribers?'

He looked at me, understood. 'They put the thing on the web after the subscribers get it, the whole world can read it. Shot in a million, digger.'

'How?'

'Well, I don't imagine these people are going to great lengths to hide their subscribers. There's probably a way to get the list. An unethical way.'

'Can you do it now?'

Orlovsky wiped his lips with the back of his hand. 'You're encouraging me to engage in unethical behaviour?'

I said, 'No. Just to get the list.'

It took him about twenty-five minutes, then he called me over. 'They're sorted by postcode for the US, otherwise by country,' he said. 'This is Australia, about thirty subscribers, I count nine in Victoria, exactly the people you'd expect: two at RMIT, two at Defence Intelligence, three at Monash, one at Deakin, one at the eye and ear hospital. Not people working on games, I'd say. Not officially.'

'Depending on what's in the post, check them out tomorrow,' I said.

Later, I showered in the slate-floored chamber where water could be commanded to come from above and below, from every side at any temperature and velocity. Then, in the big, pale room, I climbed between linen sheets that smelled of sunlight and went to sleep, instantly. And in the dog watch of the night, the dream came, the dream that was a version of reality but in which I floated freely between points of view, now myself, now a spectator.

It always began in the room in the sad little house, the odour of lifetimes held in the layers of carpet and underfelt, in the old newspapers down there on the floorboards. Seventy or eighty years or more of dust and spilt food, spilt liquids, ground-in coal ash, the urine of dozens of long-dead cats. 'We're going out now, Dave,' I say. 'Get up.'

He looks at me, wild face gone, years gone, a sad and chastened boy now. 'They'll kill me,' he says.

'No they won't. I'll be with you.'

'Kill me,' he says. 'Won't let me live.'

'Not while I'm with you.'

'Look after me?' he says in a tiny voice.

'Yes. I'll look after you.'

We go down the passage. I feel the old sprung floorboards bounce, feel the rotten stumps move. Dave is ahead of me. At the front door, I say, 'Open it.'

He opens it, stands, looks back at me. And I am seeing myself from outside, looking into the dim doorway, seeing myself, shirtless, sweat in the hollow of my throat.

'It's OK,' I say. 'It's OK, I'm with you.'

He puts out a hand to me. I sigh and take it and we go out onto the verandah together, grown men holding hands.

It is dark, no moon, no lights on in the street. I am straining to see beyond the low hedge and front gate.

At the steps, the spotlight comes on, night sun, impossibly bright light. Dave jumps, startled, lets go of my hand, turns, tries to hug me, bury his head in my shoulder.

I hear the sound and I feel the shot hit him, feel it through his bones, feel it through his arms clinging to me.

'Oh Jesus, no,' I say, holding him, feeling the strength leave his body, having to hold him up, feel his warm blood on my face, taste it on my lips, go to my knees with him.

And I hear myself saying, 'No, Dave, not me, not me.'

Then I am myself, looking into his eyes, seeing the reproach in them, no anger, just hurt and betrayal. 'You knew,' he says and he begins to cough, to cough up blood.

I see myself lay him down, stand up, see the blood on my bare upper body, my hands. Police are coming from everywhere. In the gate, Hepburn appears, black overalls, Kevlar vest, Fritz helmet.

I walk towards him.

He backs away. 'Frank, the bloke was . . .'

I take two big strides, get to him, grab him by the throat with both hands. I feel the squeeze, my thumbs digging into his windpipe, my will to kill him. He tries to spear my arms apart with his palms pressed together but I butt him in the face, hear the sound the cartilage in his nose makes as it is crushed.

Then I woke up, the dream always ended there, woke me. I got up, went downstairs, found Orlovsky's no-name cigarettes, sat in the dark and smoked and brooded. Waiting for the light.

LAUREN GEARY stood in the library doorway holding the envelope, uncertain of whom to give it to. It had been delivered just after 10 a.m. and brought from the gatehouse by a waiting security man.

We had been in the library since 9.30 a.m., Tom and Barry, Stephanie, unable to meet my eyes, Graham Noyce. Pat Carson was next door, waiting to be told. Orlovsky declined to be present. 'I hate stuff like this,' he said.

'Frank,' said Tom.

He was in his position, standing behind Stephanie. This morning, he was smoking cigarettes, had smoked three while we waited.

My duty. I made the demand, I could tell them the result. I had no quarrel with that, only regret and fear.

I took the envelope from Lauren Geary, got a finger

in behind the seal, ripped it open, took out the contents, a photograph, not a big print, a 4x3, something like that.

I turned it over.

Anne Carson, Anne Carson's head above the copy of the previous day's *Age* she was holding under her chin. Both her little fingers were visible, her left one in a neat, clean bandage. She looked clean too, her hair damp and combed off her face, comb marks showing, clean and unafraid, something unfocused about her eyes.

But alive.

'She's alive,' I said.

'Thank God.' Tom closed his eyes, brought his hands up and made a steeple with his fingers, put his forehead to his fingertips for a second. Then he touched Stephanie's shoulder, a father's touch.

'Tell your grandfather,' he said and held out a hand for the photograph.

'Good call, Frank,' said Barry, not loudly, moving to look at the photograph.

'She looks fine,' Tom said. 'She's OK, we can get her out of this. Get her out. Yes.'

I left the house, walked slowly back to the Garden House, enjoyed the misty rain on my face, the smell of the newly dug beds on either side of the brick path. The gardener I'd seen the day before was resting a foot on a fork sunk deep into the dark soil.

'Good soil,' I said. 'Making the beds bigger?'

'Mr Pat Carson went to Ireland last year,' she said, as if that were explanation enough. What did that mean? Corin would know.

Corin. I hadn't phoned her the night before. I'd said, I'll phone you tonight. Why had I said that? What would I have said to her? After one sandwich, one round sandwich with a hole in the middle, eaten in her vehicle?

Not hearing from me wouldn't have bothered her. She probably thought: Thank you, God, the psycho hasn't called. Soldier-cop psycho killer. Self-confessed.

I stood on the terrace at the French doors, cleaning my shoes on the bristle mat. Orlovsky looked up, put the phone in his lap. He was sitting in the Morris chair with the leather cushions, portable phone in his hand, ashtray full of no-name butts on the coffee table in front of him.

I opened the door and stepped into the warm, bright room.

'Alive,' I said. 'Yesterday afternoon, anyway.'

WE PARKED in the Carson House car park and sat there for a while in the gloom, not saying anything. Then the lift doors opened. Graham Noyce and a burly man came out, saw us, walked over.

'You cannot believe,' Noyce said, 'how hard it is to get used money. The banks don't want to give you used money. It's pure luck we've managed to get this sum.'

The burly man was carrying a briefcase: two hundred and fifty thousand dollars in old fifties and hundreds.

Orlovsky coughed, the cough of someone who wants to say something. 'Knew the right people,' he said, expressionless voice, 'you could've bought this cash for a unit. Anywhere. Eighty grand unit.'

Noyce glanced at Orlovsky. 'Knew the right people?' he said. He looked at me. 'We'd appreciate it if your associate doesn't put this job on his CV.'

I took the briefcase. 'It isn't over yet,' I said. 'And when it is, no one may want to put this job on their CVs.'

The instructions at 11.30 a.m. had been clear:

Two hundred and fifty thousand dollars in used fifties and hundreds in a briefcase. Be on the corner of Little Lonsdale and Swanston Street at 3.30 p.m. and you'll get your instructions by phone. When we have the money and know that you haven't tried to trick us, we'll call you and tell you where to find the girl. If you do anything else, try anything, she dies. Understand?

I said yes.

Orlovsky dropped me in Little Lonsdale and I walked to the Swanston intersection, conscious of the weight of the case. An early twilight was settling in, thin rain being blown down the tatty street, everyone hurrying to be somewhere else. I watched two haggard boys across the street making a drug sale to a lanky young man in a good suit: a hit to see him through the night shift in some twenty-four-hour office, hunched over a screen.

The phone vibrated at 3.29 p.m. my time.

'Yes.'

'Go to Museum Station now. Take the escalator down. Wait near the escalators at the bottom. Put the briefcase between your feet. Someone will approach you and say, "Anne sends her love". Got that?'

'Yes.'

I walked up the street thinking, we haven't been dealing with crazies or the Russian Mafia or the same people who kidnapped Alice. We've been dealing with small-time opportunists, people who somehow got hold of an advanced voice-changing device. They panicked at the MCG, realized that with the notice we had, we could trap them. Throwing the money to the crowd wasn't planned. It was an improvisation.

Mid-afternoon, no rush for the trains yet, half an hour before the early leavers came out of the office blocks. It seemed no more than a day since I'd come up from the depths of Museum Station carrying Vella's package. How long ago was it?

I entered the cheerless, echoing structure, paused only briefly at the top of an escalator, watched the iron stairway moving down into the cavern blasted from the rock. It was a long way down, and steep.

On the stairs, going down, the briefcase heavy in my hand.

No one waiting at the bottom. The person would be nearby, somewhere in sight of the escalators, waiting for a man with a briefcase.

I looked back, up the steel stream. No one had

joined me on the escalator. They'd picked a quiet time, they knew this station, the table of its human tides.

Why did they want me to wait? Why not tell me to put the briefcase down, get on an up escalator? Thieves, that's why. They'd lost the money at the MCG. It would be a painful thing for them now if some lurking kid saw me move away, leave the brief-case unattended, grabbed it and ran. They could hardly chase him. No. Better to have me wait, guard their money. Hard-earned money. Blood money.

I reached the bottom and stepped off, walked a few paces, stopped, put the briefcase between my feet, looked around.

No one coming my way.

They were watching, a final check to see that I was alone.

I turned back to face the escalators. People going up, the stairs I'd left still empty. At the top, far away, a tall person pushing someone in a wheelchair was looking down. Didn't they have lifts for wheelchairs? It couldn't be safe coming down this steep stairway, thousands of interlocked steel knuckles moving.

I looked around again. Where was the pick-up person? Looking at my watch, pointlessly looking at my watch, feeling a little tremor in my throat, looking back at the escalator, looking up, at the man with the wheelchair, it was a man, bearded, our eyes met in the way of animals, me on the canyon floor, him on the rim.

Our eyes locked and his mouth opened, opened in his beard, I could see the pink of his mouth, pink like a rose, and he shouted:

'HERE'S YOUR LITTLE SLUT, YOU CARSON BASTARDS!'

He pushed the wheelchair, pushed it and kicked it.

Pushed it into the canyon, pushed and kicked it onto the moving steel steps.

For a second, it was airborne, came down on its rubber tyres, bounced, lurched sideways, came upright.

I could see the person on it, someone in a heavy coat, camel-coloured, a coat with a hood, a duffel coat, you didn't see duffel coats these days ...

I didn't think, ran, ran for the escalator, saw the wheelchair lurch forward, begin to topple ...

Saw the person on it, the hood falling off the face. Dark glasses.

The dirty-blonde hair, the lock falling forward ...

I was running up the moving stairs, against the stairs, running towards the wheelchair coming down, an impossible gap to bridge, the chair toppling, hitting the side of the stairs, bouncing across to meet the other side, Anne thrown about, thrown forward, not falling out, held by something, dark glasses off her face, in the air . . .

Her eyes were open, pale eyes.

The wheelchair was in the air, one wheel on the rail, people shouting.

I could save her, stop her fall, if I could get there, get a hand on this chariot.

Running uphill, the wheelchair above me now, going into space.

I stumbled, falling, falling away from her, falling away from Anne, my arm out, my despairing, clutching hand.

And then I touched a wheel, grabbed it, pulled the chair down, pulled it on top of me, pain as it met my face, my teeth, my throat, going over backwards, holding on to it, sliding, pain in my back, agonizing pain, sliding, under the chair, head lower than heels . . .

We were at the bottom, Anne and I, thrown across the threshold onto the tiles, the chair on my chest, screams, my scream, the screams of others, still in my ears.

I fought clear of the wheelchair, got onto my knees at her feet.

People still shouting.

The hood was over her face again, her head lolling.

Please God, not a broken neck, not now.

I put my hands to her head, pushed it up, my fingers too big, too callous, pushed the hood away from her face. I pulled away the scarf around her neck, a woollen scarf, blood-red.

Her mouth was open slightly, an unlipsticked mouth, pale, paler than her face. A child's mouth.

And her eyes were open, held open, taped with transparent tape, only the whites showing.

I touched her face. Cold, cold beyond warming.

Behind me, close, a woman screamed, a scream that resonated in that cold canyon, went to the walls and multiplied, came back and went up to the far roof and there expanded, grew and grew and formed a parachute over us, a canopy of livid sound, gradually turning to echo.

I pulled the hood back over Anne Carson's face, gently, gently over the lock of hair.

Then I sat back on my heels and began to cry, just small sobs, nose and throat sounds at first, soon the other sounds, the sounds we cannot make, cannot call forth, the sounds that make themselves, that speak of pain and horror and helplessness and injustice, speak of regret, of the regrets. All the regrets.

And so it ended, in a tiled space, pitiless light, pale people all around. A man and a wheelchair, a girl in the chair, bound to it, dead. The man on his haunches, weeping, keening.

FROM THE windows of the homicide squad offices, you could look down on the lights of St Kilda Road, make out the Shrine of Remembrance where the flame never died, see the dark expanse of Melbourne Grammar's playing fields. It was a quiet office, smelling of instant coffee, of too-pungent aftershave, of roll-on deodorant applied too lavishly.

'So basically you found the sellers of the vehicle,' said Detective Senior Sergeant Vella, 'and ruled out the driver and the locksmith boyfriend.' He was sitting opposite me, across two desks, two of the half-dozen plastic-veneered desks pushed together to form a dumping ground for files and folders and boxes.

'Basically,' I said.

'Leaving only five security guards, two other drivers, gardeners, cooks, cleaners, disgruntled employees past and present by the hundreds, and so on.'

'I wasn't hired to conduct an investigation into everyone in the Carson empire,' I said. 'I was hired to hand over the money. How many times do I have to say that? Want me to say it again? I was hired to hand over the money.'

'But you did start your own little investigation.'

'We were waiting. I had nothing to do.' My face was aching, my whole head, my neck and shoulders. 'Got any aspirin?'

Without looking, he opened a drawer, found a foil strip, threw it at me. I broke out three, washed them down with cold tea from a mug labelled Fuck Off, This Is My Mug.

Vella's eyes were closed and he was rubbing his temples. 'Jesus, Frank,' he said, 'I don't know. How could you let these people not call the cops? You had a duty to walk out of there and call us, tell us there's been a kidnapping, fuck what the family wants, a fucking crime committed.'

I thought about this, looked around the big room, only four people in it, looked at the newspaper posters on the bile-coloured walls, the files on the floor, the objects in labelled plastic bags, the death masks in a glass case, the board listing homicide cops long dead.

Vella waited, sad expression.

'I had no such duty,' I said. 'They called the cops

once before and that girl's only alive because of luck and her own efforts.'

'This Noyce says you talked to the girl in England, to this one's mother, he's got a bill for surveillance on Barry Carson's son. What's the result of all that activity?'

'Nothing.'

'Just passing the time?'

'Yes.'

'Nothing of any use at all?'

'No.'

Vella pointed his long nose at the ceiling and sighed, scratched his head with both hands. 'A week behind,' he said. 'She could be alive today. Now from one end, we have to chase up every fucking Tarago in Melbourne, visit every fucking opshop that might ever have sold a duffel coat, ask ourselves where this arsehole got a wheelchair. And from the other, we've got a whole fucking small town to interview and that's only the beginning. Two crews on it, fourteen people, and it isn't enough.'

'Are you finished?' I said.

He got up and came around the island, made a space on my desk and sat on it. Not looking at me, looking at the man sitting off to my right, he said quietly, 'You get that thing to work?'

I nodded.

'See anything?'

'No.'

'Looking for anything in particular?'

'No. Just looking.'

'Fuck, Frank, I'm compromised here. Who else knows?'

'One person, there's no risk there. Forget you gave it to me. I've forgotten.'

A thin-faced man appeared in a doorway. 'John,' he said, 'the Tarago's clean, been gone over with meths, they think. And the wheelchair was stolen from Prince Alfred last Saturday.'

'Things just get easier and easier,' said Vella. 'Tell me if you think of anything. Want a cab? Your face looks terrible.'

The cab dropped me at the underground car park entrance. I walked across the garden and into the main house through the side entrance.

The house was quiet, smelling faintly of lavender wax. I went past the library, heard low voices, the smell of Tom's panatellas. The door was ajar and I caught a glimpse of a fat ankle on a knee, a lurid homicide tie, a scalp gleaming under a homicide haircut.

The study door was open. I didn't knock, stood in the doorway. Pat Carson's chair was swivelled to face the French windows and his secret courtyard, only the top of his head visible.

'I'm sorry,' I said.

He didn't turn, didn't say anything, moved his head slightly.

I waited a while. Then I turned and left the house, went to the Garden House and packed my things and Orlovsky's. As I closed the front door behind me, I smelled cigarette smoke.

'Frank,' said Stephanie Carson, face flushed as if from exercise, girlish in a poloneck sweater, 'it's terrible to say this at a time like this, but, the other night, you won't . . . they'll kill me.'

'No,' I said, 'I don't remember the other night.'

She flicked her cigarette away, didn't look where it went, didn't care, came up to me, a hand behind my head, on tiptoe kissing me on the lips, a full, sucking, wet, lascivious kiss, moved her head, teeth against mine, pressed her tongue into my mouth, pressed her pubic mound against me.

I pulled away, picked up the bags and walked, drove out of the basement car park in the old Alfa, aimed for home. Such as it was.

ALL THE WAY, Stephanie on my lips, her perfume in my head, I thought about something I had said to Orlovsky on the day he fetched me from my helicopter trip to see Anne's mother:

This thing isn't going to have a simple ending because it doesn't have a simple beginning.

I'd known that then and I knew it now, and I knew nothing more than that. But what did the beginning matter? The end was all that mattered. Had I caused the girl's death on the morning I talked the Carsons out of bringing in the police? That depended on whether the police could have found her before the kidnappers killed her.

But how could I be sure they always intended to kill her? What if my demand on Wednesday provoked them into killing her? These were not sane people.

There were no answers to these questions and there

was no point in asking them. But and but and but. In the same circumstances, Katherine Carson had blamed Barry for what happened to Alice.

As the Carson family now blamed me. And from the beginning, I'd known the risk I was taking.

If it goes wrong, it'll somehow be my fault. And I'll blame myself too. For not having the brains to walk out now.

That was all I had to blame myself for: not walking out when I should have. What would they have done? Hired someone else? Brought in their international security consultants?

All I had to blame myself for? *All?* Vella was right: my duty had been to leave the Carson house that night and tell the police that a girl had been kidnapped. The trail was fresh. An hour would have produced addresses for every Tarago ever registered in Victoria and, in a few hours more, the field narrowed to perhaps twenty per cent of them.

In the cold and sordid apartment, too cold to take off my jacket, I lay on the sofa and ate old salt and vinegar chips, chips so old they could have been made from papyrus, drank wine left open in the fridge for I didn't know how long. Too long, much too long.

When the wine was gone, I thought about going out for more, hunted without optimism in the kitchen cupboards, experienced a miracle, found a bottle of

Johnnie Walker Black Label in a box, gift-wrapped in striped paper, tied with a green ribbon. Little Morris had given it to me, the day I went to hand in my resignation, to short-circuit the procedure that began with my hands around Hepburn's throat. 'Everyone put in,' he said. 'They asked me to say, why is it you can never do a job properly?'

I had come home and stuck the package somewhere, anywhere, out of sight, didn't want to know about it, about no longer being a part of something bigger than myself.

Anne. Dead how long? She had been cold, icy.

Not a night to think about that. A suitable night to drink this expensive whisky and think about other things. Try not to think about anything would be better.

The room began to warm, my aches diminished and I felt a numbness stealing over me, half-drunken numbness. I kicked off my shoes, put my glass on the floor, folded my arms, closed my eyes, could have gone to sleep, was going to sleep.

Vibration in my chest. Insistent.

I sat upright, clutched myself.

Noyce's tiny weightless mobile, not given back, not left behind in the Garden House, throbbing in my inside pocket.

I got it out, with difficulty, squinted at the buttons, pressed the phone symbol.

'Yes,' I said.

The voice. Croaky John Wayne and awkward Jimmy Stewart and shy Alan Ladd and dry Randolph Scott, all in it.

'Tell the Carsons it's not an eye for an eye. We want more than an eye for an eye. Worth much more than one Carson slut. Tell all the Carson sluts that.'

I should have rung Vella. I didn't, put the lights out, lay in the dark and sipped whisky till sleep threw itself over me like a blanket.

IN THE NIGHT, the dream of Afghanistan, one of the dreams, the one in which I am trying to get to Cowper, liquid-eyed Cowper, who is screaming, the scream of a child, calling for me. His captain. If I can get to him, I can save him. There is no logic in this, it is a dream. I am crawling towards him, gunfire, pieces of the helicopter burning around me. I am burdened by a weight, it holds me back, I move with agonizing slowness. Then I realise what the weight is: my legs are missing, a large part of my legs, well above the knees. I am having to haul my body without help from my legs. And at the moment of this realization, pain floods through me and I know that I cannot save Cowper because I am dying very quickly.

I woke up, still there, still legless and bleeding to death on that dark Afghan plain, sat up, pushed away the blanket, felt for my knees, found them and lay back, exhausted, as wet as if I had been swimming. Eventually, I fell asleep again, but a fitful, fearful sleep this time, broken by the slam of a car door, a snarling cat skirmish, an alarm trilling far away. When I could see the dark behind the blind fading to grey, I got up, put on a tracksuit and runners and went out into the cold, near-empty world. It had been weeks and all the bits of my body that needed regular moving had stiffened up. For a while, everything hurt, my back, ankles, knees, but by the time I reached the Esplanade, I had found my stride, the pains were down to tolerable levels. And, gradually, the chemical balance in my bloodstream seemed to return to normal, my skin stopped feeling stretched like kite paper, my jaw stopped clicking.

Running, early misty rain on my face, thinking, unable to stop thinking.

Tell the Carsons it's not an eye for an eye. We want more than an eye for an eye. Worth much more than one Carson slut. Tell all the Carson sluts that.

A grievance against the Carsons. Hatred, enough to kill an innocent girl for. Madness. Hatred turned to madness. What were the Carsons being blamed for? An eye for an eye. For a death? The death of someone in a part of the Carson empire, the diversified Carson empire, now not just a construction company but the owner of shopping centres and retail chains and big pieces of other companies? Industrial accidents? A death on a building site? Presumably there'd been many people killed over the years. Deaths for which the Carsons could be held directly responsible.

Anthea Wyllie. The Altona nurse who vanished after seeing Mark Carson. Jeremy Fisher gave Mark an alibi. Was there a family who didn't accept that, who thought Mark was responsible? What was it that made a rich city lawyer give his services to the needy in a distant suburb? Was he in search of prey?

Did this mean Anne had been chosen simply because she was an available Carson, female Carson, because the kidnappers watched the school and followed Whitton's car? Cars – he used three Carson cars. Chosen because she was the easiest Carson child to get to. Anne Carson was a soft target, walking down Revesdale Road alone, flushed from whatever took place in Craig's yellow van, going into an alley. The other children were too young or too old, were elsewhere, far away. Anne's younger sister, Vicky, went to an exclusive primary school, a walled school, driven in a minibus with five other rich children. The driver and guard came from a security firm.

That would be a hard target.

I ran out of legs on the home stretch, had to push myself, to ignore the body's protests, to strive to hold the pace and not to weaken. Once I'd found satisfaction in that, asked it of others, *demanded* it of others. Not any more. Proving yourself to yourself, to others above you and below you, that came to an end in fire and blood and broken bodies.

At the apartment, I showered and shaved, put on a shirt laundered by the Carson housekeeping staff, grey flannels cleaned and pressed. Then I drove to Acland Street, bought the papers and had breakfast, no relish in the eating of it after I saw the front-page headlines, the grainy photographs lifted from Museum Station's security cameras. Both papers carried sequences of pictures of the wheelchair on the escalator and blurred enlargements and a police artist's sketches of the man's bearded face, full on and in profile.

This wasn't going to do Detective Senior Sergeant John Ricardo Vella and the combined crews of the homicide squad any good. Fourteen, he said. They could activate all fifty-six members and it wouldn't do any good. Take away the beard and you had nothing. I wouldn't be able to pick him out of a line-up and nor would anyone else. Not sensibly.

And I'd seen the man in the flesh. I'd met his eyes, looked up, across a long divide, seen a pink hole of hate open in his beard. The city was full of tall men with beards. I looked out of the window, looked across the street expecting to see one. And I did, froze. Then I recognized him, he was a journalist, a football writer, he found poetry and pathos and lessons for living and dying in young men chasing a ball. At the end of his right arm was a child, fighting like a fish, padded and capped and ecstatic at being with him in the street.

Where was he yesterday, in the afternoon? Parking a people mover in a parking bay for the disabled near Museum Station?

I didn't read the newspapers' text. What could they tell me that I didn't know or didn't want to know? The last segment of toast and poached egg, I left it on the plate, ordered coffee, went outside and rang Detective Senior Sergeant Vella. He answered with a sound made in his throat, the sound an animal might make, rolling over in a narrow and dark cave heated by its own blood, a sleeping animal disturbed by something.

'I didn't think about Noyce's mobile,' I said. 'Nor did anyone else. How's that for being sharp?'

'What?'

'They rang last night, said, "Tell the Carsons it's not an eye for an eye. We want more than an eye for an eye. Worth much more than one Carson slut. Tell all the Carson sluts that."'

A silence.

'Say it again.' The animal was fully awake.

I said it again.

'Eye for an eye?'

'Eye for an eye.'

Silence. 'Means what? In your judgement?'

'I presume that they blame the Carsons for a death. You'd want to be checking all deaths in the empire since at least 1990. Can't be that many.'

He coughed. 'Four at one go on the Coniston House site. Crane fell over. That'd be '91, '92, around then. Where are you?'

'Borscht in Acland Street. Something else. There's a woman, a nurse, Anthea Wyllie, disappeared in Altona in 1988. Last seen talking to Mark Carson. I'd look at the family, friends. Hard.'

'Wyllie? Spell that.'

I did so.

'Don't go away. Someone will come for the mobile. The beard. False, you reckon?'

'The bathroom fittings bloke in Revesdale Road says the driver who pissed him off had a beard. The young offsider says the man next to the Tarago in the lane had a big moustache.'

'Bloke who sold the Tarago says a beard. So it would have to be full beard, moustache only, back to full beard. If it's the same bloke, that says you saw a false beard.'

'It's possible. Like some bad cop movie.'

'My life's a bad cop movie. Not improved by people like you.'

I went inside and drank lukewarm coffee and waited. Not long. A green Falcon double-parked outside and the passenger came in, a woman in black who looked like a tired netball player. She walked straight to my table, knew me. I gave her Noyce's vibrating phone.

'It needs a charge,' I said.

'Don't we all.' She took it and left.

My phone rang. I went outside. Running my life from a place that served breakfast.

'Frank?'

Corin.

How can you identify someone from one word they say? Probably by intonation, a Tone and Break problem.

'I've been meaning to ring,' I said.

'That wasn't you on television last night, was it? At Museum Station?'

Her tone was tentative. She wanted me to say: No, that wasn't me. Wasn't it awful?

'I'm afraid so,' I said. 'That job's over.'

As I said it, I thought, the matter-of-fact, just-another-day-at-the-office attitude, that's a bad mistake.

She didn't say anything. I could hear her breathing

and I knew what she was thinking: How do I extricate myself from this? I don't want to offend this person, he might . . .

'I'm going to the country this afternoon,' she said. 'My brother's got a few acres, he's planted vines. Somehow, I'm in charge of them, I'm the de facto viticulturist, he's too busy, too tired, too hungover.'

'Good,' I said. 'That sounds nice. Enjoy yourself. I'll give you a ring some time. Or you could give me a ring.'

'Can you come?'

A man popping up like a cork, breaking the surface, tanks shrugged off, weightbelt jettisoned, taking air into empty lungs. 'Today? Let me think, yes, I think I can fit that in.'

'It's staying over,' she said. 'Tonight. Pretty primitive.'

'Primitive? No spa bath?'

'No.'

'Well, I don't know. That sort of back-to-nature stuff has its appeal for me. What time? My vehicle or yours?'

'Around four-thirty. It's the bulk-manure mover, I'm afraid. I've got to take bags of things. What's your address?'

For a second, the sky lightened, it seemed as if

the sun was coming out. In the midst of death, we are in life. Not a sentiment my mother would have approved of.

THE LAND was on a hillside, reached by a lane where half a dozen old elms had gone feral, produced hundreds of suckers that formed an undisciplined hedgerow.

I got out in the near dark to open the gate, a vicious thing of twisted pipes and rusted wire that resented being unlatched and fought back as I dragged it through long grass.

Corin drove through and parked inside an open hayshed, a roof held up by massive eucalypt trunks. Beyond that was an old stone and brick barn, a long building with a loft door at one end. I closed the gate and walked down the track to join her, breathing out little ghosts of steam.

'Welcome to Nightmarch Hill,' said Corin, opening the vehicle's back door. She was in her work clothes. 'Named for Phar Lap's brother.'

'He'd be as well known as Elvis's brother,' I said.

'Elvis had a brother?'

'No.'

'Well, Phar Lap did.' She handed me a plastic crate of food. 'Nightmarch. A man called Crossley bought the whole hill after he won twenty thousand pounds on him in the Epsom Handicap in 1929. It's all broken up now but this bit kept the name. Don't know why. The house is on the property next door. Dump the stuff at the door. I'll get the generator going.'

She went around the side of the barn. I had everything at the side door of the barn when a diesel engine began to thump. Corin came back and opened the door, went in and switched on lights.

It was one large space with a brick-paved floor, a makeshift kitchen at one end, a collection of old chairs around a drum stove, a Ned Kelly, at the other, and a long table with benches on either side in the middle. Next to the table, a wide, sturdy ladder went up to a hole in the wooden ceiling. Three new French windows and a door had been knocked into the north wall.

'The bathroom's through the kitchen,' said Corin. 'You'll be pleased to know there is one, complete with Scandinavian composting toilet.'

She'd been strained on the trip, arriving three-quarters of an hour late to pick me up, taking four long calls and making two in the ninety-minute drive. At one point, she said to a caller in a calm voice, 'David, I understand your concerns but I assure you that I'll meet the deadline.' Pause. 'Yes, the start has been slow.' Pause. 'No, I cannot bring them in over the weekend.' Pause. 'I'm sorry your client won't be impressed.' Pause. 'No, I did not give any commitments on progress. My commitment is to a finishing date, that's not going to be broken.' Long pause. 'David, for fuck's sake, the job'll be done on time if I have to build the fucking walls myself and lay the turf by fucking moonlight.'

'Sorry about that,' she'd said to me. 'Losing control. Two big jobs and three smaller ones on the go. Been flat out for weeks, six days a week. I promised myself this afternoon off, got on the road at seven this morning to do it.'

Now she said, 'The bedrooms are upstairs. Well, put it this way, upstairs is where you sleep.'

I carried my bottles of wine and the food crate down the room and put it on the kitchen counter.

'There's a bit of light left,' she said. 'Come and look at the vineyard.'

We went out of the north wall door onto a terrace. The day had been clear and to our left there was still a glow in the sky, like a fire burning on a long front, far away. Close-planted rows of small leafless vines began a few metres from the barn, ran down the slope away from us towards a dense line of bare trees. The sound of water moving came up the hill.

'There's a winter creek down there,' said Corin. 'Some years it runs well into summer. You can swim in the pools.'

I hadn't stood next to her before. She was tall, straight-backed and I could see her profile against the light. She looked at me, I looked away, caught.

'I picked grapes when I was a kid,' I said. 'The rows were further apart. And the vines.'

'You're an observant student,' she said. 'What my brother is attempting to do here has nothing to do with conventional viticultural practice. It has to do with viticultural stupidity. He found Shiraz vines with the smallest fruit in the world and planted them close together. The idea is to put them under stress. Benign stress, they call it. Then you only allow the vines to produce small amounts of fruit. And, by hand, you pluck off half the leaves. With me to this point?'

'No. Then what happens?'

'If the theory's correct and your site aspect's perfect and the soils are right and the temperatures are optimal and the rainfall is what you need, and the birds haven't eaten all your mini-berries, then you get small amounts of highly concentrated fruit. You crush it and let it ferment with the wild yeasts. That's like sending your precious children out to play with wild dogs.'

'I'm beginning to see the charm of this,' I said.

She looked at me and smiled, nodded.

We stood in silence, looking out on a world leaving our sight, just touching, feeling through the fabrics that enclosed us that we were touching.

Suddenly, it was dark, black, the far line of fire gone, extinguished, the world constricted, stopping where the tongues of light from the windows ended. No sound but the generator's pulse and the moving water, winter water, urgent, going somewhere, irritated by banks and rocks and roots and trailing branches.

'A fire and a drink,' Corin said, all the tightness gone from her voice. 'A cross-trained person like you could light the fire. It's stacked, I do it before I leave. Obsessive-compulsive.'

We went inside. I knelt, scratched a kitchen match, put it to the Ned Kelly. It sniffed at the flame, drew breath, exploded, sucked oxygen out of the room.

'First fire, then drink, then art,' she said. 'That's evolution. In shorthand. I've brought this frozen stew thing. Make no claims for it, emergency rations, meat and veg. I cook a huge amount of it so that I can forget about cooking. Come home and be a vegetable.'

She fetched a red cast-iron pot, put it on the Kelly.

I opened a bottle of white and we sat in the old armchairs, deep in the sag, generator thumping softly, fire making throaty noises, both comforting sounds.

'Seeing you on television, that was awful,' she said. 'I wanted to ring but I couldn't bring myself to. Have they found . . .'

'No, not yet.'

'The job, it seemed to have gone beyond mediation.'

'Well beyond, into the wild blue yonder, in fact. I don't want any more jobs like that. I'm better at dealing with hundred-kilogram men trying to strangle me. That's straightforward, not a lot of ambiguity.'

'You have a turn of phrase for a man of action,' Corin said.

'I read a lot, books on propagation, soil structure, that sort of thing. Tell me why you're in a position to take your students away for the weekend.'

'Why?'

'Why you aren't married to some restaurant designer.'

She laughed. 'Married to the job, that's why. The moving of the earth, the transforming of nature.'

I waited.

'I had a long relationship, I hate that bloody word, I had an affair with a married man that went on for seven years. Hard to believe anyone can be that stupid.' She got up and lifted the lid on the pot, stirred the contents. 'He was always on the verge of leaving his wife and kids. It was just months away, just some final thing that had to be done. In the school holidays, his wife and kids would go to the house on the Peninsula and I'd see him every day except weekends. I think it was those times that kept me in a state of stupidity. It was like being married to him.'

She sat down again, drank wine, met my eyes. 'You don't want to hear this kind of stuff,' she said. 'Let's talk football.'

'What happened?'

'I'll give you the closing scene,' she said. 'We sometimes went out to dinner with another couple, she was a friend of Don's, that was his name, Don. I think he'd slept with her in the distant past. The guy was also a married man, also an architect. One night, we ate in a hotel in Collins Street, it was always hotel restaurants for some reason, less likely to bump into people you knew, I suppose. The other couple had had a fight before they got there, the air was crackling. The guy got smashed in about half an hour, Don was keeping pace with him. Then the woman just got up and left.'

Corin paused for breath. 'I don't know why I'm telling you this,' she said. 'It must be the mediator in you.'

'Go on. The woman left.'

'Yes. More drink, they were both pissed. And then, and this is it, the bloke took out his wallet and showed Don a picture of his kids. He was misty with pride and love. And Don, he got misty too and he took out his wallet and found a picture of his kids. They sat there looking at the pictures of each other's families. Two proud family men. I had an overdue moment of blinding clarity, got up and left and I never, never saw him again. Put the phone down on him twenty times, wouldn't open the door to him. That was that.'

'Then you married the job?'

She smiled. 'I had a few toyboys first, dabbled in boytoys, but they're ultimately unsatisfying. Now I'm happy just rearranging things. The surface of the earth. Your turn. What happened to you?'

I thought about it, tried to sum it up. 'I had an army marriage first. It lasted fifteen months, of which I was home for about fifteen minutes, not all that time at once. Then when I was a cop, I married an accountant, I met her when she did my tax return. I was home a bit more for that marriage but not much and I wasn't wonderful fun when I was.'

It was her turn to wait. 'So?' she said.

'She met someone she liked, a bloke with a normal job, likes to go to the movies, listen to music, read.

He runs a paint shop in Doncaster, sells paint. Divorced. His wife went off with a house painter. Also a tax client of hers.'

'And you hate the bastard.'

'No. Well, I did for about five minutes after she told me. Four minutes. Three. Then the beeper went and I had to say, sorry, I've got to go to Werribee to talk some whacko out of murdering his whole family. That took most of the night and then we all had a few drinks, had a beer breakfast, and she'd gone when I got home.'

'To the paint man?'

'Yes. I see her sometimes. I've been to their house. They invited me before Christmas. To a barbecue, mostly accountants and house painters. She's happy. He's got time for her, talks to her like a friend, asks her what she thinks. You can see how they are together. No jagged edges.'

I finished the wine, got up and poured more into the glasses. 'Walking away from me, I can't fault that decision,' I said. 'The me I was then, anyway. I'm a different me now, a mellow and relaxed person in a stress-free occupation.'

That amused her. I was an admirer of her smile. And to provoke it was heaven.

We sat in silence for a while, looking at each other, smiling. Then we got on to other subjects, laughed, drank more wine, ate her delicious stew. It was after eleven when Corin said, 'My bedtime. We who work with the earth go to bed early. And tomorrow we prune. Savagely.'

'I'll just sit here for a bit,' I said. 'I'm too mellow and relaxed to move. Is there a torch? I'll put the generator off. I've done that.'

'I don't doubt it.' She found a torch, put it on the table, went to the bathroom, came back face shining. 'When you get to the top of the ladder,' she said, 'there's a landing. Your room's straight ahead. Spartan. But you'd know about spartan.'

'I'm trying to forget about spartan,' I said. 'Goodnight.'

She touched my shoulder, her hand lingered for a moment, I could smell her perfume, then she left, walked up the ladder as if it were a staircase.

I drank a last glass of red wine, took the torch and went out to the generator. It shut down reluctantly, in the manner of diesel engines, thumped, thumped and gave a last few thumps, and all was still, black and still, no sound but the rushing sibilance of the creek. For a while, I stood outside the barn, in the dark, part of the quiet, listening.

Inside, the big room was warm, warmth that went up your cuffs, down your collar, the only light coming from the stove, a soft yellow light. I missed Corin, hated the idea that she'd left me, didn't want to go to bed, poured another half-glass of wine, put a last log on, sat down by the fire, thought about how I didn't want to go back to the city, ever.

I didn't hear her over the crackling in the stove. She came on bare feet, down the ladder and across the space behind me, walked around in front of me, a tall woman in a white shift, pulled it over her head, warm light on her breasts, on her belly. She knelt astride me, took my head in both hands, kissed me, drew my head to her chest, buried my face in her warmth, in her skin, in the smell of her, took my hand and pressed it on her.

Later, lying in Corin's bed, up in the old hayloft, still the lingering scent of dry hay, my head on her breasts, I said, 'This is a bit of an adventure for me. Just being alone with an attractive woman. Well, any woman really.'

'I feel betrayed. I was told that mediators took vows of abstinence. That's why I felt so safe inviting you for the weekend.'

'No,' I said. 'Those are gladiators. It's to save their strength for the combat.'

'Oh shit,' she said.

'It's all right. Mediators only proceed by consensus. They're bound by the oath of consensus.'

'That sounds like something from school history.

In 1202, Magnus IV broke the Oath of Consensus and invaded Sangria.'

I kissed the soft skin under her chin. 'Mountain stronghold of the Vodka Martini people. You're right.'

The next day, we awoke in the same state of mind we'd gone to bed in, then we washed and ate. She taught me how to prune, and we pruned savagely. Light rain fell on us, stained our clothing. For lunch, we grilled venison sausages, dark tubes she'd brought, ate them with mustard on rolls. Back to work. I caught her eye from time to time, she looked at me, I couldn't read her look. Could be interest, lust, regret, could be, Oh shit, what have I got myself into? Sex conquers nothing, explains nothing. She waited for me to finish my row.

'So,' she said. 'See you next year.'

We showered, drank and ate, made love in her bed, went downstairs and ate some more, made love in front of the Ned Kelly, went up the ladder. I kissed her and held her and slept as if cleansed of everything that stained me.

In the city, outside my apartment block, a dirty rain falling, leaning in at her window, I said, 'So, another toyboy dabbled with. Now it's back to changing the face of the earth.'

She put her hand under my chin, kissed me on the mouth, a kiss to remember. 'Yes,' she said. 'In one weekend, I've had the army and the police force. Know anyone who's been in the air force and the navy?'

'I'll ask around,' I said, 'and call you.'

I watched her go, waved, felt a stabbbing sense of loss.

ORLOVSKY SAID, 'I've gone back to that subscribers' file, the one, you know?'

'Yes.'

'Saw you on TV about fifty times and it made me think.'

'What?'

'The first time, I only pulled the current list, the paid-up people.'

'So?'

'I went back, found all the subscribers they've ever had. I've got other names now, subscribers who dropped off. There's a definite civilian here, no public service, academic connection I can find.'

'In Melbourne?'

'Eltham, yeah.'

'You at home?'

'Perfectly.'

'There's something else. I'm coming over.'

Orlovsky lived in Elwood, in half of a house on a respectable middle-class street. Amid the Volvos, his vehicle stood out like a garbage scow in a pleasure-boat marina. As I walked up the path to the porch, he opened the front door. We went down the passage into a big north-facing room furnished with a trestle table holding an array of computing equipment, a desk chair, an old armchair covered with a sheet and a television set on a coffee table against the wall. Like the rest of the house, the room had an air of monastic tidiness.

'This gets more professional-looking every time I come here,' I said.

'Strictly a recreational user.' Orlovsky walked over to the table and pointed at a monitor. 'This's the baby,' he said.

A name and address were highlighted on the screen:
Keith Guinane
7 Scobie's Lane
ELTHAM 3095
VICTORIA
AUSTRALIA

There was also an Internet address and what was probably a subscriber code number.

'Subscriber in '97, '98,' Orlovsky said. 'No one's heard of him. I rang around.'

I sat down in the armchair. 'This is going to be tricky,' I said. 'But first, we've got SeineNet sitting in a Carson computer. The bloke who gave it to me's very nervous. Can you get rid of it without going back there?'

Orlovsky nodded, sat down at the keyboard and went to work. I went into the kitchen and tapped some water from the earthenware filter barrel, had a sip. It tasted worse than water from the tap.

'Ready to destroy here,' Orlovsky shouted from the back room. 'No last requests? Never have the grunt to run this thing again.'

Glass at my lips. Keith Guinane of Eltham.

'Try the name,' I shouted back. 'Try the subscriber's name.'

I was in the computer room doorway, when Orlovsky said, 'Jesus Christ, come here.'

On the screen was the heading GUINANE, *CASSANDRA (CASSIE)* and the date 12 May 1986. Under it were menu boxes, dozens of them.

'Who's Cassie Guinane?'

Orlovsky clicked on a box. A colour photograph of a young woman appeared, dark shoulder-length hair, a strong face, good-looking. She was sitting at a table, wearing a low-cut dress showing a deep cleavage. A dinner party, a celebration of some kind, perhaps a wedding reception or a twenty-first birthday.

The people on either side of her had been cropped out but you could see a man's shoulder and a bare arm.

The text beside the picture said:

Cassandra (Cassie) Natalie Guinane, born 17 October 1962, Eltham, Melbourne

Occupation: Postgraduate student

Last seen: Swanston Street, outside Newman College, University of Melbourne, apparently waiting

Time: 7.20 p.m.

Date: 12 May 1986

Dress: Long dark coat over jeans and polo-neck sweater

'Any Keith Guinane?'

Orlovsky went back to the menu, clicked *Family* under *Interviews*. Three names came up:

Guinane, Keith Allan, brother

Guinane, Lennox Pearse, father

Guinane, Victor Martin, brother

'Is this stretching coincidence or what?' said Orlovsky.

'Bring it up.'

It took almost three-quarters of an hour to skim the Guinane material in SeineNet, me sitting on a kitchen chair next to Orlovsky. When we'd finished, he made espresso coffee and we sat outside the kitchen door in the late morning sun.

'Buggered if I can see how this can tie in with the Carsons,' said Orlovsky.

'Not exactly your innocent, Cassie,' I said.

Orlovsky sniffed his coffee. 'Costa Rican blend. Produced by slave labour, no doubt. She was twenty-four. They found four blokes she'd possibly screwed. That's not setting any records. For a male, they'd probably have turned up six times that many.'

'And that would be for an underachieving wimp like you. It's not the number. Only one of them was under thirty-five. And that was when she was twenty and he was thirty-four. The lecturer was twice her age.'

For a moment, my mind went to a lecturer, a landscape design lecturer. I shook the thought away.

'Women find maturity appealing,' said Orlovsky. 'Real maturity, that is. Men grown out of childish pursuits like playing with guns, playing cops-and-robbers, that sort of thing.'

'I find that hard to understand,' I said. 'Anyway, she liked older men. Which may be hugely significant or mean absolutely piss-all and I'm sorry I raised it.'

'Hitting on the name when you're interested in voice systems, finding it in SeineNet, it's one of those coincidences,' said Orlovsky. 'Weird but there's weirder, much weirder.'

'Don't tell me about them. How's your neighbour?'

I'd briefly met the woman who lived in the other half of Orlovsky's house. He seemed to be on more than neighbourly terms with her.

'Gone white-water rafting in New Zealand.' A pensive note in his voice. 'With her upper-level management colleagues. Bonding, they want them to bond. Costs the company four grand a head.'

'Should make them all join the Army Reserve,' I said. 'It's free and I gather they bond like two-pack adhesive. Can't separate them. After dark, they become inseparable.'

He laughed but it was a duty laugh. 'I think she may be entering a bondish phase,' he said, not looking at me. 'I can't quite work out what to do. Don't know where to go from here. If I want to go anywhere.'

This wasn't standard Orlovsky talk. There was vulnerability in his voice, the way he moved his shoulders, his head.

'Things can dry up in you,' I said. 'That's the worst of the life. You don't learn to live with women. You learn to shut them out. It's not a good way to be.'

We sat in the weak sunlight, a still winter's day, smog haze building up over the city, drinking Costa Rican coffee. Dun-coloured sparrows who would inherit the earth in partnership with the cockroaches walked right up to our feet. Orlovsky lit a cigarette, exhaled. The smoke hung in the air, didn't want to fade away.

'Well, you'd know,' he said. Barrier up, the standard Mick back in action. 'Twice married. Unsuccessfully.'

'You can't be married twice successfully unless they leave you for health reasons. The first one was just practice. It doesn't count, shouldn't be recorded as a conviction. Listen, Mark Carson. He'd be in SeineNet. The missing woman in Altona. Last person to see her.'

We went inside. Orlovsky called up a Find box, typed in *Carson, Mark* and clicked. The program replied with a list of references found: one in the Alice Carson investigation under *Family*, and references in the Anthea Wyllie investigation under the interviews with Mark, Stephanie Carson, Jeremy Fisher and Moira Rickard and in the investigating officer's summary.

'Let's see Jeremy Fisher,' I said.

We read the transcript of the interview. Jeremy said that he'd heard Mark leaving shortly after the last client left the Altona Community Legal Centre. A matter of minutes afterwards, he thought.

Under the transcript, the interviewer noted that

Jeremy had rung him two hours later to say that he'd remembered that after hearing the client leave, he'd gone to the filing room to look for something. It was after he was back in his office that he heard Mark leave. As he'd been away for at least fifteen minutes, Mark must have been in the building for about twenty minutes after his client left.

We went to the investigating officer's summary. He concluded that Anthea had been abducted while walking from the legal centre to the hospital, a distance she could have covered in less than fifteen minutes. He noted Jeremy Fisher's change of story but said there was no reason to doubt him. Fisher and Carson denied any discussion of their statements. Carson's sister, Stephanie Carson, said in a statement that she rang her brother at home that night around 9.30 p.m. and spoke to him. He said he had just come in the door. The timing matched Jeremy Fisher's revised estimate that Mark left around 9 p.m.

Two days after Anthea Wyllie disappeared, the investigating officer concluded:

Anthea was probably abducted within ten minutes of leaving the legal centre while walking to the hospital. She would not have got into a vehicle driven by anyone she did not know and trust. We have conducted fifty-eight extensive interviews and done 171 alibi cross-checks and have not produced a suspect. It is likely that she was abducted by force by a stranger/s and the investigation will have to be broadened to take in that category of known offender.

There were several more investigation summaries. The most recent review said:

There are no grounds for optimism concerning this investigation. It may be that in time some evidence will come forward to assist.

'Touched by tragedy, Keith Guinane, Mark Carson,' said Orlovsky.

'Fuck tragedy. Get them up again, the Guinanes. And for Christ's sake don't destroy this thing.'

'Sir.'

The father of Cassie and Keith and Victor Guinane was Lennox Pearse Guinane, an architect of a practice called Sitesong. There was an address in Heidelberg, a phone number. A file note recorded that Lennox Guinane committed suicide in 1988, two years after his daughter's disappearance.

'Get Lennox,' I said.

The database recorded that Lennox Guinane had a conviction for driving under the influence and convictions for assault and illegal possession of firearms.

'An armed and violent architect,' said Orlovsky. 'You'd have had a lot in common.'

'I COULDN'T change the name from Sitesong,' said David Klinger. 'Appalling name but it was there before I was. I've lived with it all these years. Used to be very trendy.' He sniffed. 'Trendy. Not a word you hear today either. We were a bit trendy, a bit fashionable then.'

He drank half a glass of white wine, glass the size of a cricket ball. 'Len was a guru, one of the mudbrick gurus.' There was no admiration in his voice.

David Klinger, all that remained of the architectural practice of Sitesong, was a man having a go at defying age. He was well into his sixties, shaven head, rimless glasses, thin body in a black T-shirt and black jeans. We were sitting at a table in his studio upstairs in a square tower attached to a house. Half a cheese and lettuce sandwich lay on a large white plate, next to it, two open bottles of white wine, one half empty.

A drawing board with a plan on it looked over a golf course.

'Very much gurus,' I said. 'Both of you. That's why I was keen to do something on your practice when this assignment came up. I was thinking along the lines of short biographies with details of major works.'

'Len's been done,' said Klinger, filling his glass. 'A student at Melbourne Uni did a Master's thesis on the mudbrick pioneers. What's her name now? Kilpatrick, Fitzpatrick, something like that. They'll all be in there, Knox, Len, the others. Visionaries, all of them.' Much less than admiration in his tone. 'Mind you, I've never seen it. She promised to give me a copy, spent bloody days here, let her see all the sketches, plans, everything. Never heard from her again. That's bloody gratitude for you.'

He studied me, narrowed eyes. 'You're from where?'

'Burnley, part-time.'

'Teach architecture there now?'

'It's a landscape design project,' I said. 'We're encouraged to see the buildings as part of the land-scape.'

Klinger nodded. 'Enlightened of them. I did a bit of teaching at Melbourne, place was full of career-change hopefuls. Didn't have a clue what they were getting into, most of them, not a clue. This practice's been going since 1956 and on average I doubt whether we've made more than the basic wage. People don't understand that. Bloody brickie makes more, much more. Go and be a brickie, that's what I used to tell them. They didn't like that.'

'I'm holding on to my day job,' I said.

He was studying the view without seeing it, glass in one hand, tapping the bony knuckles of the other on the table. 'Well,' he said, 'Melbourne Uni will let you see the thesis on the gurus, get what you need out of that.'

'I've seen the thesis,' I said. 'But what I wanted to do was talk about your partnership. I wanted to talk to you about how you worked together, how you influenced each other.'

Klinger laughed, it turned into a cough. He stilled it with wine, a little warmth came into his gaze. 'Won't have a drop? The Queen Adelaide, all I can afford these days. Price of wine's bloody outrageous. Influenced each other? I don't know about influencing Len. I'd studied in Europe, of course. Len never left Australia, very narrow was the guru.'

'So you brought a wider vision to the practice.'

He drank wine, turned his lips down. 'I was younger,' he said. He burped. 'Excuse me.'

'That would've made a difference.'

'Nothing made a difference to Len. He was a bull-dozer. Get in his way, he'd go right over you, didn't give a damn. Got into these fearful rages.'

Klinger finished his glass, filled it, most of the bottle gone. 'Didn't drink before sundown in the old days,' he said. 'Can't stay awake long after sundown now.'

'Lennox had a bad temper?'

'Tantrums. Like a child. Ellen told me, that was his wife, died in an accident. Tragedy. I loved that woman.' He fell silent, stared at his glass. Then he looked up. 'What was I saying?'

'Ellen told you . . .'

'Yes, the tantrums. Len's father was the same. Ellen's father-in-law. He was a doctor, used to rage at his patients, felt they were letting him down. Ellen said he went to see a patient in hospital one day and shouted at the poor fellow so violently the man had a heart attack on the spot.'

'That kind of thing can run in a family,' I said. 'Did he pass it on to the children?'

Klinger sighed, sipped. 'Sure you won't?'

'Perhaps half a glass. That would be nice.'

'Excellent.' He was pleased to have drinking company. 'I'll just get a glass. Frank, it's Frank, isn't it?'

'Yes.'

'David. Call me David. No one's ever called me Dave. I wouldn't have minded that. Dave.'

He went to a cupboard in the corner and came back with another goldfish-bowl glass, splashed it three-quarters full.

'What were you saying?'

'His temper. Passed on to the children?'

'Ah, the children.' Klinger's good mood dimmed a little. 'The twins, well, they were a worry from early on in the piece. There's something about twins, something mysterious, I don't know. They were both late developers, didn't start talking properly until they were, oh, five, thereabouts. But they had this private language, they made these sounds, not quite words. Word-like sounds. Only to each other, didn't respond to their parents or to Cassie for ages, more or less ignored them.'

'That would be a worry,' I said.

'Yes. Ellen took them around the medical profession, they weren't any help. As usual. Len of course was too wrapped up in himself to take much notice. And then one day Keith, right out of the blue, started talking to Cassie. Advanced speech too for a child. Ellen came around here, she was in tears. Tears of joy and relief. I cried with her, I can tell you. And a few days later, Victor started up, also to Cassie.'

I drank some wine. 'So they were fine after that?'

Klinger shrugged, drank. 'Brilliant, both of them. Reading like teenagers at six, playing the piano by ear. Writing stories, plays. Then Victor attacked a girl at school. He was about eight. She'd been taunting him but he didn't do anything, not in class. He waited until playtime and he called this little girl around a corner of the building and attacked her. A serious attack, an assault. Premeditated assault. That was the real concern. He beat her with an empty soft drink bottle, got her down and rained blows on her. A teacher was there in seconds but the girl had teeth knocked out, her whole face was a big bruise. She was in shock, had to be taken to hospital. No one had ever seen an eight-year-old hurt someone else like that.'

He shook his head. 'Terrible. Murderous streak, that would be from his father, no question. Len had a conviction for assault. Knocked an electrician right off a building, he fell twenty feet. And that was the one that ended up in court. There were others. I was scared of him, I don't mind saying that.'

I said, 'Someone mentioned an illegal firearms charge.'

'Didn't put that in the thesis, did she?'

'No. I heard it somewhere.'

'Len started going weird after Ellen's death. Survivalist rubbish, Indonesian invasions. Built this bunker, year's worth of food, even bloody cold storage, some silent fridge thing he devised. And this in bloody Eltham. Hardly your backwoods mountain hideout, huge city on the doorstep. But it wasn't a logical matter.'

'Illegal arms. What was that?'

'Part of the lunacy. Len bought guns from a bloke in Fitzroy. Back then, you could simply have applied for a licence, they handed them out like lollies. But the conspiracy theory said the traitors were going to give the Indonesians a list of all the people who had licensed firearms. So you had to have unlicensed guns, then the Indonesians wouldn't know and you could take to the hills of Eltham and fight back.'

'He got caught?'

'He had them in the four-wheel-drive and he got stopped for drunken driving. They separated the charges.'

'I sidetracked you,' I said. 'You were talking about Victor at school, the assault.'

'School wouldn't have either of them back. They'd had complaints about Keith too but not about violence. I never quite gathered what, Ellen didn't want to talk about it. That was unusual, we talked about everything.'

He drank, reached for the bottle, topped up our glasses. 'I'll get the cork out of another one, just in case,' he said.

He got up and went to a small fridge I hadn't noticed, opened the door. It was full of wine bottles on their sides.

I said, 'What did the twins do about school after that, David?'

He was applying a sleek black device to the top of a bottle. 'Ellen taught them at home. Had to, no school would take Victor. That School of the Air stuff the kids in the bush do. And Cassie, she was five years older, very smart, behaved like a real teacher. That went on till Ellen's death. They were eleven then.'

Klinger turned his back to me, holding the bottle in one hand, the corkscrew machine in the other. 'That was the biggest waste of a human being I know of. Ellen's death.'

There were tears in his voice, probably in his eyes. He didn't want me to see them, but he wanted to tell me.

'On the Eastern Freeway. Drunks in a stolen car, bloody police chasing them at a fantastic speed, car came right across the middle, over the dip. Head-on collision.'

Nothing I could say. I looked at his back, at the rigid set of his thin shoulders under the T-shirt.

'I loved that woman. From the moment I came into the room and saw her. The first time. The day

I came for the interview with Len. Loved her. She loved me, you know. Loved me.'

I drank, waited. Klinger put the corkscrew down, pretended to be looking in the fridge, wiped his eyes with a knuckle.

'Don't know why I'm saying all this,' he said. 'Not the vaguest idea. To a total stranger. That's probably why. I don't think I've ever said that to anyone. You're a good listener, Frank. It is Frank? Names just come and go.'

'Frank. So Ellen taught them at home?'

'Yes. Then Cassie had to do it. They didn't need much maths teaching, taught themselves after a while. Len bought them a computer, pretty new then, computers, and the twins were off, writing programs, all that stuff I don't understand. Obsessed by it.'

He came back with the bottle, not too steady now. 'That's also from Len,' he said. 'Obsession. The man didn't have interests, he had obsessions.' I held out my glass and he poured. 'Good to have company. Get used to being on your own but it's not good for you. Not for men. Women, they seem to handle it better. Unfair, really. Another bloody mystery.'

'What did the twins do when they finished school?' I said.

He sniffed. 'Nothing. Same as before. Stayed at

home and played with the computers. Made money out of it by then though.'

'Money? How?'

'Games. They write games. Is that what you say? *Write* games?'

I had a big swig of wine, felt acid rise in my gullet, felt the muscles of my back and shoulders tighten.

'Write, yes, that's what you say,' I said. 'They write games?'

'They make up these computer games. Beats me how you do things like that with numbers. Anyway, they do. Make quite a bit. Not surprising, they're good at making up things. Even when they were little, they were always making up things, putting on plays, getting dressed up.'

'They write commercial computer games?'

'Somebody bought the games. I suppose they still write them. I've lost touch since, it's been a while, six or seven years. Can it be that long?'

Klinger fixed me with an inquiring look, as if I knew the answer to his question.

'Lennox died in 1988, didn't he?' I said.

'Died? Killed himself. You could see it coming from the day Cassie disappeared. I went around there once afterwards but I didn't have anything to say to them. Victor would only speak to Keith and Eric, and Keith never said much, sits and looks at you with this smile.

And the place is like a shrine to Cassie. She was everything to them. Not just a sister, everything. They worshipped her.'

'Who's Eric?'

'He was a labourer on a house we built out in Coldstream, didn't have any family, and Len took to him, brought him home and there he stayed. Like a slave, really, didn't get paid, board and lodging, did all the work, built mad underground bunkers, fixed cars, anything. He's a bit simple. Good with his hands though, fix anything, any machine. And he can cook, God knows where he learned that. Fancy things too.' He shrugged. 'He loved Len, the children. Happy slave though. Like a Labrador.'

He sniffed, looked into his glass. 'Cassie stayed here for a while when she was in her second year at uni. Had to get away from home, she was being smothered by them. But Len kept turning up, taking her back. She was scared of him.'

Klinger took a sip of wine, his sips were getting smaller, stared out of the window, blinking, not seeing anything he liked.

The day had turned, night in the wings, shadows on the golf course now, golfers walking behind their giant elongated shapes. From this height, the bunkers were half dark, sinister hooded eyes.

'Yes,' he said, and there was something different

in his voice, 'she was scared of him. Very scared. Scared of the twins too later on, when they were grown up. It became a very strange family, Len and Cassie and the twins and Eric. Very strange. Cassie was like the mother, no girl should have that sort of burden placed on her. Unnatural. The whole thing was unnatural.'

I waited. Klinger wanted to say more, moved his lips twice, licked his lips, fought off the desire to speak.

Finally, he said, with a small smile, pride in the smile, 'And she still went to school every day, driven by Eric, got good marks. Amazing, an amazing person. Could take up burdens and put them aside, come back to them. Like her mother. One never ceases to wonder at the strength of some people.'

He stood up, now distinctly unsteady. 'Well,' he said. 'It's been a long day for me. Frank. Show you out. It is Frank, isn't it? Didn't get anywhere, from your point of view. Come again, we'll have another session, talk architecture. Aalto was my hero, I had a model of his church, do you know the church? Imatra? Lovely building. Len smashed it to bits one day, in one of his rages.'

I went ahead, down the steel spiral staircase, fearing for his safety behind me, down towards the client entrance at the bottom. Outside the door, a brick-paved path led to the side gate.

We stood in the stairwell.

'Thank you for talking to me, Dave,' I said.

His eyes were thin, body swaying.

'Dave, no one's ever called me that. I wished at school, never mind, I don't mind being called Dave. At all. I like that. Dave.'

We shook hands. He held on to my hand, didn't want to let go, looked into my eyes.

'She's mine, you know,' he said. 'Cassie. She's ours. Mine and Ellen's. Untainted by the vile Guinane blood.'

'THEY WRITE computer games,' I said. 'They earn a living from producing computer games.'

I was back in Orlovsky's computer room, sitting in the armchair.

'That's very interesting,' said Orlovsky, 'and it supplies a complete and satisfactory explanation for Keith Guinane's interest in voice systems. It's the kind of thing you'd expect him to be interested in. It doesn't necessarily connect them with the Carsons.'

'Alice Carson said that one day someone put on a computer game for a child and it had a tune repeated over and over.'

I remembered the way her hands had moved from the arms of her chair into her lap, that I could see that she was clenching one hand with the other by the tension in her neck and shoulders.

'Yes,' said Orlovsky.

'She said she felt sick and scared. She couldn't bear it and had to leave the room. That she vomited.'

'She also said she'd never heard the tune before,' Orlovsky said, deadpan.

'It triggered a memory, something she'd closed out.'

'I thought repressed memory was a load of bull-shit.'

'Who knows? I'm repressing a lot of memories. They come out in my dreams. What about you? How can we find a game written by the Guinanes?'

'Frank, this is a waste of time. Accept coincidence. Think about it. Finding Guinane and Carson are both in SeineNet is like finding them both in the telephone directory. How many zillion names do you think are in SeineNet?'

'No,' I said, 'it isn't coincidence. It can't be.'

'Anthea Wyllie, that's where you should be looking. Have you reminded the cops about her?'

'Yes. How can we find the game?'

He sighed. 'I don't know, there'll be a fucking list of game authors somewhere, I suppose. Make some coffee. Do you know how to make espresso coffee? Is that part of officer training?'

'If need be I can make a stimulating drink from a parasitic plant that attaches itself to mangrove roots.'

'Costa Rican beans will be fine.'

I was in the kitchen watching the coffee drip into the glass jug when my mobile rang. Vella.

'I should've called you before,' he said. 'The girl was dead at least thirty-six hours.'

Thirty-six hours? I'd made the demand for the photograph at lunchtime the day before I went to the station . . .

'The picture?'

'Manipulated. Taken with a digital camera. Two pictures brought together. One of her alive holding up the newspaper. Then they changed the newspaper, put another one in its place. They were expecting you to ask for proof. So they took the picture before they killed her.'

I felt tired in my legs, in my arms, in my shoulders, tired and sick.

'She was electrocuted,' Vella said. 'Probably in the bath. There's more. Not pretty. Want to know?'

'No. That's enough.'

'Not going anywhere fast here. You got anything to add?'

'No.' What was there to tell him? That I was running SeineNet on the Carsons' mainframe and risking his job every second that it was up? And for what? I didn't know for what.

I was looking at nothing out of the window when

Orlovsky came to the door. 'Can't believe it. These things can take hours. Fourteen Guinane games registered with the U.S. Patents Office, earliest one is 1985. I might be able to find it on the net. Get most of the early games.'

'She was dead when they sent the picture,' I said. 'Electrocuted. The picture'd been manipulated.'

I looked around. Orlovsky had his forehead against the doorjamb, eyes closed. 'I'll find the game,' he said. 'Today. I'll find it today.'

'Before you do that,' I said, 'get Cassie Guinane's housemate on SeineNet.'

HER NAME was Margaret Patton then and it was Margaret Spears now and it took me three hours to find her in an expensive house in expensive Albert Park. She was very reluctant to see me.

'We've only just moved in,' she said. She was fortyish, fair and pretty, flushed cheekbones, a doll's face, a grown-up doll wearing a dress with pleats in the front. 'We got back from England three weeks ago.'

Her husband came down the passage, a tall man, sleek dark hair. 'Hamish Spears,' he said, putting out a hand. 'It's related to this awful Carson thing, is it?'

I shook his hand. 'Frank Calder. Yes, it is. I'm sorry to be a nuisance.'

Margaret Spears said, 'I don't understand how Cassandra is connected . . .'

'We don't either,' I said. 'But we think there's a possible connection. If I can have ten minutes.'

'Of course you can,' said Hamish Spears. 'Come in. I'm an accountant. Abergeldie, Smith, Alberstam. We've done some work for CarsonCorp. Shopping-centre business. Nice people to do business with.'

Carson, the magic name, opener of doors, inspirer of greed and fear.

He led the way into a chintzy sitting room with a pale rose-coloured carpet and plump furniture. 'Frank, I'll leave you two alone,' he said. 'Maggie, give Frank a drink.'

She cocked her head. I shook mine.

'Please sit down,' she said. 'It's so long ago. What can I tell you now?'

'I've read the transcript of your interview with the police in 1986,' I said. 'There wasn't much you could tell them.'

'No,' she said. 'Well, I didn't really know her. It was just a noticeboard thing. And we were both private people. To tell you the truth, we were unlikely house-sharers. She saw my notice on the board. My parents had bought the house and I needed a tenant. We weren't friends or anything. I was a bit straitlaced, I suppose.'

'And she wasn't?'

'Well. After she moved in, someone told me she'd had an affair with a lecturer when she was an under-graduate. In second year. That's not very straitlaced, is it?'

'No. Men came to the house?'

'No. Only her father. He was a frightening type.'

'In what way?'

Margaret shrugged. 'Big and angry-looking. A beard. He always seemed to be angry with her. Never came in. She'd go out and they'd talk in the street or in his Land Rover. Dirty, covered in mud. She seemed frightened of him. Terrified, really.'

'You didn't tell the police that.'

'Didn't I? I suppose it didn't seem important. They weren't interested in her father. Boyfriends, anyone I'd seen her with at uni, that's what they wanted to know about.'

She paused, scratched her hairline with perfect nails, moved her head quickly. She was uncomfortable.

I waited.

'I really didn't want to get involved,' she said. 'Frankly, the father scared me too.'

I waited, looking at her. She couldn't hold my gaze, swallowed. There was something else she wanted to say.

'I was a coward. Just a girl from the country. I didn't want the police going to her father and saying that I said she was scared of him. Anyway, I was just reading that into her behaviour, I didn't know that.' She frowned. 'I didn't know her. If I'd known her . . .'

'That's perfectly understandable,' I said, smiled at her, waited, wouldn't be the one to speak.

She exhaled loudly. 'Yes, well, about four years later, the strangest thing happened. The place next door had been standing half-renovated all the time I'd been in my house. This man who owned it, a Greek, a Greek person, he'd work on it for a weekend, then he wouldn't be seen for six months. Anyway, one day he knocked on the door and said he'd found this book in the rubbish skip in his back yard and was it mine? You know, you get burgled and they find your stuff dumped all over the place?'

'You'd been burgled?'

'Often. Well, at least twice before then. It was a diary. And it had Cassandra Guinane written on the cover. I rang the Guinanes and her brother came around and fetched it. I suppose he'd have passed it on to the police if there was anything important in it.'

'I'm sure he would have. You didn't open it?'

'Of course not.'

'Of course not. So you never actually saw Cassie with anyone?'

'No. Well, the closest was, that was months before, someone dropped her at the end of the street. It was a Sunday morning. I was going to get milk or something, the papers, and we met. She said she'd been to Mount Hotham, it was lovely in the summer, no one there.'

'You didn't see the person?'

'No, just the car. A Mercedes.'

'That's not in your interview either.'

'Isn't it?' She seemed genuinely surprised.

'No. Probably just an oversight. You forgot about it.'

Frowning. 'No. That's what they were interested in. They asked lots of questions about things like that. I'd have told them that. I couldn't not have told them that. I did tell them that.'

'Well, I probably missed it, easy to do that. Thank you for seeing me. I won't take up any more of your time.'

At the front door, she said, 'This hasn't been of any use, has it?'

'It may have been.'

Hamish Spears appeared at the end of the passage. He shouted, 'Frank, sure you won't stay for a drink?'

As I was getting into the car, the phone rang: Orlovsky.

'These boys,' he said, the faintest note of satisfaction in his voice, 'I've got the earliest game. Got a tune.'

With trepidation, I punched Barry Carson's number. He answered immediately, crisply.

331

'Frank Calder,' I said.

'Frank. You might have said goodbye.'

'I saw your father. He didn't want to talk to me and I didn't think anyone else would either.'

'Rubbish. The old man was distressed, nothing about you. You don't bear any responsibility for what happened. Risked your life on the escalator. I appreciate that enormously. We all do. Have they told you about the photograph? I asked Graham to be sure you were told. He hasn't got much to do now that the float's postponed.'

Barry didn't sound like a bereaved relative, didn't sound like someone whose niece had been violated and slaughtered.

'They told me,' I said.

'Good. There was nothing anyone could have done. Your advice was sound. Professional. We bear the blame for not taking it in the first place. See the papers today?'

'No.'

'Tom's stood down as chief executive. He's retiring, in fact. I've taken over.'

Perhaps a small dinner party to celebrate. Would he do that, the police out there looking for his niece's killers? Probably. He was a Carson.

I said, 'I'd like to talk to Alice again. Tonight.'

Silence. There was faint music behind him, voices

in conversation, as if he'd left a dinner table, was talking in the next room.

'This is in the hands of the police now, Frank. If you have any ideas, they should be told.'

I hesitated. 'This is very important,' I said. 'I've been the police, I think I can do this better than the police.'

Silence and the music. 'Frank, her mother says she's taken Anne's murder in a strange way. You can understand that. This is not a good time.'

'Good time? It's never going to be a good time. Ever. You don't have walls high enough. Did the cops tell you about the call? An eye for an eye's not a fair exchange?'

'Yes. Mr Vella told me. We've put Jahn, Cullinan in charge of family security now, Frank. Should've from the beginning, just my father's strange ideas.'

'I'll put this simply. I'm not on the payroll. I don't want to be on the payroll.'

Another silence. A long silence, the music.

'I'll give you Alice's number,' Barry said. 'It's silent, so tell her who you are straight away or she'll be alarmed. She'll talk to you. She liked you.' A beat. 'I can't think why.'

'Inexplicable,' I said. 'One more thing. Do you ski?'

'Yes. Not much any more. Why?'

'Where?'

'Hotham mostly. We've got a place up there, family place, a lodge. Why?'

'Just a survey I'm doing about the habits of the rich.'

Laugh, a small laugh. 'Frank, we're going to have to put you on the payroll. To ensure your discretion.'

At Orlovsky's house, we opened SeineNet and looked up the investigating officer in Cassie Guinane's case. His name was Terence Sadler and a file note said he'd taken early retirement in 1990.

THE PHONE in London rang and rang and rang and I knew with no possible logic to support me that it was summoning no one, ringing in a place where no one would answer it. I sat on the kitchen chair in Orlovsky's computer room, he sat at his keyboard, our eyes locked, both of us listening to the ringing.

'Alice isn't home,' he said.

When all was lost, when I was nodding at him, she answered.

'Yes.' Breathless voice.

'Frank Calder, Alice, we talked the other night.'

Deep breath. 'Frank. Oh, hello. I was getting in the car and heard the phone ringing.'

There was warmth in her voice and it warmed me. 'I know I'm not a welcome sound,' I said.

'No, no, not at all, no.' No hesitation. 'After we talked the other morning, I felt better than I've felt, well, ever, really. Since, I mean. From the day the American man left, the psychiatrist, no one ever said anything again. Everyone looked at me in a way, as if there was something wrong with me, do you know what I mean? I'd catch them looking at me in a certain way . . .'

She tailed off.

'Yes,' I said, 'I think I know what you mean.'

'It's nicer to talk when I can see your face.' She laughed. 'I always felt they didn't believe me when I told them . . . what happened. It's stupid but the more they asked me questions, the more I felt they didn't believe me. They asked me the same questions over and over.'

'Yes,' I said. 'They were scared they'd missed something.'

'I understand that, why they'd do that, they have to do that, but I was just a girl. And I was young for my age, I think. When people keep asking you the same questions, you think they want different answers. Your answer's not good enough. You're not telling the truth. Am I sounding stupid?'

'Makes perfect sense to me.'

'My father's like that. There's a wait after you say something. And the man with the beard and the soft voice, he scared me so much, I can't tell you. I didn't know what a psychiatrist was. It was like . . . it was the beard more than the voice. Lie down and relax, he said, that was the most awful thing he could say . . .'

This was another Alice, an Alice released from bondage.

She said, 'Frank, it's a terrible thing to say, when I heard about Anne, I had this thought, not really a thought, a feeling, well, a thought. I thought: now they'll believe me, now they'll believe me. Is that awful?'

'That's not awful at all, Alice,' I said, 'that's got nothing to do with awful. People can only pretend to understand other people's pain. And they can only do that for a while. Then it annoys them, they think: how bad can it have been? If you talk about it, they want you to shut up. If you don't, they think you're sulking.'

I looked up and met Orlovsky's eyes, he looked away.

Alice laughed, a laugh of relief, tension dispelled. In the trade, if she was holding a gun on people I'd have taken that as a good sign.

'Alice,' I said. 'I want to play something to you, I want you to listen to something. May be nothing, probably won't mean anything to you, just a silly hunch. Can I do that?'

'Of course.' There was a firmness to her voice, an adult, grown-up firmness.

I held out the telephone to Orlovsky's machines, gave him the nod.

A hippety-hoppety tune, a childish tune, a few bars, repeated.

I put the receiver to my ear. 'Hear that, Alice?'

The line was open. She was there, you know when someone is there.

Silence.

'Alice?'

She made a sound, a tiny sound, a sound in her throat, and put the phone down.

After a while, I put my phone down. Orlovsky had his elbows on the table, chin on his hands, looking at me.

'The authors, they'd have written that tune, would they?' I said.

He nodded.

'What's the game called?'

'Shooting Star.'

'Nice name.'

'Yes.'

'Tomorrow,' I said. 'Early. I want to see them.'

'See them? Are you mad? If all this means anything, they're crazy kidnappers and murderers. For fuck's sake, go to the cops, tell your mates what you know.'

'No,' I said. 'I want to see them. This happened on my watch.'

'So did Afghanistan. You planning on going back there? Have another crack at them? Bring the boys back to life?'

I looked at him for a time, then I said, 'We'll need some ID.'

'I'm going along, am I? That's taken for granted?'

'No,' I said. I got up. 'I'll drop the pay envelope around.'

I was in the passage when he shouted, 'What kind of ID, you bastard?'

It was 10.30 p.m. when I rang the Carson compound. The switchboard spoke to Stephanie Chadwick, put me through.

'Hello, Frank,' she said. 'This is a nice surprise.' She'd been drinking.

'Stephanie,' I said, 'does the name Cassie Guinane, Cassandra Guinane, mean anything to you?'

'No,' she said. 'No, I don't know the name.'

'She was in your class at school.'

'Was she?' She laughed, an uneasy sound. 'Lots of unmemorable girls in my class. Why?'

'I think her brothers may have kidnapped Anne. And Alice.'

I heard her draw breath. 'Have you told the police?'

'No. I don't want to yet, not till I'm certain. Sure you don't remember her? Tall, dark, pretty?'

'No. Well, perhaps vaguely. The name.'

'I'll be in touch.'

'Yes. Goodnight.'

Sleep was hard to come by, my nights with Corin seemed to be in the distant past. I thought about the Carsons, their laundered clothes, their Italian soaps and French butter, their Jamaican coffee beans freshly roasted each morning. I thought about Pat not acknowledging my presence and Stephanie's lascivious kiss and pelvic thrust and Martie Harmon's story of Mark salivating at the memory of seeing women abused. I thought about the security men patrolling the walled compound and the Carson child taken from them and put to death. And I wished I had never heard the name Carson.

I left my bed long before dawn, no rest in me, and ran down the snakeskin streets. See them. See the Guinanes. What *was* the point? The point was to see if my skin tightened, to see if I was in the presence of people who murdered a girl in a bath, of a man who pushed a dead girl through the streets in a wheelchair, pushed the wheelchair down an escalator.

That was the point. That was the point.

ON THE way, too early to pay the call, we parked in Eltham's main street.

Orlovsky lit a cigarette with the slim stainless-steel lighter he'd always had. Then he had a thought, offered me the packet. I took one. He lit it, regretted it instantly.

'That's not good,' he said. 'You shouldn't smoke, I'm not comfortable with you smoking.'

I knew what he was talking about. I'd taken a cigarette off him on the night C Troop went to hell.

'Omens now,' I said. 'Mick, it's just a fucking smoke. Why don't you get your palms read? Palms. Soles of your feet. You could get your dick read. There must be some meaning there.'

He blew a thin stream of smoke at me. Contemptuous smoke, his composure regained. 'Flippancy,' he said. 'You cloak yourself in flippancy.'

Then he changed tack. 'Ever given your command instinct any thought? What it might stem from?'

'I have,' I said. 'It stems from a fear of being led by idiots. The only worse fear is of being followed by idiots.'

Cigarettes didn't last long, promised more than they could deliver. I'd forgotten what hot and acrid teases they were, tiny unbalancing hits. I threw the end out of the window.

'Time to go. Think like an inspector.'

The house was hidden from the road behind a dense screen of mature gums. A long steep unmade driveway curved to the right. We drove up and parked in front of a low building surrounded by vine-covered pergolas built from massive timbers. There was no garden, just native plants everywhere, many close to death.

'Do inspectors have the power to hurt people?' said Orlovsky. 'Like tie them up and torture them?'

'I don't think so.'

The front door was huge, double doors, metal-studded, probably saved from some public building hammered to fragments by the wrecker's ball. I rapped a tarnished brass knocker in the shape of a clenched fist.

We waited, quiet here, no sounds except birds in the gum trees, waited.

I dropped the knocker again, once, twice.

The lefthand doorknob turned and the door opened, just the width of the opener's face.

'Yes?'

A tall man, in his thirties, thin, clean-shaven, long hair combed back, dirty fair hair, touching his shoulders. I looked into his eyes, didn't feel anything.

Orlovsky said, 'Mr Guinane?'

'Yes.'

Orlovsky offered him a card. 'We're from Powertron, your electricity supplier.'

He looked at it. 'Powertron? The bills come from EasternPower.' He had a thin, scratchy voice.

'They did. EasternPower is now Powertron. Your bills will come from Powertron from now on.'

He gave Orlovsky the card back. 'OK. Is that it?'

'Well,' said Orlovsky, 'we've got a problem. We don't have any power usage pattern for this address.'

'What?'

Orlovsky ran a finger along his upper lip. 'It's a bit embarrassing but before we took over, EasternPower managed to wipe the consumption records for this whole area. So we don't have any record of your power usage over the past few years. The pattern of usage.'

The man opened the door a little wider, shook his head, impatient. He was wearing an old sweater over a T-shirt, camouflage pants. 'So? We're not behind. The bills get paid on time.'

Now Orlovsky scratched his head. 'They do, yes, that's not the problem. May I ask, are these domestic premises?'

'Domestic premises? Do you mean, do we live here?'

'Not business premises? Industrial?'

'What's this about?' He was annoyed now, not just impatient, getting angry.

'Mr Guinane. Mr K. Guinane, is it?'

'Keith, yes.'

'Mr Guinane, these premises use far more power than we would expect from domestic use,' said Orlovsky. He coughed. 'Now the usual practice in these cases is to notify the police, but . . .'

'The police? What for, what are you talking about?'

'We don't wish to do that because of the embarrassment it can cause. And because we don't have the usage records, we thought . . .'

'Notify the police about what, for fuck's sake?' High voice, loud.

'If we can be satisfied that you are using the power for some legitimate purpose, then we can simply note that.'

'What's illegitimate?'

Orlovsky coughed again. 'Well, for example, people

growing certain kinds of plants under lights tend to use large quantities . . .'

The man smiled, a smile in which he didn't open his lips.

'Oh Christ, is that it? You think we're growing dope. It's computers, we use half a dozen machines.'

We both smiled back at him. 'Right,' said Orlovsky, 'right, computers, that makes sense.'

'Yeah,' said the man, 'that's it.'

'Could you just show us that?' said Orlovsky. 'We have to report that we're satisfied the usage is for legitimate purposes.'

'You're like an arm of the fucking cops,' Keith Guinane said. 'Come in, I'll show you.'

As he opened the door, I saw movement in the second doorway along the passage. He led us down a wide passage with a polished concrete floor, mudbrick walls, doors opening on both sides at the end. The second door on the left was open. He went in first.

It was a big room, dark, heavy curtains drawn. There were benches along the inside walls and on them computing equipment, screens glowing with coloured images of people running, all slightly different. At first, I thought they were photographs but there was something of the comic strip about them.

A man was standing in the right-hand corner, his

back to a screen. He was the double of Keith, right down to the clothes and the long dirty hair combed back.

'This is my brother, Victor,' said Keith. 'These people are from the electricity company,' he said to Victor. 'We're using so much power, they thought we were growing dope under lights.'

Victor laughed, a screeching sound. 'Growing dope under lights,' he said, delighted.

It was like rewinding a tape, playing it again, listening to the same speaker.

... *growing dope under lights*. Rewind, play: ... *growing dope under lights*.

Alice on the monitor in the television studio:

Not similar, the same. At first, I thought it was someone talking to himself, having a conversation with himself.

'Well, that's all we need, Mr Guinane,' said Orlovsky. 'I can see where the juice's going. Sorry we had to bother you, but you can understand, there's not many houses pulling this kind of current.'

'Yeah,' said Keith Guinane. 'I know. Just doing your job.'

He went out first, then Orlovsky.

The door across the passage was open. I had a moment to see a section of wall. It was covered with photographs, at least a dozen framed photographs of different sizes, some of them school photographs, class pictures, all arranged around a big picture of Cassie Guinane. On a table in front of the pictures, a candle was burning, a candle in a silver candlestick on a small table covered by a white lace tablecloth.

There was something odd about the school photographs.

I took an extra pace across the passage, focused on a picture of girls in school uniform.

A girl had been blacked out.

In every school class picture, a girl had been blacked out.

It would be Stephanie Carson. Stephanie Chadwick.

We went down the passage, walking behind Keith Guinane. On the way, I put out my hand and touched the wall, ran my fingertips along it.

Mudbrick, mud-plastered mudbrick.

Adobe.

... *and I thought they were lovely, adobe, sort of Moorish-style and we unpacked and I went to have a shower and I got out all wet, water in my eyes and I had to steady myself and I touched the wall ... Repulsive, revolting, the feel of it ... I ran out, I didn't have anything on, I think I was screaming, I gave my mother a terrible fright ...*

Alice, talking to me. How long ago that seemed.

WE FOUND a place in Eltham to have coffee, waited for it in silence at a table on the pavement, Orlovsky smoking.

'The voices,' said Orlovsky. 'Remember what Alice said about the voices?'

'I remember.' I got out my mobile and rang Enquiries, got a number.

And she still went to school every day, driven by Eric, got good marks.

'Yes,' said a woman in the school records office after I'd lied to her, 'Cassandra Guinane was a pupil here. She finished in 1979.'

'Stephanie Carson?'

Pause. 'Carson. Yes, finished in the same year.'

'Was that a large class?'

'No, about twenty.'

I said thank you. The coffee arrived. Orlovsky took a sip, looked disapproving.

'Tastes like something made from a parasitic plant that attaches itself to mangrove roots,' he said.

I was thinking: This is the moment to ring Vella, meet him, lay it all out. The moment to stand clear, leave it alone. My watch is over.

I hadn't killed Anne Carson. There was never a moment when I could have saved her, never a moment when anyone could have saved her. She was doomed the instant the Guinanes decided on her, decided that she would be the next sacrifice to the memory of Cassie.

But why the Carsons? Was it possible they thought Mark took Cassie from them? Mark was probably an abductor and a murderer, had probably killed Anthea Wyllie, got his sister and Jeremy Fisher to lie for him, give him an alibi. Jeremy Fisher's career had gone like a rocket after he lied for Mark. Tom Carson had moved all the CarsonCorp business to Jeremy's firm, Jeremy was in charge of the Carson stock exchange float, a man grown rich on the Carsons.

Did Graham Noyce know about Mark? Who knew what Noyce knew? He fixed things for the Carsons. He didn't want me near Mark. Because of the float, he said, didn't want any bad press about a Carson, any Carson.

And Barry Carson? Barry didn't mind me having a look at Mark, encouraged me. Barry hated Mark, wouldn't be in the same room with him. Perhaps Barry was less worried about a Mark Carson scandal because he didn't mind the float prospects being hurt. Was he the person cultivating the idea that Tom was too old to lead the company into its new public incarnation? Tom thought so.

But none of that mattered. The Guinanes had killed a girl. Done things to a terrified girl and then electrocuted her, executed her.

Had they done it in the shrine to Cassie?

Why was it a Carson girl?

It didn't matter. Time to go. Back to Afghanistan. *You planning on going back there? Have another crack at them? Bring the boys back to life?*

'I'm going back,' I said.

Orlovsky was looking into his coffee cup. 'I don't feel inclined to pay for stuff like this,' he said. 'What?'

'I'm going back.'

He fixed dark eyes on me, ran fingertips over his lips. 'To what end?'

I didn't want to answer the question. It wasn't reasonable to want that man in the camouflage pants, those men in camouflage pants, weak chins, mocking eyes, to want those men to tell me what they'd done, to show me where they'd kept the girls, to show me where Anne's hair got wet before they took her picture, where they'd combed it, to show me the bath they electrocuted her in, to show me where they kept her body, kept it cold.

But I wanted them to do that, the Guinanes.

I'd put my hand out to her, touched her lovely face, felt the cold.

What had David Klinger said?

... even bloody cold storage, some silent fridge thing he devised.

Orlovsky said again, 'To what end?'

There was no reason in it. I had no explanation to offer.

Orlovsky saw that. I saw it in his eyes.

'Take a cab home,' I said. 'It's on the house.'

We sat there looking at each other.

'Just don't fucking smoke,' he said. 'No fucking smoking.'

WE DIDN'T go to the impressive front doors this time. We went around the house, going fast on the dirt, making a noise, took a hard right at the back of the sprawling building, another mudbrick building to the left, braked to a stop, came out of the car at a fairly efficient speed, not in condition for this kind of thing, crossed the space, ran over the terrace towards the back door.

Not an old door this time, an ordinary door, four panels, also saved, scrounged from some other life, tried the doorknob.

It opened.

A kitchen, huge, smelling of bacon, the scent of bacon fat, the smell of morning.

A man was sitting, leaning a little to the left, at a long table, a wooden farmhouse table, a shearers' table, built to seat twenty people. He was in his fifties, strands of grey hair combed back over a freckled scalp, a nice face. The plate in front of him held scrambled eggs, bright yellow. Free-range eggs.

Eric, the man Lennox Guinane adopted. Eric, who could fix anything.

The hole was in his temple, just in from the ear, a small hole, not even a hole, just a dark dent.

We didn't pause, went through a door into the wide passage, me first. The electronic humming of computers, otherwise silence.

Victor Guinane lay over his keyboard, shot from behind, upwards from the base of the skull, his brains on the wall above the monitor, still moist.

Keith Guinane was in the shrine to Cassie.

He had been on his knees in front of the table, the table that held the candle, when he pressed the muzzle of the pistol into the soft skin under his chin.

The flame in the candlestick on the lace-covered table was flickering in the last of the wax, guttering. It would die soon, no one left in this house to replace it, to keep the flame of remembrance alive.

TWO AND A HALF hours' drive from Brisbane, we parked the hire car on a green hill beyond Maleny, got out and stood in the sunlight looking over the landscape. Below us, in a paddock bordered by hoop pines, grazed a herd of Jersey cattle, stomachs full as blown-out cheeks.

'Pretty country,' said Orlovsky. 'I could live out here, grow avocados.'

'Forget it,' I said. 'You're an urban creature, an expert on coffee. Besides, they don't need legal drug distributors around here. They grow their own. Time to go.'

The farmhouse was at the head of the valley, a handsome white timber building on stilts, verandahs on three sides, an elaborate portico. Behind it were outbuildings, all painted white, a water tank tower, not high, and a stand of trees.

We drove over a juddering cattlegrid and triggered some kind of alarm because I could see the white front door of the farmhouse go dark. Someone had opened it and was watching us come. Then the door closed, the space went white again.

The long driveway led past a pond, a big pond with an island and rushy banks and a jetty where a rowboat was tied up. Four horses, one a yearling, watched us from their post-and-rail paddock beyond the water.

As we neared the house, I could see into an outbuilding with horse tack on a rail, saddles, bridles, see a fowl run beyond that, washing on a line, a garage with three vehicles, a Mercedes, a four-wheel-drive, and a ute with a flat tray, two bales of hay on it.

'Park at the front door,' I said. 'There's someone waiting.'

We drew up on the gravel, got out.

The front door opened again and a man came out onto the verandah, a tall man in his sixties, country clothes, close-cut grey hair and a handsome face, a handsome sardonic face.

'Frank,' he said.

'Nice place this,' I said. 'Nice country.'

A woman came through the door, also handsome, late thirties, a few strands of grey in her dark hair, dressed for riding, checked shirt, khaki breeches. She went to stand next to the man, put an arm through his, looked at us, not smiling.

No one said anything. I heard footsteps on gravel and a girl, a young woman, came around the corner of the house carrying a saddle. She was lovely, very like her mother standing on the verandah above us, but with a trace of her father in the mouth.

'Hello,' she said, friendly, a country person. She hadn't noticed her parents on the verandah, saw them out of the corner of her eye, looked up in alarm.

'What's wrong? Dad?'

'Nothing, Mel,' said Tom Carson. 'Just surprised to see our guests. Frank Calder, Michael Orlovsky, this is my daughter Melissa. Come up, gentlemen, come inside, time for a drink.'

For a moment, I didn't move, stood there looking at Melissa's mother, holding Cassie Guinane's eyes, hearing Christine Carson's voice:

Stephanie found her father screwing her school friend in the tennis pavilion at Portsea, did you know that?

Then I said, 'Just a quick one, we're just passing through, a plane to catch.'

VELLA RUBBED his eyes, rubbed the bridge of his long nose.

'You could've saved me a lot of pain,' he said. 'Lots and lots of pain.'

'I didn't know anything. Just a collection of feelings, bad feelings. It's easy to get bad feelings when you hang around the Carsons.'

'Oh, you knew plenty,' he said. 'All you had to do was mention the fucking Guinanes, point to them, and we could've gone around there, just a social call, kicked the shit out of them.'

'Is that how it's done? On the basis of exactly nothing, get a warrant to go around and kick the shit out of people who might be totally innocent?'

'All we needed was a warrant to look inside the computers. For a Carson abduction-murder, any fucking magistrate will give you a warrant to look inside a computer. Anybody's computer. We'd have found the photographs.'

We were in a smart pub in South Yarra, looking out over the Botanical Gardens, watching rain falling on runners, drinking Heineken. Vella finished his, motioned for two more.

'And that brings me to the point again,' he said. 'Why? Why did the mad fuckers do it?'

'I don't know. We didn't get to them because of motive. We got to them because of their voice-changing machine.'

Lying, lying to a friend, a man who trusted me, put himself at risk for me.

The beers came. Vella waited, then he said, 'These pricks in Forensic are slow but they get there eventually.'

'Get where?'

'There's skin under Keith Guinane's nails, some other signs. He put up a bit of a fight till they had him in position.'

I thought about sitting in the comforting study with old Pat Carson, the drop of whisky glowing gold on his chin, the pleasure in his voice as he said:

Had a bad accident later, Mr Ashley Tolliver, Q fuckin' C, two years later, a good time later. Just lost control of the car. Mercedes, mark you. Into the sea. Down there other side of Lorne, the cliff's steep, go

off the edge ... Never walked again, they say ...
No respect. He had no respect.

Who had organized that? Tom and Noyce?

It would be dark soon, the park was full of shadows, the day was sliding out of reach. I thought about the guttering flame on the table in the shrine to Cassie. It would be long dead now, in a silent house.

'Without shedding of blood is no remission,' I said.

'What?'

'Just something my mother used to say.'